Regret

Regret

By

Brad Windhauser

A Star Publish LLC Book
http://starpublish.com

Regret ©Brad Windhauser 2007

Regret is a work of fiction. All incidents and dialogue, and all names
and characters are products of the author's imagination and are not
to be construed as real.

ISBN: 1-932993-82-7
ISBN 13: 978-1-932993-82-0

Library of Congress Number
LCCN: 2007906039

Edited by Janet Elaine Smith
Cover Design by Star Publish LLC
Interior Design by Mystique Design
Author photo by Jessica Puma

Published in 2007 by Star Publish LLC
Printed in the United States of America

This book is dedicated to Dr. Judith Vanderbok, for encouraging me to write; to Janet Heilke, for telling me I had hidden talent; to Mel Freilicher, for giving me the courage to write about the things that I care about most; and to Lisa Zeidner, for teaching me how to put it down on the page.

Though this book may be "morally ambiguous" to some, the lesson encourages your ability to live the life you want to, becoming the person you were born to be, and not run from anything that anyone tells you is "wrong," or chasing someone else's version of what success means. When we hide from the scars of the past and turn from the life we know to be true in our hearts, we create conflict in not only our own lives, but also in the lives of everyone we touch.

Life is too short not to be happy.

The only emotion more powerful than love is regret.

Part I

Chapter 1

Rolling this plan into motion would erase everything about William's past. His son's death taught him that achieving understanding arrived by way of sacrifice. And now he stood, watching the materialization of his calling with the beginnings of his work finally arrived, feeling his confidence bolstered to new heights at his own success. As he surveyed his future, his immaculately polished black shoes stirred up dirt and dust as he strode across the concrete floor of the warehouse. He leaned down to make sure none of the dust had settled on his dark suit trousers.

Though bigger than he envisioned needing, the building's vast space would not go to waste, William vowed. He would find a far better use for these walls than housing those weekly "counseling" sessions that had far outgrown their usefulness. Even though his superiors would expect that they happen under this roof, he would find a better use for his time than continually perpetuating comfort to people who needed more than words. William knew that this day would mark the beginning for so many that languished in sadness.

"Now, this states that you intend..." William Thompson had completely forgotten that he was not alone when the realtor rudely interrupted his musings.

To expedite the realtor's exit, William turned and snatched the outstretched pen: "All I need to know is that you made the changes we discussed." William looked up, hoping to find the expression that countered his expectations. Any good businessman would long ago have abandoned this bumbling idiot. Two properties had fallen through, due to the realtor's inability to follow through with aggressive offers, and his inability to make prompt phone calls had cost William half a percentage point on his payments, as well as a quarter of a point up front. Although William prided himself in having patience with those that needed pushing along in life, even he had his limits, and the realtor was quickly raising William's blood pressure.

"Yes, well..." The realtor stammered like a man intent on making his case, but only took a moment longer to find his efforts useless. "The changes are in there, just as you requested, Mr. Thompson." William noted the growing guilt in the realtor's face and plunged his attention to the document in hand. "About the issue with the bank—I wanted you to know that I made every effort to secure..."

William, eschewing any interest in hearing about the past, waved off the realtor while he signed everywhere the Xs were marked. He handed the document over and swung his back to the presence that had quickly outstayed its welcome.

"Great. I will fax your copies over to you. Oh, could I get a business card or something to attach to this? We like to keep complete files for all our clients."

William anticipated showing off his new business cards, but had not imagined this to be the place. He wondered if a layperson would share his conviction that the cross looked better in black, as opposed to the gold leaf embossing of the original design his superiors suggested. William, however, felt a solid black background and a smaller cross might be more appropriate, more business friendly. After all, he wasn't into beating people over the head with his religion. He passed the card over his shoulder, without looking to see the reaction.

"All right, Mr. Thompson. Here are your keys. You are all set."

William held his palm open over his shoulder and waited for the deposit. In another moment, the soles of the realtor's shoes told William that he was wise enough to show himself out. William double-checked the departure out of the corner of his eye.

Alone finally. William turned his attention to mapping out the space. In the front section was an area for couches. In case any of the people that signed the checks came around, they had to put on the appearance that this was a place of warmth, a place for people needing shelter or solace of some kind to come and feel loved. Well, he had already played that hand and witnessed how ineffective that game could be. In the back were a few small rooms hidden from view where the real equipment would stand, waiting to play its part. William would have to devise, later, how best to justify their place. He did not doubt his ability to do so. He had faith.

Now, if only his faith would turn out to be properly placed in Isaac, whom William had selected for the trial run tomorrow night. Isaac would be the best indicator of their success or failure, for he needed the most practice. As such, his success would bode well for the future. Doing so also offered the perverse pleasure of seeing if Isaac would actually pull through, like someone watching a pigeon flap along the street with a wounded wing, taking bets to see if the bird would actually take flight before the oncoming car ran it over. Although he should be above such pleasures—given the fondness he had developed for Isaac—William could not hide his little school boy giddiness.

Isaac stood in line, wondering if dark slacks would have been a better choice than the light khakis. Had he used too much gel in his cropped hair? William and Scott had told him it was for his own good that he go first, that it would strengthen his character and build his confidence, but Isaac was not sure he was the right man for the job as he looked around at the guys clad in tight black shirts and matching jeans, bobbing their heads to a melody that he was sure wasn't there. Isaac hoped the lighting inside was as dark as he remembered so nobody would see how nervous he was. He knew he was doing the right thing, but it sounded like such a better idea when somebody else was getting it done.

Once inside, he parted the faded purple curtains. The music assaulted his senses, overtaking his eardrums with such ferocity that he closed his eyes and sucked in his lips as if he were being invaded through every possible orifice. He plugged his ears and eased his fingers out slowly and raised his eyelids again to watch the lights dart along the walls. When he had adjusted to the sound, the smell enveloped his nostrils causing him to tug at his nose like a runner would after drudging through a thick screen of heavy dust. He loosened his shoulders and thrust his arms at his side. He looked around to see if anyone else noticed but each gay guy, oblivious to everything but his own desire to have fun on a Saturday night, sputtered around carrying on like a dog that had grown accustomed to, and almost proud of, the scent of its well-worn beds. Isaac stepped forward and felt like he was wading through a shallow pool, unsure which shore to move towards. A sea of men toppled over one another on the large dance floor to his right. There was a bar lining the far wall but there didn't seem to be any place to stand and the noise would be even more unbearable closer to the dance floor. Then there was a smaller dance floor separated by a solid wall. As he moved closer towards that area, it seemed to be a little more contained and not quite as deafening. He turned around and saw a cozier section of the bar where more properly-dressed men milled about carrying beer bottles, pausing to talk to others who were seated in high-back chairs or mingling with the pool players. That room seemed to provide the most comfort.

It seems more like a coffee house than a bar, he thought as he edged closer to that room. People disappeared through the back corner. Isaac discovered that the doorway led to the smaller dance floor and he found his way back to his starting point, past the suspended televisions which played gay porn—*they can play this in here?* he thought—that he only stopped to look at for a moment before reminding himself that he still had his coat on.

After he had checked his coat, he made himself comfortable at one of the bars and ordered a lite beer. He looked at the men standing around him and wondered if the beer in his hand helped him blend in. Everyone had their shirts opened or off completely. Isaac unbuttoned the top two buttons and smoothed out his shirt. *There, that's better*, he thought. *Maybe I should fold up my sleeves.* He gave each cuff two folds over. *Maybe I should untuck my shirt.* He gave the shirt a tug. *No, no, that does not look right.* He tucked the shirt back in. *Maybe another button down on the shirt.* He went down another two, stood for a moment, looked around for a consensus, and then buttoned three back up. *There, that looks better. Maybe...no, no, just leave it,* he thought, taking his beer back in his hand while shoving his free hand into his pants pocket and taking a breath to relax. Perhaps he was not cut out for this. Even though he had received encouragement leading up to that night, he wondered if he should have come after all. But showing up empty handed and giving Scott an opportunity was enough of an incentive to push through all his doubts. He sipped his beer and made room for another man to step up to the bar.

While Isaac occupied himself with watching the pool game, one of the players made eye contact. He walked toward Isaac, with his cue stick in hand, clutching the skinny end.

"Now, there, that's better," the man said and pointed at Isaac's smile.

"Sorry, I'm...I'm just a little new to this." Isaac pursed his lips and shifted his body weight from one leg to the other. *Take the first one and run with it,* he thought.

"Everyone's gotta have a first time, if this is your first time..."

Isaac nodded yes. It felt like the first time, anyway. He remembered when it had been his first time. When he had felt so ashamed. Now he couldn't help feeling guilt—guilt over what he had been made to feel was right for him to do—but he just couldn't justify it. He kept telling himself that there were just some things he didn't understand and that he needed to do what they told him and things would work out.

Holding out his hand to Isaac, the guy said, "My name's Benny."

Isaac shook his hand hesitantly, then Benny tightened his grip ever so slightly.

"That's better, that's better. Now we're getting somewhere, Mr. First-time."

Isaac smiled, then surveyed the room. He was sure everyone had stopped what they were doing to watch this meeting take place.

"What's your name, Mr. Brown Eyes?" Benny's eyes trailed Isaac's everywhere they peered. Isaac faced Benny and shook his head a bit, as if tripped up by the question,

"Isaac. My name's Isaac."

"Okay, then, now come on over here. I'll let you meet some people that I happen to call friends." Isaac wondered if someone a little less amicable would be a better choice. Isaac felt a little guilty as he watched Benny's ass—pressed tightly in his faded pair of jeans—strut to the bar. "The first one will be the hardest," he had been told.

"Can I get you something to drink? I think I have some good German Pilsners in the fridge." Isaac removed his coat, hung it in the closet, then shut the front door. He had not had a visitor to his apartment in a very long time.

"Yeah, I'll take a beer if you got it." Benny slid out of his coat and set it in Isaac's outstretched hand.

Isaac offered Benny a seat on the futon and scurried to make neat the top of the chest that acted as a coffee table. Benny laughed and expressed his indifference to the state of Isaac's apartment, but Isaac felt like he needed to keep moving. In between excuses, apologies flooded his mind. *Calm down, calm down,* he thought. When he felt confident that Benny had settled himself comfortably, he made a beeline for the small kitchen just off the front room.

While plucking two glasses down from a cupboard, Isaac heard a slight rustling so he poked his head out of the cubbyhole of a kitchen. Although Benny had disappeared from sight, his shadow painted him in the small hallway that led to the bedroom.

Concerned that he might move further down the hall, Isaac called out, "If you want, I have some books on a shelf in the hallway leading into the bedroom. That is if you wanted something to look at while I'm in here." He ducked back into the kitchen and mumbled, "Please stay put for at least a moment."

He hoped Benny wasn't tempted to come back into the front room. Maybe he shouldn't have said it the way he did. Maybe Benny thought he shouldn't be looking around and had come back to the futon. *Why'd he have to be so cute? I should have remembered that they told me to try and find someone for the first time that isn't cute, someone you won't have any chance of getting attached to. That'll make it easier.*

Isaac opened the door of the refrigerator and grabbed two beers. His hands quivered as he struggled to pop the tops off, using an opener that was fastened to the side of one of the cabinets. He fumbled in his pockets for a capsule, sealed in a plastic bag.

"You have an interesting assortment of books. Kinda hard to figure out exactly what your tastes are," Benny called out from the hallway.

Isaac struggled with the bag. "Yeah, well, I guess I, ah, like a little bit of everything." Separating the plastic rails, he turned the bag upside-down and begged the pill, with tensed lips, to tumble down into his palm. He balled up the empty bag in the palm of one hand and shoved it into his right pants pocket. Then he pulled the capsule apart, spilling the whitish powder into one of the glasses. His eyes darted around for a safe place to ditch the capsule. For some reason, the trash can didn't feel like a good idea, so he moved his hands to the rim of the sink and let the plastic fall. He turned on the faucet to help the process along.

He reached for one of the beers that was starting to perspire down its own bottle and emptied the majority of it into the glass with the powder. The head of the beer rose and he swirled the liquid around. He then poured out the other beer before the first head had a chance to settle.

Holding tightly onto the ends of the kitchen counter, he closed his eyes. William had said that was the thing to do. We had to. It will be difficult, but it will eventually straighten you out. *I have to be strong.*

Isaac opened his eyes when he heard the soft creaking of the hardwood floors. *He is coming back.* Benny entered the doorway before Isaac had a chance to make his way out into the front room. He had such a nice smile—such a nice smile on such a nice man. William would be proud of him and it would silence Scott's opinion that he wasn't up to the task.

Isaac held out the beer, and Benny took it with his right hand. Benny reached out with his left hand and cupped Isaac's neck with his long, strong fingers. Those fingers kneaded Isaac's neck, while pulling Isaac closer at the same time. "You sure you are okay with this? You look a little nervous." Benny's eyes followed Isaac's, as they looked everywhere except at Benny's face. When he eventually looked back, their eyes met and Isaac blushed and stifled a small laugh at not being able to compose himself.

"I hope you like the beer. It comes highly recommended from a close friend who knows about these things." *Please let this end soon.*

Benny smiled and removed his hand from Isaac's neck. "Yeah," taking a long drink from the beer, Benny assured Isaac, "that'll do." He wiped the foam residue from his upper lip, using his forearm. "You're still so tense. Relax a little. I won't bite." He took another drink from his beer. "Can we sit, or do we have to stand up all night?"

Isaac smiled and nodded. He gestured to the futon and Benny turned and took a seat. While Isaac scoured the surface of the chest for a coaster, Benny held up a plastic disc. "Looking for this?" He smiled as Isaac took it out of his hand and placed it under his glass of beer on the chest.

Benny reached out and caressed Isaac's cheek. Isaac's skin bristled with a unique sensation at Benny's soft, gentle touch. Isaac bit at his lower lip and turned away as casually as he could. Benny took the hint, but moved his hands onto Isaac's tense shoulders and went to work. "You know, Isaac, it really seems like you're uncomfortable with this, so maybe I should go. I don't want to make you do anything you're not cool with."

"No, I'm okay," Isaac assured him. With that, Benny leaned in and kissed Isaac's neck.

This should last for another ten minutes. I can stay strong for ten more minutes, he thought. Benny's soft lips pressed into Isaac's neck and Isaac felt his body go a little flimsy, as he couldn't deny how good it felt to finally be kissed again by another man. Isaac couldn't remember how long it had been.

When Isaac regained his senses and guessed that enough time had passed, he tensed up again and Benny drew back. "Maybe I should go, Isaac, and we can meet up some other time." You could see the resignation in his face, but in a moment's time, that shifted, as the muscles in his face relaxed and Isaac knew the drug was strengthening its hold.

Isaac felt like he could take a little control. "I don't want you to leave; I want you to stay. I have to do this—for me." He tried to grin, but it came across as forced. Benny didn't bother to smile back. He moved his hand from Isaac's neckline and pulled down some gelled back short bangs. Benny's eyes drooped; you could see the fight in his beautiful eyes. They still held that sparkle as they fought. He attempted to articulate, as a mildly intoxicated driver might towards an officer, "Do...do you...can I use your bathroom? I'm feeling...feeling kind of light headed. I think I just need...just need to get some air, or, walk around...or something."

Isaac sat back, retreating to one end of the futon, as Benny hobbled to his feet before his legs failed him. Isaac prayed the neighbors below him did not hear the thud Benny's body made on the hardwood floors. The worst part was over. Benny brushed the sides of his face with his hands, like someone checking to see if the mosquito they felt had drawn any blood, and then hoisted himself up using the arm of the futon. After another moment, the battle within Benny's body ended and he slumped down.

Isaac tried to lift Benny's limp body, but faltered, so he grabbed him by the ankles and eased him down the hall, so as not to create any more noise for the neighbors. When they reached the bed, Isaac set Benny up and leveraged him until he was lying flat on the mattress. Looking around his bedroom, Isaac pulled down both shades to give himself some privacy, then got to the task at hand. Benny gazed up at Isaac, with his eyes partly opened and his mouth wide. Isaac rushed over and shut the eyes and carefully closed the jaw. *He was such a nice man, and so beautiful,* he thought. No, he shouldn't be thinking those things, cutting himself off. He had come this far.

Isaac closed his own eyes and repeated in an inaudible whisper, "Forgive me, Father..." When he was finished, he motioned his fingers in the form of a cross over Benny's body. He leaned down and rolled Benny's sleeve up past his elbow. Scott didn't want to have to roll up any sleeves back at the warehouse, and Isaac didn't want to cause any problems.

Isaac got up from his squatting position and fetched his beer from the front room. He came back to the bedside and sat Indian style, studying Benny's limp body. Noting the time on the electronic alarm clock by the bed, he took a finger and felt for a pulse on Benny's neck. It was faint, but still there. It would be safe to move him now. He pulled the phone down to the floor and dialed the number he'd been trained to remember.

An alert voice answered on the other end. Isaac felt his own voice wobble, "Yes, I have one. In my apartment...okay...okay...I know... I'll be waiting." Feeling that he had spent his whole life waiting, Isaac wondered when he would finally get to where his patience had been promising him for some time.

As the warehouse door rose, intermittent cars whisked by on the neighboring freeway. Isaac fidgeted in the front seat of the van every moment of the ten minutes it took to reach the northeast part of the city.

Isaac got out of the passenger side when Matthew Coddling, decked out in his faded navy blue Dickies pants that made him look like an auto mechanic, brought the van to a halt safely inside the concrete walls. Isaac wondered why William avoided asking him to cut his bleached-out hair, but then he figured that William saw a need in the look.

Two men were busy unloading Benny by the ankles as Scott strode in their direction. Isaac felt himself tense up like a mailman approached by a Rottweiler, and questioned—as he did almost every time he came into contact with Scott—what was it, exactly, that William saw in this criminal?

"Take that one to the back room and lay him up on the table," Scott, looking like he had just woken up from a nap and thrown on whatever was laying on the floor, barked to the two men who were ambling along with him. "Actually got one, eh?" It took him a moment to start something, but Isaac's successful completion of the mission afforded his spirit some confidence, allowing him to hold Scott's beady little stare without turning away.

Scott choked out some guttural noise, then turned and scampered off with an unnerving authority. *One day*, Isaac thought, *you will not be held in such high esteem.*

Isaac turned towards Matt. "That one," pointing in Scott's direction. "I doubt he even cares what we are trying to achieve by doing all this. I wonder if he even understands that we are trying to help people. I'm sure he just enjoys it all." Matt made no response, but smirked and walked in Scott's direction. *They all hate me*, Isaac thought.

In the back of the warehouse, Scott clicked on the hanging light fixture over Isaac's contribution to the cause. He used two fingers to feel for a good vein, shaking his head, amazed that Isaac had remembered to fold up the sleeve. *Maybe he can follow directions,* he thought. Satisfied with the vein he found, he turned toward a small table that hugged the wall behind him, took up a syringe and inserted an empty vial. He dipped the thick needle into the vein and watched as blood slowly rose in the vial.

Drawing his fingers away from the arm, he allowed himself to softly caress the soft skin. Everything he had learned over the past year had taught him to resist temptation and he had overcome his predilection towards men, but there was something in the way the body looked at peace—so quiet, so innocent. Scott surveyed the still body until he fixed his gaze on its groin. *How long has it been since the sight of another man's cock excited me? Why did none of the other bodies arouse me so?* Cautiously, he extended his hand, inching up the leg, then turning his hand inward to the thigh and stopping just short of the crotch. He brought his hand up slowly and reached for the zipper. Then he paused, bowed his head, took a deep breath, and recoiled, withdrawing his hand and covering his mouth, while looking down scornfully at the body that had tempted him.

Scott composed himself. He shut out all emotion, feeling neither pity nor remorse, as he exhaled, impatiently waiting for the vial to be filled. After another minute, he plucked out the full vial, placed it on the counter, and left the needle dangling from the arm. He took a marker, scribbled a number on a piece of masking tape and stuck the tape around the vial of blood. He struggled to untangle a tag from a bunch in the drawer of the table and wrote the corresponding number on it. He turned around towards the body, disgusted as he realized he would have to remove one of the shoes to place the tag on a toe. Not bothering, he grabbed a finger and twisted on the thin wire fastener. He then jerked out the syringe and tossed it on the table, stopping when he noticed a small trickle of blood on to his shoe. He brushed it off and was glad it left not so much as a mark on his shoe.

Now that the blood was drawn, they could put the fag on the table out of his misery permanently. He would round up Matt and hand him the clean-up work. Matt had said he wouldn't mind being the one to administer the lethal injection to finish off the job. He actually seemed like he would enjoy doing it. Scott had to appreciate the joy with which Matt was diving into this whole thing. Dedication was so hard to come by these days.

As he passed through the doorway, Scott knew that having to test for AIDS was going to get old quick.

Chapter 2

Those with power within the Church took a shine to William for several reasons. William swaggered with a salesman's ability to make anyone buy anything but he emanated a slight vulnerability that put to rest any inkling that the tall man with ominous eyes looking down on you could ever do anything to make you distrust him. William had felt entirely lost until he found his way to the Church, and he himself would have believed anything you told him just to make him feel included, to give him an incentive to mask the gash in his heart left by the loss of his family.

This recent trust placed in him gave William the courage to carve his own niche in the Church. He had no idea what that niche would entail, that is until his work led him to counseling troubled souls, and further, when a number of those men suffered from a burden, one with as much weight as he had once endured: their sexuality. When William saw the pattern congeal, he appealed to his superiors to create a community outreach group to target the seemingly increasing numbers. With his powers of persuasion and his own budding feelings of being "saved"— albeit for different reasons—William knew he could talk to these troubled men—some young, some old—so they too could find a resolution within themselves. When William's numbers swelled, requiring several groups a week, his superiors declared success, and William was trusted, even admired, for his dedication.

As the months bled into years and the same faces returned, seemingly unconvinced or carrying on as if saddled with a greater burden than the one with which they entered, William felt the ping of failure prick his skin. He knew he had to retool his plan of attack, for he knew that the end goal—to cure these men—was correct. He believed in his mission but needed to find another, more direct way to achieve success. He would not let anything turn him from what he understood to be his penance for his part in his youngest son's death; he would save hundreds, perhaps thousands, as a penance for failing his own family.

Almost all the men who had sat across from William, sharing their sins, had left a haunting impression on him. Few gave him the impression that talk alone would help them. They needed a stronger hand. *One*, he daringly thought, *stronger than faith*. This conviction, which he believed God had presented to him, compelled him to take a more drastic step. But he could not do it alone, and as he rolled his options around in his head, he felt he could corral some of his counselees into helping him. Some did not seem so receptive to the opportunity, since William could only be vague about the operation, but one man jumped at the chance to take a firm hand in his own destiny. This man, Scott Everett, sat across from William in the warehouse office, assisting William in going through stacks of medical journals.

"Remind me again what we're looking for." Scott's voice carried the tone of a toddler asking how far the family car was from the final destination on a long road-trip.

"Now really, Scott, try to pay attention this time. What I want..." Isaac barged in through the door, late. Scott threw him a stern look. William enjoyed the gentle sibling rivalry that had grown between them. William counted on Scott to work with Isaac much like an older brother, charged with making a man out of his younger brother.

"I'm sorry I'm late, I got held..." There was no need to let Isaac finish the sentence. Paying attention to his excuse would only encourage his behavior.

"That's fine, Isaac. Take a seat so we can all get started." It would be necessary to reprimand Isaac for his tardiness, but to do so in Scott's company would only discourage him. There were some things that were better left done in private. William sat back in his chair and stroked his freshly-dyed brown beard. He thought getting rid of the gray looked more professional. Even though he couldn't do anything about his severely balding scalp.

"Now, you two, here's what I'm looking for. Comb through these pages and create a list of any articles that seem to deal with anything vaguely homosexual in nature, in terms of research. Once we get through the initial phase, I'll fill you in from there. Understood?" They both nodded.

"Isaac, you look confused." It was true; the confusion in his eyes betrayed him. Even when he said he understood, William had been around him long enough to know that in half an hour he would ask for further clarification. William was hoping to avoid that scenario.

That same desperate stare drew William to Isaac in the first place. That painful defeat, resting in his pupils, asking for help. That look, and so many like it, convinced

William that the Church's ways were too slow moving. Whenever he wavered in his resolve to see this project through to success, William only had to have Isaac and his stare to remind him. As a businessman, William understood that one person could not do everything; you needed a team. Although he had the utmost faith in God, he realized that maybe prayer was not as strong as the ways and manners of science, and only by bringing the two together could true success be achieved and maintained. Indeed, maintenance had been the true hurdle. This project would find the bridge to the scientific world that would solve the problem that prayer and faith alone could not.

"So, anything related?"

"Yes, that's it. Anything related. And if you're not sure, write it down anyway. Understood?"

"Yes." Isaac turned to Scott, who shook his head in disappointment, but that would be something Scott would hopefully get out of all of this: patience. *And maybe some compassion,* he thought, *but I will feel success at just patience.*

"And Scott, I almost forgot, where is Matthew?"

"He said he doesn't do paperwork."

Matthew was new to the fold, a friend of Scott. William contemplated whether to be annoyed or not, but quickly decided that every team had its members specifically geared towards certain jobs. Matthew would fulfill his. Perhaps it was best to leave him in the dark on some of the ins and outs of their purpose. He did not seem to want to know too much. Perhaps that was the advantage to having him in their small group. Keeping it small kept it easy to dissolve.

"All right, then, carry on. Let's see how fast we can finish this tedious task."

The hours raced by for William. Every page, every article, every name attached as author presented an opportunity, the answer to which they searched. Compiling his list brought back memories of his sons, seated at the dining room table scribbling out their Christmas list. For a brief moment, he remembered the last time he had stood in the doorway of the den and looked on as his sons wrote away, oblivious to his company, unconscious of the sparkle in their own eyes as they wrote out the things that would bring them joy, the things they wanted more than anything, the things that were like dreams just waiting to be fulfilled, the objects that seemed out of reach, objects that required someone else to deliver them.

William felt the need to set his pencil down for a moment. He looked up across the desk, and Scott and Isaac were fidgeting, cracking their knuckles and trying to massage their hands, as if the task wore on them. Perhaps skimming through the plethora of black type on white paper did not hold the same allure for them. He peered down at their lists, shorter than he had hoped, but they would have to do. Both of them followed instructions well, or so it seemed. William could tell by the scratched out names that both came across repeats and kept a tight list, a narrowed pool from which to draw. Anyone that could publish more than once would not be out to make a name for himself, having already created a foothold in the field. William sought someone who would be so willing to create a name for himself that he would ask few questions.

Scott looked up and locked eyes with William. In another moment, he pushed his chair back and stood up. Scott had either finished or felt that he had wasted enough time at the table. Either way, William would have to be satisfied. Their operation was in its infancy and required a stronger foundation before either Scott or Isaac could be pushed too hard. Scott's talents clearly lay elsewhere, but expanding his horizons in small doses would prove to be a good lesson in the long run. Whether he would ever appreciate remained to be seen. For now, the present proved a more pressing matter. Evaluating Scott's findings, William ascertained that Scott's work proved satisfying enough, at least as far as he could tell. William nodded at Scott, answering the unspoken question, and Scott departed as quickly as he had arrived hours earlier.

Isaac exhaled sharply at Scott's exit, as if he had been holding his breath these past hours, but Isaac abruptly followed suit and took to his feet. William guessed that Isaac had finished some time ago, but neglected to leave for fear of Scott's ridicule for doing a haphazard job. Isaac would have to learn to have more confidence in himself. That would be what he would get out of all of this.

"Is it all right if I go now?" William wondered if Isaac shouldn't stay around to help put the lists together to save on time.

"Have you finished your stack to your satisfaction?" William tried the indirect approach of appealing to Isaac's lack of confidence to see if Isaac's self-confidence would improve. His punishment for lack of assuredness would be to stay around and help. William would put the decision in Isaac's unsuspecting hands.

"Yes, I think so." Isaac handed over his pad of paper, but looked away in the process. A partial improvement.

William gazed over the list. He was unsure of how well Isaac had performed his task, but he decided to let Isaac off the hook. After all, he needed to make sure that this job would be done right. "Enjoy the rest of your day, Isaac." And with that Isaac turned and left the room.

Now all William had to do was sift through the names, whittle down the list to find those who had only published once, then go back through that pool to determine which of those men's works seemed to be the most in line with what he needed. William arrived at the name more quickly than he expected: Dr. Stephen Riles.

Isaac stepped into the late afternoon air. The sun had shifted in the sky; nightfall was not far off. A cool breeze coursed through the buildings and he wondered how much a walk through the city would ease the weight on his mind. William's plan came together quickly. It seemed that before he knew it, his part played out. He could shrug off the incident of a few nights ago, but how much success would he find in the future? That nagging voice in his head caused him to question his role in all of this. William trusted him, placed his judgment in him. For that, he was eternally grateful. But should he take William's word that this was what God wanted? And should he still feel this weight once he started down this path? Was this God's will? Perhaps he had not been a believer long enough to understand how things worked, but he prayed the understanding would present itself soon, for he grew weary of his own tentativeness.

Isaac traipsed through this unfamiliar neighborhood on his way to the subway. He paused when he happened upon the door to a church. He reached out his hand as he climbed the stairs to the door. He felt like he needed a confession to rid himself of the guilt that constrained him. As he stood clutching the brass handle, he couldn't help but remember the time he had reached for another church door and where that had led him.

He felt like had been in this situation before, some years before, in fact. As the fall leaves floated down from the trees, something in the air told Isaac that he needed a change in his life to squelch the hollowness in his conscience. And so he turned down Walnut Street and paused before the imposing, deep red-stained wooden doors of the church. Isaac stood, humbled, before the seemingly impenetrable entrance, questioning whether he should attempt to step across the threshold, or whether he even had a right to. He wished the voice he had been hearing for months would coax him into action, but no murmurings rumbled in his head, a sign he took to mean that he had to make this choice on his own. But fate would not wait for him to make the decision on his own, for someone came to the door and invited him in.

"Oh, hello, young man. What can I do for you?" Isaac turned from trying to see if anyone on the street was watching him. The priest standing in the doorway eyed him curiously and Isaac felt like the priest was judging his skinny frame. People were always judging him with their eyes.

"Oh, I...nothing. I think I made a mistake." But before Isaac could turn, the priest clasped Isaac's hand and stepped down to his level on the street.

"Now, then, son, it doesn't have to be hard. Won't you come inside and talk a while? Maybe we can find out what brought you here." Energy surged through the priest's grasp and Isaac felt compelled to trust his direction, so he followed when the priest led the way into the church.

Walking into the church that day brought a relief, created a safety in which Isaac could unload his anxieties and his fears, all the while crying helplessly in one of those deep-stained wooden pews. The priest refrained from judgment as he held a hand on Isaac's back. For those fleeting moments, Isaac felt a hope that he had never known, as if everything would truly right itself in his world.

The priest did not take Isaac under his wing for long. Isaac soon found himself referred to someone who would "be better able" to help him. He was always being passed off to someone else. He felt a need to turn from the Church that day, feeling like the priest had abandoned him. But that initial sense of safety compelled him to see this through so he went along, enduring the one-on-one sessions that were the best way to start. Apparently, the man Isaac knew as "William" felt it best to keep him sequestered from everyone else. Isaac's disdain for being made to feel different lost out to the promises that touted William's ability to work wonders with people. So Isaac sat, allowing William to lead every counseling session, his advice unchecked and unchallenged.

"You can change, you know, Isaac." There was something encouraging in William's voice, but Isaac had not seen the hope of which William spoke.

"I don't know how. All I know is that I'm tired of hurting, tired of feeling like a freak, tired of not knowing where I belong." Isaac choked the words out, but he wasn't sure they were his own. They were somewhat coached out of him—words he had overheard from other members of the outreach group when he came early for his own sessions so that he could provide what William sought from him. The words seemed to provoke the empathy Isaac needed.

William wrapped his arms around Isaac, pulling him in close, and encouraged him to let it all out. "You belong with us now, Isaac. We will show how you can change."

As he let that memory pass out of his mind, Isaac felt a surge as he recalled how much strength he drew from that promise William promised. *A change is possible.* After that first night out, however, Isaac was not so sure the change would be one he could embrace. Isaac had waited for some tingling while he sat staring blankly at Benny's limp body laid out on the bed, waiting for the pick-up, but nothing came over him, nothing but guilt, and a little regret that maybe he was more lost now than ever. Gone now was that initial euphoria he felt when he first entered the group, the one that succeeded in turning the tide of sexual desires cresting within him. He bonded with these kindred souls as they worked through their misery together. William's new group offered an even better sense of inclusion. Not only was he conquering his demons, he was also using his strength to help others. His life now had purpose but when he entered that bar that night, he felt the old feelings of self loathing return in slow waves. Watching Benny lying on the bed, he caved to the feeling that he might be in need of some stronger encouragement. William's words had not taken hold as strongly as predicted. He wanted to be able to show William, and to a lesser degree the black-hearted Scott, that he was up to the task, that he was willing to do whatever it took to be able to change.

That courage seemed so very far away now. Resolved to enter the church door, spurned on by his conviction and belief that he had made the right decision back then—or at least been made to believe so—Isaac tugged at the door, but could put no force to the grip that held the handle. It would be so much easier if someone came along, noticed his presence and invited him in. Committing to walking into the church on his own involved too many consequences, but reflecting on the courage it had taken to walk into the bar the night before... Isaac felt a sudden surge of gumption and strolled into the church. And as he approached the confessional booths, a priest was stepping out, making eye contact with Isaac.

"Oh, hello, young man. Are you here for confession?"

"Yes, I uh, well, I'm not sure if..." Isaac could feel the priest's pity descending onto him.

"Very well, young man. Please have a seat, and if you would, just wait a moment. I will be right back. I have to use the restroom." The priest continued on his path and Isaac watched, debating whether he should take the offered seat. As the door closed behind the priest, Isaac couldn't help feeling as if he was again being passed over for something more important. That must have been the sign that he was not meant to sit for confession and that he had to work things out on his own, that he needed to be the man William always told him to be. If he was to sit and speak, he would be what Scott constantly ridiculed him for being—weak. No, he must go, leave now. He committed to William, someone he trusted and, right or wrong, he needed to see this through for the flicker of possibility that William would be right. William must know what he was doing, for the Church would never back him otherwise.

Without waiting for the priest to return, Isaac coasted over the hardwood floors and stepped back out into the crisp autumn air with a slightly renewed conviction that he would ask fewer questions and try to roll with whatever William or Scott put in front of him and commanded him to do.

29

Chapter 3

John Thompson enjoyed the relative silence at his desk the best way he could. He pretended the clicking, tapping, and clatter of voices echoing off the water-stained drop ceiling overhead did not exist. Of course, the chomping of ice across his desk, the incessant cracking created by his partner Glenn Baker blended in, but managed to stick out for no other reason than its proximity to him. In a way, John found the noise soothing, like the snoring of a lover sleeping next to you for so long you grew to depend on it for reassurance.

But some sounds stood out for their distinctiveness and only took a moment for John to place them: the sound of heels on linoleum, the sound of more work coming his way.

"Come to bring us some presents, Rachel?" John massaged his forehead and his cigarette dangled from the side of his mouth, the ashes falling onto the page that gave him a subtle pain in reading.

"How'd you know it was me, John?" He pictured her tilting her head in eager anticipation of the sarcasm that was about to spew forth.

"Are you kidding? We could smell you from across the room. Must be that cheap perfume you insist on wearing. Right, Glenn?" John's eyes never left the pages on his desk.

Glenn played with a pen in his hand, clicking the top up and down. "Nah, not me. I couldn't smell ya. But damned if the lights in here didn't get a little dimmer on account of your tits taking up all the room in here." John raised his head and caught Glenn's smirk in appreciation of his own self-proclaimed wit.

Rachel embodied the type of woman John loved being in the company of: strong- willed and able to roll with the punches, waiting for the right moment to retaliate. "You two couldn't do better than that? Must be losing your touch."

John loved the fact that she welcomed the opportunity for men to fawn over her looks, then watch their faces as she shut them down.

Glenn sat up and eased his chair around the edge of his desk. He set his hands on Rachel's elbow. "Ah, come on Rach, you know we love you. We just love it when you come and see us...and show us your tits." He smiled like an adolescent asking for his first kiss. John wondered if that line had ever worked for Glenn. He was sure he had heard something similar pass around him at a gay bar at one time or another. But then again, half the time you didn't have to ask to see it.

Rachel shook her head and looked down at John for some help. She coughed in lieu of speaking.

"You're on your own, Rachel. You know he has a crush on your tits—I mean, on you." John smiled.

Looking down rather pathetically at Glenn, who still tugged gently at her arm, she said, "And your wife married you. Poor, poor woman." She shrugged off Glenn's grasp and walked over to John. She pulled out his chair, and he leaned back. She slouched down, casually tossed the folder on John's desk, then stood perfectly erect, proudly displaying her double-Ds. "Now you two get some of my crap. My boss says that these should go to you because there might be something to these missing persons reports that spell out a little pattern. So, have fun. Less paperwork on my desk and more on yours makes me a happy girl. And Glenn," she pointed to him and he leaned forward with a smirk. She came in close to John and thrust his unsuspecting face into her chest, holding it there. "If you were half the man that this one is, you might get a little piece of this one day."

John struggled out of her grasp without much fanfare, and a few other heads in the office shook at the spectacle at the end of the room. She stood up, satisfied with her performance, and started to walk away.

"Hey, how come the gay guy gets all the fun?" Glenn watched her saunter past their desks and called out "Bye" as she passed. "Hey, I could be... Ah, forget it." He turned back to John, who worked to straighten his thinning hair, and stroked his gray-tinged goatee. "You're a bastard."

John couldn't help feeling that Glenn had issues with his 38" waist on a 5'10" frame and replied, "Oh, get over it. She'd never give anything up to you even if you weren't married."

"Yeah, but a guy can dream, I guess." He paused and eyed the folder that John had just opened. "What'd she bring us, more milk carton stories?" He reached for the coffee getting cold in front of him.

John pulled his chair in close to his desk and thumbed through the report pages while he reached for a fresh cigarette. Flakes of freshly lit tobacco fell onto the pages and picture from the first file, clipped to the outside of the folder. John wiped them away with the side of his hand, without bothering to look to see if he had gotten them all.

Glenn craned his head over the desk. "Careful. I don't think that guy would appreciate you spilling cancer all over his face."

John gave the picture a good blow and scattered whatever flakes might be left. He shot a look at Glenn, then flipped open the folder and ran his finger down the missing person's stat sheet. When he found what he was looking for, he flipped the folder shut. I don't think Mr. Benny Telluride is going to mind much." John scooped up half the stack and handed across the desk. "Here, join the fun."

The past few hours proved to be tedious, but any grunt work on the beginning of a case always yielded more bloodshot eyes than leads. "Got anything yet?" John reached for his cigarettes. He had read somewhere that you would stand a better chance of quitting smoking if you put off smoking to only when you had time to sit and enjoy it. He had always told himself that he'd quit by his 30th birthday, but that date had come and gone. *I'll give myself until 35*, he thought, as he sparked another one up.

"Nah, not too much to go on." Glenn waved the smoke out of the air, away from his face. "Why do you people insist on always having something in your mouth?"

If you swat at a bee, it'll come at you with more force, with more intentions of stinging you. But left alone, it'll buzz around your ear a few times, then fly on to someone else. John rather enjoyed the buzzing of Glenn's comments in his ears.

"I got a few links. Out of the six I have here, four were last seen leaving Woody's, 12th Air or Key West."

"Aren't those some of your clubs?" Glenn asked.

John thought of a way to rib Glenn for knowing the names of some of the lesser-known gay clubs around town, ones he would never admit to being in, for any reason, but abandoned the opportunity. Glenn would claim professional need, on account of being a good cop. Numbers was the only one mildly worth visiting and the only one most people—gay or otherwise—would know offhand.

"Nope, I hate those fucking places." Though seen as a hypocrite by some, John used the bars when he saw no other way to date an interesting guy. Gay Bingo wouldn't cut it. But once he became happily spoken for, he gladly found better uses for his time, though he had to admit that he missed going out once in a while. Those times, however, were farther and farther between.

"No wonder this guy disappeared. If I was him I would have headed south and hoped I could find some money to get my face made over." Glenn had long abandoned compassion in favor of his own sanity. Every cop dealt with the brutality of their job in different ways, and unless you worked law enforcement, you didn't understand the attitude for what it was.

John rolled his eyes and chuckled. He let the phone ring a third time before he answered it. "Thompson."

The officers needed a good five minutes to get enough leverage to free the body from the branches. John couldn't remember the last time he had seen a victim fished out of the water. He felt a slight shutter reverberate through his bowels. He fought the vague percolating memory down from the depths of his subconscious, succeeding before the picture splashed across his vision as he moved his eyes from the water and focused keenly on the tight iridescent shirt that managed to look dry as the water glided off of it.

Before one of the men carrying the gurney could zip up the body bag, John motioned for the photographer. "Get a shot of his face, with his eyes open, for me."

The flash bulb exploded and Glenn strolled back over as John stood up.

"What do you think?" Glenn folded his blank notepad and tucked it in his pocket.

"We'll give it to the coroner to turn over something, but if I had to guess, probably some unfortunate queen OD'd on something." Glenn eyed John curiously. "The shirt he was wearing...had to be gay to wear that." As much as John repelled the gay stereotype, instances like this put it in his mind that sometimes it was justified. What a tragedy it was to have another kid lose himself in the downside of the "gay scene": the drugs. Cases like this reminded him of one of several reasons he held all "those" clubs in disdain; they fed this lifestyle, whether they admitted it or not. But then he had to remind himself that this shit went down just as easy in straight clubs across the city. He felt some kind of pride in pulling Kevin out of that mess on the West Coast. Kevin couldn't appreciate the upside of life, surrounded by all that bullshit.

Watching the ambulance trickle into traffic, John attempted to light his cigarette, with the wind picking up over his shoulder. All around him, the rustling of the red, yellow, and faded brown decorated trees surrendered their leaves to the ground waiting underneath. The image of the guy's eyes hung in the front of his brain. He seemed to recall a similar gaze sitting on his desk in that pile. *What was the connection?* he wondered. He stared off, watching the leaves continue to fall. His eyes floated back to the river and he could feel emotions welling up within him. He tried to think of other things, things he needed to get done, errands, birthdays...and then the date rolled in his head.

In a few months it would be twenty years. Twenty years ago he had frozen and let it happen. His little brother died because he could not act. John stood there, gazing off at the water. When his mind drifted farther down that emotion, he abruptly collected himself and squelched the feelings. Glenn searched around for any other random signs of an altercation, anything that might help. John gazed once again at the falling leaves. A few cascaded down and made subtle ripples on the water's surface and coasted downstream. John felt his eye sockets moisten. *What pretty leaves. What a waste,* he thought, as he turned away from the water and stomped his way to the car, stepping over and through the dead leaves.

Chapter 4

Something, anything. Dr. Riles scanned the paper's headlines. *Nothing.* Not one thing to distract his mind from the hours he had to kill before the meeting he hoped would change his life, and his family's as well. To top it all off, he had let his morning coffee grow cold. He would have to dump it and pour a fresh cup. *Dammit!* Should he just head into campus early? Without security around he would have to try and hunt someone down. He did not want to have to work that hard. Hopefully, this Isaac person could make good on the sketchy details he had provided over the phone. His glasses fogged a bit. He tried to control his exhaling. At last, fruit of his labors: an inquiry into the work outlined in his first published medical article. It came just when he was about to relinquish all hope of establishing a name for himself within the academic community, no longer happy with an article here and presenting a paper there at some conference. Finally, if all went well, he could make a name for himself that would echo beyond a mention in the faculty newsletter. Someday his name would be a headline in the paper. His sweating grip was bleeding the newspaper thin. He eyed the clock and waited for the second hand to pass over the five before he looked away again.

Across the quiet table, Barbara Riles cleared her throat and reached for her steaming cup of chamomile tea. In the 22 years they had been married, he had never seen her touch another flavor. He had almost forgotten she was there, as he watched her fiddle with her pencil over her crossword puzzle. Studying her long curly hair, draped over her white robe, something did not seem right. The chestnut color was new. His circular glasses slipped down his nose as he squinted. "I think I like that new color of yours."

She lifted her eyes without moving her head. "What?" The muscles in her face tightened and a slight red powdered her fair skin.

"Your hair color. I like the change." She had to appreciate the compliment.

"I changed it two weeks ago."

His smile relaxed as an appropriate response eluded him. The color in her cheeks subsided to a subtle pink. She picked the most peculiar things with which to get annoyed. Discouraged by his honest mistake, he felt that now, perhaps, would not be the best time to mention all the potential in store for him with his meeting later in the day. She would probably question him, asking him for details he would not yet know, then smirk while scolding him for getting his hopes up. No, he would keep it to himself. He folded his newspaper in half and looked at his watch. His wife's eyes hadn't left him. They were studying him. 7:25 would not be too early to leave. Traffic might actually delay him, throwing off his projected arrival time on campus. Had she really changed her hair color two weeks ago? *Focus, focus— this afternoon, this afternoon.*

"I must be off, Barbara."

"I'm picking up Tommy today. You'll be home by 7 for dinner?" Her eyes followed him to the door.

"Oh, yes, yes, by 7. I had almost forgotten. Of course I will." As he shut the door behind him, he mentally jotted down "home by 7." Hopefully, something more pressing on campus would not materialize to detain him later than that.

"Come in." Though the incessant clamor that typically existed outside his hallway was pleasantly absent, the knock at the office door grated on him like moving inches a minute along the expressway.

"Dr. Riles?" The shaky voice indicated he would have to explain another term grade. Why students could not learn to accept their shortcomings in his class was beyond him.

"Is this a good time? Perhaps I should come back some other..."

If you are going to the trouble to disturb me... The moment he raised his head he felt like a common idiot for having allowed the appointment to pass out of his mind. Clearly the individual was no student of his, dressed in a suit, although the tie was not tied by someone who had ever worn one before. *Breathe; this is your moment.*

"Hello. Isaac, isn't it?" Half rising from his chair, Dr. Riles extended his hand. "You'll excuse me; my busy work often gets the best of me." As he settled again in his chair, he couldn't help feeling an increased disappointment over Isaac's appearance. Though he staved off a mental picture of who might knock at his door, even so, Isaac would not have been that image. Isaac appeared a little underweight for someone with whom Dr. Riles would be working, for example. Clearly, someone with Isaac's financial backing could afford a

BRAD WINDHAUSER

suit that fit properly in the shoulders and manage a respectable haircut now and then, yet Dr. Riles reminded himself not to be too critical when meeting a person for the first time. The misplaced comment about Barbara's hair that morning had awakened some need for stronger scrutiny.

"So, you said you represent a special interest group with an interest in some of my work?" Better to rip right into the present's wrapping without bothering with the card.

"Yes. We are a small group here in the city, but we have connections throughout the United States." His eyes bounced off every wall, like a student avoiding the question Dr. Riles had just posed.

"Does your organization have a name?" Perhaps square one would be a more comfortable starting point.

Oddly caught off guard, Isaac hesitated through "No, not really. We are a small group working within the Church."

The Church? "I'm sorry. I was under the impression that you represented a special interest group." Dr. Riles' project began to turn brown and wither in his mind.

"Well, yes, we're a special interest group through the Church; however, that doesn't mean that we are not prepared to finance your research." He stammered, like a student presenting on a topic with which he had not properly researched.

Still, the word "finance" breathed new life into the leaves of Dr. Riles' project. "Oh, okay, then we are on the same page so to speak. You do understand my trepidation when you mentioned the Church. The research I'm looking to undertake requires somewhat extensive funding." Dr. Riles pushed his glasses back up onto his face from the tip of his nose. "You mentioned on the phone that your group..." he used his fingers to mimic quotation marks "would have no problem procuring an ample supply of bodies that are not only HIV negative, but also confirmed gay men."

"Yes, that's right." Isaac's anxiety eased out of his jaw.

"You didn't seem too concerned about establishing this, but I must again make it clear that for my research to be given any weight I would have to know that these men were gay while alive. How is it again your organization can guarantee this?" An unacceptable response would send his house of cards crashing down. His chest tightened like a member of a crowd holding his breath, waiting for the pitcher to hurl that fast ball across the plate. Choke up, wait for it.

"Well, you see, we provide an outreach program for gay men who are coming to us for help, to find God and renounce their lifestyle. We cannot, you understand, save everyone in time and, unfortunately, some have chosen to take their lives while wallowing in their own despair. At first we didn't know how best to serve these people, but after learning about other similar organizations around the country with similar tragic cases, we became determined to not have these lives lost in vain. The families shared our convictions and pushed to have their loved ones' bodies donated to science so similar souls would not meet the same end. We believe that if a genetic source can be located, then a procedure could be developed to fix this affliction."

Somewhere in Isaac's rambling rested a legitimizing of the bodies, and that's all that mattered. Whatever their motivation, Dr. Riles wanted to make sure this would all be on the up-and-up to legitimize the findings he knew lay within his reach. As long as Jesus would be writing checks, he would be more than happy to cash them.

"That is why we sought you out."

"Okay, well, this is what I need to have happen at this point: I will need to work with someone on your side. I assume that would be you?" Isaac nodded. "I have to put together a proposal. You understand that since this is a university, there is a review board that would have to approve an undertaking of this kind. When did you foresee putting things into motion?" Dr. Riles pulled out his calendar and thumbed through the days. Christmas break loomed on the horizon. The proposal would have to come together fairly quickly, but the review process would prove time-consuming and tedious as usual. "Hopefully we can have everything together so we can have our proposal before the board in three weeks time. I trust your schedule is flexible?"

Isaac nodded.

"I will need all the proper documentation on the test subjects, complete with death certificates, and a signed waiver by the families of the deceased authorizing the donation, as well as affidavits from them attesting to the lifestyle of the deceased. You have all of this lined up?"

Isaac nodded. Dr. Riles hoped he wasn't wasting his time. "Great. Well, if you would just leave me your phone number..."

Isaac interjected, "Oh, I'll have to get back to you. We're still getting the lines set up. You know the phone company."

At the pinch in his lungs, Dr. Riles paused. His mind painted a picture, and when he wasn't comfortable where that road in his mind may lead—away from his funding—he reminded himself of his own experiences with public utility companies. "Sure." And then a curiosity crossed his mind that he could not prevent from crossing his lips. Isaac was obviously getting a little fidgety and he should just let him go on his way, but he felt compelled to ask, "Isaac, what's the Church's interest in all of this?"

Isaac breathed deeply and Dr. Riles could have sworn he had just asked a Miss America pageant contestant to think about what she would like to change in the world.

"Well, as I said before, Doctor, we believe that discovering the answer for sexuality will spare a number of people from meeting the fate of those that will be delivered to you."

"Oh." At least he had an answer.

"And you, Doctor?" His voice warbled as it delivered the question.

Although Dr. Riles was sure Isaac asked to be polite, Dr. Riles responded with, "No interest. I have no opinion whatsoever. But, to be honest, with all that is going around in the medical community regarding genes, I think it is a crime to not let people come to the decision about their own lives until they have had a chance to live them. What I'm doing would give people an option. Should I feel differently?"

Isaac took the business card Dr. Riles offered and placed it quickly in his pocket. He stood for a moment, unclear as to what constituted a question and what qualified as a rhetorical statement. Dr. Riles would never get his answer from Isaac, and felt defeated in not having his response critiqued; since Isaac had been the first to hear the justification. Dr. Riles desperately wanted some form of feedback so he could fine tune his remark.

Across town, while drudging through the coroner's report, something about the picture of the corpse's face that lay next to his stack of files did not sit right with John. A drug overdose did not fit what his instincts told him. How could this kid—whom he determined to be around 23—have been anesthetized? He closed the report folder and plucked up the picture, studying the eyes that stared back at him blankly. Shifting some of the reports around, he tugged out one of the missing person's reports Rachel had handed him yesterday. He flipped the cover over and compared the picture in his hand to the recent photo offered by the family. There had to be a pattern here—some sense. Did positive HIV status have anything to do with it? John tossed the photo into the folder, closed it and plucked out two different folders, placing them side by side.

Glenn looked over from the brim of his diet soda can. "Getting somewhere with the milk cartons?"

"Maybe. You seen my lighter?"

"Check under the stack. What are you thinking?"

"The only thing these guys have in common is that, well, first, they are all twenty-something to early thirty-something men, last seen at a gay bar, except this one. No one remembers where they last saw him, but they are sure it wasn't at a bar when we asked yesterday. His close acquaintances also didn't appreciate insinuating that he might be gay, either."

"Which he probably was."

"Right. So, they're all gay, presumably, and they were probably all seen at some sort of gay establishment, but where are the bodies?"

Glenn shrugged.

"Then this one turns up. He's got track marks, but no trace of drugs, at least not the recreational kind, but he does turn up HIV positive."

Glenn nodded, which meant he was still with him.

"So what does it mean? What's missing here? Why these guys? And why did we find the one who was HIV positive in the river?" John held his cigarette while he massaged his forehead.

"I don't know, John, but what I do know is that I'm going to go home to my wife, cook her some dinner, and if I'm lucky, get laid before setting my ass in front of the TV with a cold beer. What do you think of that?"

"I think your wife is a lucky woman to have a husband like you."

"If you were smart, you'd knock off early and take care of some business of your own. You know, your wife?" Glenn tugged at his pants and dusted off his jacket. Sitting on his ass more each year was showing in his gut. John thought he should invest in a belt, or at least find clothes that suited his body type. Perhaps he was just putting off thinking about Kevin, who would not mind being referred to as "the wife." Comeback or no? *Decisions, decisions.* He wanted a smoke, bad. "I'm leaving soon too." The truth was all relative.

"Yeah, you do that," and he walked away from their desks. John returned his attention to the case files in front of him, feeling lucky that he had a man at home who did not need constant attention and who understood the importance of John's job.

As typically happened to him, time got away from John as he continued to pour through the stack of reports, indifferent to Glenn's departure hours ago. He leaned back in his chair to stretch out his back. Figuring it was some time around 6:30, he turned to the window only to realize that the sun had set without him. Checking his watch, he was sure 9:17 could not be right but feeling his stomach growl, he was inclined to go along with it. He sipped his cold coffee, then snatched up a cigarette. Alone in the office, he could steal a good smoke without hearing about it. He took a long drag, then yanked up the phone, dialed his home number, and waited to hear Kevin's warm voice.

The first ring.

The second ring. He removed the cigarette from his mouth, exhaled, then ashed in the littered ashtray. *Come on, come on. Pick up the phone. You said you would wait for me.* The third ring. He turned and turned his cigarette, fashioning the ash at the end into a small cone. *You are going to be so pissed at me, aren't you?* The fourth ring. Click. "You have reached 617."

John set the receiver down and massaged the back of his neck with his right hand, took a deep breath, then reached for his cigarette. *You should have been home when you said you were going to be, shouldn't you? I could always meet you two out. Maybe I should just go home and have some flowers waiting for you. Nah, nothing's going to be open now. Ahh, fuck it, you're out having fun with Eric without me. It's better if I'm not there anyway, so you can catch up, isn't it?* He took a long drag from his cigarette and swiveled in his chair, returning attention to his caseload, counting on Kevin not to care about his absence.

All the energy Kevin had bottled up billowed out of him as he swiveled and swerved like a chugging smoke stack to the tune the DJ spun for the packed dance floor. The sweat, the liquor, the men, the music, and his oldest friend in the world...what more could a guy want? The bodies gyrating into one another surged as one, and they offered up their glistening limbs like a congregation raising their arms to receive the Lord's Prayer that exploded from the speakers overhead. For Kevin, it felt good to be out and about for the second time in nine months. Maybe with Eric back in town, Kevin could grow to like the East Coast after all. Maybe all he needed was a good friend.

The beat shifted when the DJ mixed in a new track. Eric stopped moving, as if culminating a strenuous aerobic workout. He let out a loud shriek in a high pitch that failed to garner any sort of reaction. Putting his arm around Kevin, he said, "Come on, Big Girl needs a cocktail. She was over this song last year." The two maneuvered their way to the nearest bar.

"What does a girl have to do to get a drink in this town?" He arched his eyebrows and cocked his head. He was airing out his tight couture shirt while reaching into his designer jeans—bearing a label that Kevin had never heard of—for his wallet.

"Hey, hey, look who's here. If it ain't the queen bitch of them all." The bartender laid out a hand for Eric. Eric met the shake and capped it with a kiss on the bartender's cheek. "And you," pointing to Kevin, "how're you doin'? You lettin' this one get you into trouble?"

Kevin smiled. "Not yet. How are you doing?" What was this guy's name again? They had been introduced the last time they were in.

"Not too bad. You know, my joints are a little sore, but can't complain too much." Both Kevin and Eric looked at him questionably. "You know, it's this medication I'm taking for my skin; it dries out my joints and makes me all sore." He rotated his shoulder and massaged it a bit, trying to evoke some sympathy. Admiring the pecs that tented through the shirt, Kevin promised to devote a good chunk of tomorrow to the gym. Perhaps getting a job as a bartender would force him back into the gym on a regular basis. Suddenly, his pants did not have enough give in the waist, and as he ran his hand across his stomach as subtly as possible, he wondered whether his barely noticeable belly that he wasn't quite used to was protruding too far out. *God damn late night pizza.*

"You're such a fag, Donnie," Eric said, smiling.

"You wish. What'll it be tonight? Sapphire Martini and a Southern and coke?" Both nodded.

"Make sure I see shingles riding on top of that bitch." Eric's voice attracted some attention, and even if he had noticed, he would not have cared. His mannerisms invited attention and garnered scowling looks, as if he were beneath the other gay guys around him, but the spectators would never understand that Eric did it all for attention and he was actually much less of a mess than his behavior indicated.

"Is there any other way to have it?" Donnie went to work on the drinks while Eric looked on with admiration. He valued a good bartender almost as much as he prized a good tailor.

"How does he remember what I drink?" Kevin asked Eric.

"It's his job. That's how he makes all his money, remembering what the bitches drink."

"I still don't understand why a straight guy would work here." While Donnie scooped ice in the glasses, he winked at Kevin.

"Agreed. He just works here 'cause he knows who has the money in this town. It's all about milking the disposable income. Look around. How else are these guys going to spend their money? They can't afford surgery yet." Eric felt proud over only needing a slight peel in his early thirties and not having to put it on layaway.

Donnie placed the drinks on the bar. "15."

Eric handed over a twenty. "Thanks, Donnie."

"You boys have fun tonight."

Taking up his drink, Eric directed, "Let's grab a seat and settle in a bit."

They found a high table off one end of the dance floor. They set their drinks down and made themselves comfortable in their chairs. Eric waved to someone on the dance floor.

"Who's that?"

"Mike." Eric sipped his drink and grimaced, as if his drink was stronger than expected, if that were possible.

"I didn't know he was going to be here tonight." Kevin sipped his drink. Obviously Donnie had made Eric's a touch stronger, for his proved just right. Maybe Donnie did know who had the money and who didn't.

"I told you we were meeting my boy here tonight; he just got here early."

"Who's he dancing with?" Kevin asked as Mike gyrated into view.

"Who cares? He's cute." Admiration had long replaced jealousy in Eric's relationship.

Kevin couldn't help wondering what John would do were he to see Kevin getting cozy with some other guy. He scuttled that scenario, confident that that would never happen anyway. "Doesn't that bother you?" He tried to imagine what it would be like to see John dancing with some stranger, and he wasn't happy with the image.

"Please, you know we are always looking for a third." Eric's voice was as affected and concerned as a cashier at a department store on Black Friday.

"You bitches are crazy."

Eric had read a book touting three-way relationships and bought into the idea immediately. He and Mike had been holding auditions every so often over the course of their two-year relationship, but no one ever made it through probation. They tended to ride their prospects a little too hard. "Seriously, I will hear none of your close-minded attitude tonight."

"I don't think wanting to have a one-on-one relationship is being close-minded."

"That's the breeder in you talking. I mean, really, we spend all this time coming out of the closet, then we spend the rest of our out lives trying to get back into it. Why should we conform to what straight people deem appropriate? It's all about love, girl." Eric followed Mike's every grind. "I just hope he lands this one."

Realizing that he could care less who Eric fucked, Kevin's mind quickly drifted to John, and he felt a surge of longing for his boyfriend. Although watching Eric take in the dance floor, he realized how miserable John would be right now. Clearly, Kevin's night was going better than it would have been had John showed up. Yet, wishing he could unbutton his shirt and tuck it into his waistband, disregarding John's frowning on such a move, it was all he could do to hold back the fact that, present or absent, John seemed to prevent him from being who he was. Maybe it was a good thing that John was pulling yet another one of his long nights at the station. At least he could speak freely with Eric and getting out on the town felt good. Kevin could not recall the last time he and John had cut loose. Maybe what they needed in their life was something like Eric and Mike had. They seemed happy. He couldn't recall hearing about any major drama.

Eric slinked along to the music, perhaps gearing up to slide right in between his boyfriend and their future friend for the night. A ping of sadness flooded through Kevin and while watching Eric act like a cheerleader, he longed for John to cut back on his hours, giving them some time alone like there used to be in their first year together in San Diego. Damn Eric for causing him to drudge up all these feelings. The breath of fresh air Eric provided only stirred up doubt about the future of Kevin's own relationship. When he pursued those emotions a touch further, he pulled back, telling himself he was still adjusting to the East Coast and only needed time. He wished someone would tell him exactly how much time "it" would take, for his patience grew thin. Kevin watched the ice hug the outer rim of the glass as he swirled his drink around.

Eric took another sip from his drink, then raised it up, spilling a little in the process. "Damn! Here, cheers." Their glasses clinked delicately enough not to spill any of Eric's drink. "So now, when are you gonna leave that man of yours?"

Feeling a rehearsed response trickle up in his throat, he replied, "We're not breaking up; you know that."

"You could do so much better than that tragic mess of a man you got." Eric turned to the traffic passing along their path. Kevin looked over and smiled. *Typical.* Eric avoided eye contact in favor of inspecting the action below the belt.

"Girl, don't worry about John. Everything's fine." Convincing enough? Kevin had heard somewhere—perhaps from some positive thinking guru—that the more you say something, the truer it becomes. He had invested too much into his relationship for things to come apart after all he had given up by relocating. Eric was unfairly using everything they had talked about on the phone for the past few months against him. Maybe cutting back on the stream of info would cut down on his ability to become a target.

"Please, he moved your ass out here after treating you like shit back in San Diego under the pretense that he had changed; and now, as always, all he does is work. He doesn't pay attention to you, and more importantly, he doesn't treat you the way you deserve to be. You're my girl, and I hate to see anyone not treat you well." Taking another big drink from his glass, he added, "This cocktail is absolutely fabulous, by the way."

Kevin stared down at his drink, letting Eric's words flow over him, soaking in them in the way he liked to stand in a hot shower for a good ten or fifteen minutes longer than usual when the air in the apartment was too cold. Hearing someone on his side felt far too good to question his perspective. He and John were meant for each other. They were just going through a lull stage. Everything would be fine. He was just depressed from not knowing anyone in the city. Now that Eric was here, everything would work out fine. These thoughts had to be true; for he could not swallow that he had wasted so much of his time—and his heart.

"But seriously, don't worry about that man of yours who could not even bother to show up tonight. If we're lucky, we'll get you someone to take your mind off of him." Eric's smirk spelled drama for Kevin. Kevin would soon learn to get rid of his conscience—or what he had been told that pesky little weight on his shoulders was—as Eric's line often went. Entertaining the idea of cheating on John fell in line with nodding for the mechanic when he said you needed a new air filter when you changed it the last time you were in. Let the wind blow, pick up a scrap of paper or two, then watch it settle.

Eric's ears perked up to the sound of the familiar beat from the speakers overhead. Putting both his hands on Kevin's arm, he said, "Dance floor!" Eric gulped some more of his drink down to make it dance-floor ready before leading the charge through the crowd to Mike and his new friend. Among the mass of bodies, a little circle formed around them, with Kevin just on the outside. He watched, with a slight tinge of admiration, as both Mike and Eric went in for the kill.

On his way to some refuge at the back bar, Kevin's eyes locked onto a nice hunk of a man who was staring back. When that body came trotting over with his water bottle in tow, Kevin found out quickly that he was a little more tipsy than he had thought; the white socks with black shoes confirmed that his judgment was clearly impaired. Walking away would have been too rude and bothering to exchange words would hint at something he couldn't stomach on his best day. As the guy stopped just short of Kevin's personal space, there was something endearing to his geeky-ness. He did seem a little cute, if not a little pathetic.

"Hi."

"How are you?" This was going to be painful. Where was Eric when he needed him?

"Do you come here often?"

This could not seriously be happening to him. "Actually, no. I just stepped away from my boyfriend on the dance floor for a moment." The loud music tended to curtail any long drawn-out conversation and those who had been in the scene long enough knew when to answer questions before they were asked. Kevin hoped "boyfriend" would end the conversation right there and then.

"So what does your boyfriend do?"

Just his luck, a thick headed one. "Well, he's a..."
Kevin felt an arm come across him from behind.

"Hi, honey." The body to the arm circled around and
Kevin was sure his eyes were continuing to fuck with
him. This is the type of thing that never happened to
him when he was single. Encouraged by the alcohol in
his head, he figured, *fuck it, why not?* "Oh, hey, Hon,
this is..." He turned.

"Isaac, my name's Isaac." The geek stiffened up like
a soldier called to attention.

Kevin could not get a finger on what that smirk on
this savior's face meant, but he did seem to be enjoying
this, that much was clear from the way he shook the
hell out of Mr. White Socks' hand. And with that, the
man known as Isaac walked away.

Though the guy yanked his arm away, Kevin wanted
to tell him to leave it for a bit. "You looked like you could
use some bailing out." His soft smile and piercing brown
eyes, even in the dim light, suggested that he might
deserve a drink.

Kevin laughed. "Yeah, thanks."

"I'm Josh." Josh caressed Kevin's palm with his
finger. While their eyes locked, a swell of guilt built in
Kevin's throat. "You're cute."

Kevin blushed. "Thanks. I have a boyfriend."

"Yeah? Where is he?" Josh's confidence oozed from
every pore, while his cologne tantalized Kevin's nose.
Kevin stood in the company of a pro, and not the kind
that asked for money.

"Actually, he's probably at home at this point." *Fuck
it. Why not flirt a little?*

"Too bad for him. Lucky for me."

"What makes that lucky for you?" Might as well let
the fish flap around on the deck before you club it.

"'Cause I get to stand here holding your hand while you tell me how unhappy you are with your boyfriend, and maybe if I am even luckier, I'll be buying you a drink by the end of the night." Kevin let his eyes fall to their joined hands and felt a subtle comfort in seeing their hands resting on top of one another. His automatic pilot kicked in: "I don't think so." Nonetheless, it was good to feel wanted.

"Really?" Josh responded like someone successfully with his foot in the door.

"Yes, really." Kevin took a sip from his drink.

"Then why haven't you asked me to let go of your hand yet?"

It felt so comfortable that he hadn't felt the need to reclaim it. Guilt compelled him to retract his hand and Josh relinquished it willingly.

"You want to dance?" He didn't look like the type that wanted to dance.

Kevin had thought about going back out, but he didn't want company, at least not the kind that tempted him. "Nah." Wait, he walked back here for something.

"You looked like you were having fun out there a little bit ago."

Imagining Josh doing the watching felt somewhat stimulating, instead of the feeling of caution that such an admission should have elicited. Josh could gaze over him anytime. *How I miss being single*, this thought bringing with it a flutter of sadness. "So, do you have a boyfriend?" Kevin felt the need to dig for some personal information.

Josh laughed. "Nope." Kevin wished he heard a "Yes."

"I find it hard to believe that someone like you doesn't have a boyfriend." Kevin wondered if Josh would buy the sincerity.

"I don't believe in them."

"Don't believe in them? How's that?" This was a common response with a whole number of varying responses. He wanted to hear how original Josh's would be.

"Because someone gets hurt in the end. It's inherent in the set-up. I'm not into hurting people."

"Why does someone always have to get hurt?" It's always the single ones who bash relationships.

"That's just how it is. So, did you want to dance, or what?" Josh plunked his empty glass on the bar.

What harm can a dance do? "Sure, why not?" He thought he would get around to asking Josh why he thought he was unhappy in his relationship, or, perhaps how it was that he could tell.

Chapter 5

The stuffing that served as Barbara's comfort zone in the front room, the stuffing packed into the furniture that cradled her posture as she read, made her itch. The more she shifted to find some comfort, the more pockets of annoyance she discovered. But not just on her back; now her seat dipped too much, her position was uncomfortable if she altered her posture even an inch. Now matter how hard she tried, she could not convince her body that this chair had once been comfortable. Maybe the time she devoted to pouring through her novels and her crosswords puzzles in this corner deserved a new seat on which to sit. Perhaps it just felt different without a book in her hand to distract her. Maybe turning on the television or something would distract her from the incessant ticking of the clock over the stove. She had moved herself from hours of sitting at the kitchen table to ignore the uneaten food on the plate at the dinner table, but she hung onto the napkin ring in her hand. She passed it between her fingers as she flirted with the idea of cracking an unfinished book, vetoing that idea when she realized that she would have to do too much catching up to figure out her place in the story. Perhaps she could go upstairs and make some sense of the closet that had been begging for organization for weeks now. But all of these options deprived her of listening to the clock. Something about the ticking seeping under her skin soothed her.

Tommy had waited around after dinner as long as he saw fit, but he changed clothes and headed out the door after kissing her on the forehead. He was only home for a three-day weekend, taking a few days off from school to spend some "quality time" with the family. She wasn't sure what that concept meant anymore. The three of them together—how long had that been a distant reality? A year and a half into his college years and his visits home not only became shorter in time, but also less frequent. Stephen buried himself in his "work." What was left for her? Maintain the memories? Maybe she struggled too hard to hold something together that had long since passed its shelf life.

When the garage door rattled open, she let the napkin ring fall without realizing she had laxed her grip. The diesel engine hummed while it idled. The garage door ratcheted as it descended and the car engine cut off shortly after the door slapped the concrete. The pinging of the "door ajar" sound whispered through the house. That sound used to bring her joy, once told her that they had made it; now it reminded her of how they had lost it. She wished he would hurry up and close the door so she wouldn't have to hear it anymore. Barbara flirted with the thought of getting up and trying to look busy, but she thought it might be interesting to see if he would notice her just sitting in the dark.

Stephen crossed the kitchen and placed his briefcase and jacket on one of the chairs. She eyed him while he stepped into the dark room and felt for the light switch, taking his time, as if he were in a foreign house.

"Oh!" The light clicked on, assaulting Barbara's eyes. "There you are. I didn't see you." She made no movement. "Why didn't you say something?"

"What would you have wanted to hear?" She made her voice as derogatory as she knew how. She forced herself up out of her seat and crossed in front of him. She waited by the kitchen sink for him to apologize.

He turned on his heels. The look of confusion on his face signaled that he was waiting for her anger to subside. With his eyes on the floor, he took a deep breath, like a batter waiting to step back into the batter's box. Tommy had inherited the same annoying coping mannerism. She had hoped her son would inherit only her husband's positive traits.

He brushed his hands to his side, as if taking the hint to speak first. "I think I got it." His face lit up, even through his exhausted eyes.

Her disappointment continued on through the night. She wasn't aware that he was shopping for something. "Got *what*, Stephen?"

"I think I found funding for my project." His enthusiasm filled in the creases around his eyes.

There had been so many projects over the years. Was there a recent one? It had been so long since he had included her in the details of his "work" that she had trouble nailing down one specific project of interest of his.

"The article, Barbara. The article I just had published. The one that I had been putting together for the last ten months."

She thought a moment, and then it hit her. *That gay gene thing in the brain.* That's about as interesting as it was to her. Then she remembered why she had blocked it out. She half-heartedly said, "Congratulations, Stephen. I know you've been working very hard on it." She hoped Stephen felt the sting of her disinterest. At what point would he think of his son? Or her, for that matter?

Barbara turned on the water faucet and hoped her taking to washing the dishes would produce one of two outcomes: Stephen would remember what he missed by not being home or he would retire upstairs, leaving her to stew in her anger a little longer. But Stephen did neither. He scraped his hands along his face and took a few deep breaths. He went to Barbara while the suds bubbled up in the running water.

"This is a huge deal for me...a huge deal for us. I'll be able to go on a sabbatical and devote more time to my work." She knew the apology lurked nowhere in sight.

She knew a sabbatical spelled even less time at home. The joy came from working without the distraction of teaching. Then she remembered the last time he had found himself in this situation. She worried that Stephen was getting ahead of himself. Like so many other times, this money could fall through, leaving him back to square one.

Barbara turned off the faucet and turned away from Stephen and surveyed the house for a second, wondering what it was he might think she was missing. "I never asked you to be some famous researcher, Stephen. I only wanted a husband who was around once in a while—one that is involved in my life, like we used to be." She shook the water off her hands in the sink and grabbed the towel over the sink cabinet door. She plucked her glass of red wine from the counter and strutted into the next room.

Barbara took a seat and turned her head so she could gaze out into the night. *God damn this chair for not being comfortable any longer!* Stephen leaned against the wall that led into the room, staring at her. Words had never been his forte. She could tell that he was waiting for her to keep the conversation going. He always relied on her to keep things going. She did not turn from the darkness. He let the silence stack up for another minute or so before he gave the wall a rest, retrieved his suitcase from the kitchen and stomped upstairs. Barbara wondered if he even remembered that Tommy only had one more day home. Would Stephen be so busy working out his "news" that he would forget? And would she even bother to remind him?

Tommy heard from mutual friends that you could smoke in bars at one time. Of course he had seen it in movies all the time, but by the time his baby face and pathetic ID got him by the doorman at the bars and clubs near campus, on the two occasions he had been brave enough to scope them out, all that could prove to him that anyone ever smoked indoors was the faint smell that lingered, like a boy's junior high locker room. No one in his family had ever smoked so he was not sure about the big deal a cigarette could make to the non-smoker, but that night the gusts of smoke provided a crash course in what he quickly learned to disdain. Hopefully, Mom would not be able to smell the smoke on his clothing. He hoped she would not think it was him who was smoking. Dad would miss it. Weird, how possibly smoking cigarettes would bother her, but the fact that he used a fake ID to get into a bar would probably not faze her. He hoped that spending all his time thinking about the smoking subject would prevent him from thinking about how nervous he was to be in a bar by himself, much less at home, where he had never been out and the chance of running into a random friend was non-existent. No, it was the off chance that he might see someone he knew that actually made him made him feel like he constantly had to pee.

Tommy took up along a wall leading to the dance floor. He was sipping his drink when he noticed some guy casually strolling towards him. The guy's slowed pace meant he was cruising Tommy. When they locked eyes, the guy smiled and moved in closer. He wasn't clean-cut, the type Tommy preferred, but the spiked out blond hair looked kinda cool, plus it was nice to find someone his own height. Everyone in California seemed so tall, and it was nice to be around people who were closer to 5'9" than 6'3". His glass slipped a bit in his grasp at the prospect of carrying on a conversation. Mustering the energy to walk through the door was one thing, but talking was a little more than he bargained for, made the whole thing seem a bit—real. What should he say? A head nod worked in California. Would that work here?

"Hey."

"Hi." Tommy wished he could be so relaxed, like ordering a burger in the drive-thru or something. The guy seemed rather smooth and his conservative dress downplayed the crazy hairstyle.

"You don't remember me, do you?"

"No, I don't think so." He wracked his brain. No way did he know any gay people here.

"Jackson High ring a bell?"

The wheels started turning as images of high school memories flashed. All the close acquaintances had faded away and drifted into more casual ones, the ones he would wave to or see in class or during tennis practice. *Nothing.* "You went there too?"

The guy laughed. "Garrett. Garrett Martin. We weren't really good friends, but I was friends with Daniel Haddon on the tennis team."

Daniel Haddon. Daniel Haddon... That name sounded so familiar, but the face eluded him. *Daniel Haddon.* Why couldn't he place the face? *Think, think...Nope, nothing.*

"You might not have remembered him. Daniel was on the JV team and you were on Varsity."

That's it! Daniel Haddon. That scrawny guy on the JV team, the one with all the freckles and skinny legs. Was I ever friends with him? Just as quickly as the face surfaced, Tommy wiped it out of his mind. Tommy remembered fucking with him all the time, goaded on by the other varsity guys. He wore these prissy little polo shirts all the time. You would ask him what color he wore on any given day and he would respond with a happy, "melon," or, "salmon," as if he was happy someone noticed him. But when the answers only garnered laughter, he lowered his head and scuttled away, testing the tightness of his racquet strings with his palm along some vacant wall. A few other instances came together, but Tommy's guilt held them down. Was it ever too late to say "sorry," for he had not thought about him in a while and the memory made him hate being in his own skin, like sitting around in a wet swimsuit.

Tommy tried to play things off, as if he didn't remember who Garret meant.

"Wow! I never thought I would meet someone from high school who was also gay." Garrett seemed oddly happy to see him.

"Yeah, really weird."

Not as weird, Tommy thought, *as still not being able to place Garret.* He was nowhere in his memories, his face about as absent as the guy trying to get him to fill out yet another credit card application on campus. *Would Garrett hold high school against him? They had a bond now, right? This connection was overriding any negativity in the past, wasn't it?* Garrett's face held no animosity, as if just walking in the door was the excuse for Tommy acting like an ass those few short years ago. Without being able to articulate it, Tommy was experiencing how "coming out" and sharing a piece of what it was to once be a part of the majority and suddenly being cast into the minority. Over the course of their catching up, Tommy relayed all that he had been through, just coming out relatively recently in California, his mom being cool with it, not telling his dad, not sure if he wanted to start dating, and not sure what it was that he did not know but that he needed to find out. With all the questions Tommy had had while living in California, he never had the sense that he could approach any of his friends on that level yet, but standing across from someone whom he had known back in high school, even though there had been no history between them, he felt like he had finally met someone who would understand.

Garrett just smiled and chuckled as Tommy rambled. Tommy thought he was being made fun of. "What?"

"Nothing, nothing...you remind me of me when I came out a couple of years ago. You gotta relax and just go with it, you know, California boy?"

"Yeah, yeah, I guess."

"You know, Tommy, you were one of the most popular people in school."

"Yeah, I guess...well, I don't know..."

"Oh, come on, don't be modest. You know how bad everyone wanted to be your friend."

"I think you're exaggerating." Tommy felt ashamed for everything he had done, even the things he could not remember. How did everyone in high school really see him, or more importantly, remember him? He could really use another drink.

"Yeah, fine, be modest, but I don't know, this is kinda weird, meeting like this. I guess I made it into the 'in' crowd now." Tommy was glad that he didn't have to insinuate a friendship first. He wondered if Daniel was lurking somewhere in the club, and he wondered what he would say to him if they met again. But first things first. He was happy to have a connection to someone. As his dad always said, pursue your first finding and worry about the second later. Certain things would be said another time.

Chapter 6

Through his office window, William looked to the waterfront to occupy his mind, watching the lights of the bridge break up the calm of the night sky. He fiddled with the heavy cross around his neck and prayed his way though his worry about Isaac. The ease with which William detached himself from his work strained under Isaac's presence. Every day, the resurgence of the past called William's mind back to the family he had left behind. Pockets of time over the years had allowed him to successfully distance himself from the truth of their existence, and his failures under their roof. But the dam that held back the floodwaters of his guilt showed cracks. Through those cracks trickled water. As William stared at the drifting snowflakes cascading back and forth on their way down onto the ground, he could not restrain the secluded memory, the memory of that day when his son told him what happened. His oldest son's vivid recounting etched that singular moment of his family's life into his conscience for all eternity, crystallizing just how short, as a father, he had come up.

If only he could forget that day.

"Come on, Johnny, keep up." Danny was in one of his exploring moods as his nimble, light body seemed to float over the inches of snow as he scampered through the maze of trees.

"Danny!" John's chest heaved. "Danny, slow down. Don't run so fast. Dad said to be careful through here." John paused by a tree, reaching out an arm for support as he hunched over for a moment, unable to keep pace. Danny could be such a handful sometimes, and he never listened when he was supposed to.

John made his way into the clearing moments later, and took a deep breath when he saw Danny standing a few trees away from him. Snow covered everything in sight, drowning out all sounds with its soft blanket.

Danny looked over, parted his chapped lips and flashed his gap-ridden tiny-toothed smile. "Come on, Johnny, let's go." Danny was intent on getting to the lake as fast as possible.

"Danny, don't! Dad said it wasn't safe..." John held out a hand, but found himself his own audience. Stopping Danny was like trying to halt a charging lion, fresh from the confines of a cage, on its way to the hunt.

Danny paused at the water's edge waiting for John to get a few steps closer before he ventured onto the frozen surface. He extended his arms for balance on the slippery ice until he got a good twenty feet out onto the lake.

He waved. "Come on, Johnny. It's safe out here." He jumped up and down repeatedly on the cold surface, intent on stomping as firmly as his legs would allow. The rubber galoshes met the ice with a diffused thud each time. "What's gonna happen?"

"Danny, don't mess around," John called out, using his mittened hands as a bullhorn. "The ice could break." Even if it were not safe, he would have to do like his father and carry Danny off the lake.

"Oh, don't be such a worry wart... Nothing's going to happen. It's fun out here." He stomped his feet one more time to prove his point. Dancing around, his arms mimicked a propeller. His breath circled around him in rings over his head.

John gingerly stepped on to the frozen lake, one step at a time, his eyes scanning the surface of the lake, searching for some sign of security. "I don't know about this, Danny. I think we should go back home."

"We're fine. Dad doesn't know what he's talking about. Nothing's going to happen to us. We always come out here during the winter." The ice snapped, halting John's approach just ten feet shy of Danny. Their soft brown eyes locked on one another. Fear found its way up through John's toes, tingled through his legs, and settled in his stomach as the taste of aluminum rested on his tongue.

"Danny, step over here." John extended a hand for safety.

"I'm scared, Johnny..." Danny's eyes clouded and his lips shook. His expression went blank as he gazed down on the ice under his feet. The ice continued to crackle, the makings of a disjointed circle forming around his feet.

John turned to run off the ice. "Danny, run!"

The disjointed line of the shape thickened and formed a circle, the shattering of the ice nearly complete. Danny's entire body shook. His legs would not move. He cried and sniffled.

After running for a brief moment, John turned. He whispered, "Danny..." Danny looked up at his brother as the ice beneath him disintegrated into the icy blue flowing underfoot. John could not make it back to the body that was falling in slow motion.

Danny managed to grab hold of a side of the fragmented circle, trying in vain to clutch for some hope of safety. The cold ice took hold of Danny's little red glove as his hand slipped free, and the rushing water carried his body under the ice and off into nowhere. His red glove lay fastened to the side of the ice. John dropped to his knees in disbelief, gazing at the motionless red glove. He remained on the surface of the ice, staring off, whimpering in a low, muffled, tear-soaked voice. "Help...help..." but there was nothing he could do to help.

Of course the fallout only worsened matters, for all tragedies carry with them some level of insult to injury. The funeral, the well-wishers...every day brought a warm hand to remind William of his deficiency as a father, a reminder of how he had failed his family. From this life he would have to run, to escape out from under, and to be a man again in a different life, one that he would create for himself. But that journey had to begin somewhere, and the beginning began in his mind with the hardwood floor creaking under the weight of his heavy boots. The clearing of his throat echoed in his ears, resounding through the house like a dull bell ringing in an empty church. He resented the fact that his family—his young son as well as his wife—would not raise their voices to prevent him from leaving. Their silence ushered him out the door, expelling him for his failure as both a husband and a parent, but he understood.

That had been his state of mind then—that he was being punished—but when he entered that church for the first time and felt what he had deprived himself of for all of his life, he realized that what had once been punishment was merely a sacrifice on the part of his son, a sacrifice that placed him on the path on which he now stood. A path that included the warehouse and everything he, Isaac and Scott, and yes, perhaps even Matthew, were hoping to accomplish. He wondered, as he stood studying the snow falling over the city, exactly how far along was he on his path, and would he reach his goal soon?

William stepped away from the window and walked out of the office, peering down on the vast empty space of the warehouse floor. The plan coalesced much more quickly than anyone would have predicted, but that had been his gift—to bring together a deal quickly and effectively. While Isaac worked through all of his demons, Scott assisted—albeit indirectly—in small ways to see him succeed, much in the way he had through William's guidance. Now, Scott had embraced this healthy outlet for his anger. What Matthew got out of all of this remained unclear, but no one would argue with his contribution.

These young men were his new family and together they demonstrated William's ability to succeed. Had he brought Isaac and Scott together, an unlikely pair, to represent in some small way how his own sons might have turned out? As much as he did not want to recreate the past, perhaps it was worth creating a reminder of it. He wondered how proud his family would be of him now, if they would understand his purpose and the sacrifices necessary for progress to be achieved. He wondered, in the big picture, what would be said of him in the future. How would his legacy be made and thought of? *They will think I'm a great man someday,* he thought, *a great man indeed.*

William decided to call it a night, having completed all the necessary paperwork that existed for his eyes only. He entered his office, tucked himself into his winter coat and slung his tattered red scarf around his neck. Having that scarf around his neck, the last thing his youngest son had made for him with his little, growing hands, put everything in perspective. It was the most tangible way to remember the sacrifice his youngest son had made so William could see the light. But every time William evened out the scarf around his neck, he couldn't help feeling that even he failed to grasp God's ways at times, feeling like so much light did not need to come shrouded in so much darkness, but then again... However, with everything he had learned in the church, such things were not meant for him to decide. Some things needed to be accepted blindly. Although he never lost his ability to see, William did develop an uncanny ability to close his eyes, and close them tightly, when the time proved appropriate.

Each halfway drunk, laughing and carrying-on guy clung to John as he pushed through the annoying crowd, causing him to remember with all too much clarity why he hated coming out. He failed to understand how making an ass of oneself made for a good time, but there were a lot of traits he didn't share with his community. Still, the guy who smiled while he offered John a light for his cigarette without asking for his name provided a glimmer of hope that not every fag needed a reason to be nice. But that lone example would not be enough to squelch the fear ebbing inside of him that, with Eric now in town for a while, Kevin would slip into his old ways. John shoved that thought to the back of his mind while he stepped to the bar and ordered a beer in the hopes that a quick drink would convince him to try and have a good time, if for no other reason than to show Kevin that he still could, that is if he could locate him among the mass of bodies.

After paying for his beer, John staked out a safe place near the corner of the bar to create a good vantage point from which to scan the crowd and isolate Kevin. Checking the poolroom at this hour would be a waste of time, for Kevin took in his games early—at least he used to—before his drinks had a chance to set in, then slowly found his way to the dance floor. But then Eric's first night might throw off the routine. John wove through the club-goers until he reached the railing so he could take in the massive dance floor. Spotting Kevin among the throngs of shirtless bodies would be a challenge, or at least more effort than he wanted to put forth at that moment. He toyed with the idea of calling it a night, allowing Kevin the opportunity to summarize, in one concise retelling, the evening's uneventful details. But he was trying to make a point, a statement that Glenn's comments prompted: to show Kevin that he could still go out and be social, even if the people around him could care less. *God, how long can I take this music?*

He didn't have to wait long to spy Eric, propping Kevin up. Kevin turned to mumble something, having trouble keeping his eyes fully open, quite evident even from this distance. And as John moved in their direction, he saw a new face moving in to hold up Kevin. John kept up to date on Kevin's acquaintances, so clearly Kevin found someone new to talk to. By the way the new guy's hand ran across Kevin's face, John knew this was not the type of friend he was fond of Kevin having around. John's neck muscles tightened.

Soon he got close enough to reach out and ease the guy's hand off Kevin's chin. John realized that if he killed this guy it might look bad at work. The guy returned the gesture with a long stare, but when he figured out that John wasn't going to be nice about this, he surrendered and wisely removed his arm from Kevin. *Smart move*, John thought. The guy removed himself from the situation without comment. John didn't know what to feel towards Kevin at the moment, but he did know that Kevin's state-of-mind made an intelligent conversation pointless. Plus, seeing Eric and Mike standing right there, he didn't want to create the scene they probably had a strong hand in creating. His anger would have to wait.

Kevin slumped forward. John held him up, stepped a little to the side of Kevin and held up his head. "You okay?"

"Uh-huh." Kevin quickly rested his head back against John's chest.

Something about feeling Kevin's pathetically innocent head resting against his chest, being able to run his hands through his overly gelled hair, caused his anger to subside. In his helpless state, John was thankful he had shown up to be the one to bring Kevin safely home. That was all he ever really wanted, to be able to be the one to bring Kevin safely home. As Kevin let out a slight burp, he worried that Kevin might vomit all over him, but he told himself to stop thinking and just give Kevin this night.

The cool breeze of the night air picked up some strength while the clouds loomed overhead, illuminated by the waning moon. The air, chillier than normal for this time of year, compelled Scott to tighten his coat as he rounded the corner on his way to the bar. He hoped that some fags would not step all over his shoes as he made his rounds to find someone to take back to the warehouse. As he strode, he finally believed, once outside, the weatherman saying how the city would get cold fast and would remain so. The unexpected flurries allowed experts to predict that the city had a cold winter to look forward to. As Scott trotted up the steps of the bar, he was happy to get inside. Isaac didn't need to be the only one having all the fun. Scott was ready to show William how the job could be done right.

Part II

Chapter 7

"Okay, Mr. Thompson, have a seat or enjoy a drink at one of our bars. Your table for four will be ready in fifteen minutes." John nodded. Kevin wondered why they needed four hostesses.

Eric strutted over, his martini held with two fingers at the stem, his other hand in his pants pocket as if he were at a work social function. The venue dictated his behavior, to a point. At least he could whisper about their latest sexual conquests. Kevin hoped their table would hurry up so he could catch up on everything Eric and Mike had been through on their recent month-long excursion in Rio. Although Eric liked a striking long winter coat more than the next queen, he detested the cold and avoided it whenever he could. As a financial analyst, his work was only as far away as his laptop, and he could take that anywhere in the world. With the money he made for his clients, and the fact that his trust fund suggested that he did not have to work anyway, his company gave him a lot of leeway to be out of the office—at least for reasonable amounts of time. But apparently Eric and Mike had not stayed away long enough, for winter held the city captive, making good on the experts' predictions that the city was in for a long one. Upon hearing this news, Kevin became giddy, for he looked forward to his first cold spell the way kids wait for Santa. Kevin had not really ever been through a cold season, being from Southern California. This novelty, however, evaporated the moment the stacked snow refused to melt.

Eric did two half-pirouettes for his outfit, an obvious new addition to his couture collection. He did not bother for a comment, knowing that he looked fabulous, but then again, you can only do so many interesting things with all black.

"Hello, John." Eric extended a hand, then returned his attention to his surroundings. "This town needs more places like this."

After fifteen minutes of lobbing questions back and forth about the weather, movies, and the recent building being put up on Broad Street, the hostess relieved the tension by motioning the four men on with her menus. She sat them at a table butted up against the glass, overlooking the first floor. Kevin looked forward to people-watching almost as much as he anticipated the food people could not stop raving about. Eric cheerily took the seat across from Kevin and gave the crowd a once-over. Eric enjoyed being both an observer and a participant simultaneously.

"I'm feeling a little lightheaded. They don't play around with their cocktail pours." Eric fanned himself for a moment, then sipped his drink.

"Why didn't you get some food at the bar while you waited?" Kevin placed his napkin length-wise across his lap.

"Haven't I taught you anything? It's much more economical to drink on an empty stomach. Plus, you get to kick-start your buzz better." John flipped open his menu and examined the options with a cool quiet.

Kevin could tell he was biting his tongue, resisting the opportunity to comment that Eric need not worry about money, thanks to his trust fund, the type of comment Kevin was sick of hearing John make. At least John was trying to have a good evening by not saying anything. Kevin wished he would try harder.

Mike buried himself in his menu, doing his usual quiet act. Kevin couldn't recall ever really having a conversation with him. He wondered if that was the reason Eric and Mike had always been looking for a third party, because they had run out of things to say to one another.

"What's good here?"

Eric was like a DJ with a shopping spree at a used record store. His two favorite things were eating and drinking, in either order.

"Graham said the edamame raviolis are to die for." Kevin could taste them melting in his mouth, even though he had no idea what edamame, leeks, ginger, and garlic pureed together might taste like.

"Really? She said they were good, huh? Hmm, well, should we start with those?"

"I'll have one. I think you only get three in there, though, so make sure you ask for an extra," John said.

"Have you eaten here before?" *Oh, here it comes! Eric just has to sound so surprised, as if John lacks the taste for a place like this*, Kevin thought.

"Yeah, I wasn't sure we had, but then when we got here I realized that Glenn dragged me here for lunch about a month ago. I had totally forgotten about it when I called for reservations." John set his menu on his bread plate. He wrung his hands in a way that told the world that he needed a cigarette.

Kevin picked at the small gap between his lower front teeth. He wondered what hoops Glenn jumped through to drag John through the doors of this restaurant. John never would have entertained the idea had Kevin proposed it. He made a mental note to find out Glenn's trick. Watching John answer Eric, Kevin felt something drain out of him—that sort of dull sensation that someone with a bad back feels when they stretched the wrong way and know they will be laid up for a few days. Just like that bad back, what had been fragile would never again know the same resilience. Kevin felt the *snap* and he wondered if John had suddenly become a different person, or if he was finally beginning to see the layers of his impression give way to the man John had always been. He could not wait to probe Eric about this revelation, though Eric would probably just roll his eyes and tell Kevin to stop being so dramatic. Perhaps Kevin needed to find a better way to describe what he felt. Perhaps saying this was like seeing "Star Wars" again as an adult and wondering what had changed, because you could swear certain scenes had played differently, more brilliantly, than what the celluloid projected now on the screen.

Kevin let his mind wander to other things. To think further about a shift in his perception of John would mean that he had caught hold of something he would rather let coast on by. He returned his attention to his menu, wondering how his mouth would handle the wasabi on the grilled filet.

Once the server left with their order, Eric started up the conversation again. "So, we went to see *Cabaret* last night."

Ah, something else John avoided seeing. Kevin wondered if a double date with Glenn and his wife might be in order. That could coerce John into going. This thought made Kevin's stomach twinge with a hint of anger and sadness, for although he had no idea whether or not Glenn and Renee would want to go, he felt that Glenn's attendance would nudge John into buying a ticket. "Oh, how was it?"

"Oh, it was cute. Fabulous stage; and the music, fantastic, but you know this city—it can only be so good. Nothing like catching it on Broadway, but they did have the original Annie in it, so it was definitely worth seeing."

"I would have liked to have gone." Kevin missed the theater, or at least the idea of it. Moving East presented so many cultural opportunities that, like everything else lately, didn't seem to pan out.

"Here are your raviolis." The food runner waited while everyone moved their drinks to make room for the plate.

"That was fast." Having worked at restaurants, Kevin wondered how the kitchen cranked out the food so quickly.

"You did order soup, didn't you?" Eric looked at Mike, who nodded. In another moment the server appeared at the table, a plate of silverware in one hand and a steaming bowl of soup in the other. She set the bowl down and pulled out a spoon from the napkin that was folded carefully over the silverware on the plate. She smiled. Strange how she appeared, then disappeared, without a word. Though she clearly made sure they had everything they needed when they needed it, Kevin liked a little interaction with his server.

John grabbed the spoon and fork. He placed the fork under one of the raviolis and moved it near Eric, who lifted his plate so John could serve him. Kevin was impressed that John chose Eric first, but John probably only did it for show.

When Eric was done expressing how much he enjoyed them with a loud "Oh!" even the table behind him knew how good they were. John clenched his jaw and kept his head down. He hated being anywhere near Eric when Eric chose to revert to his club decorum.

Kevin fiddled with his chopsticks and frustrated himself to no end over not being able to get it together. Eric watched him struggle.

"Here, hold the bottom one still between your thumb and index finger and up here with your middle finger." He held his chopsticks out to demonstrate. "Take the other one and hold it firm with the tip of your thumb and index finger and move it like this." Kevin attempted to emulate. His sticks moved awkwardly in his hand. Eric smiled and looked on as Kevin attempted to take another bite. The food made its way to his mouth, but not without some difficulty. Eric snorted a bit as he bit his lip. "See, you're getting it. Just takes some practice." John was making quick work of his food without a word. Halfway through the meal, before he slid a slice of beef to his mouth, Eric dropped, "So, John, what's going on with all these disappearances in the city? There are some rumors going around that there might be some killer stalking us."

Kevin's stomach twisted. John hated talking about work and Kevin questioned whether or not Eric really gave a shit about everyone vanishing into thin air.

Kevin did not know what to think when John answered, "We haven't come up with any concrete suspects, nor are we convinced that there is anything to investigate." He loaded up his fork and drew a breath while he waited for a comment from Eric that never came. "We hear the same rumors that you do." Maybe this proved to be the part of his work he did enjoy discussing. Should Kevin have been the one to ask it, then? Did John think that Kevin did not care about what went on with his cases? All of a sudden, Kevin did not know how to react to the jealous reaction he was feeling towards Eric's comment.

"So there's nothing to all these people just dropping out of town?" Eric recoiled like a person who had been told that the sale had ended hours before arriving at the store.

"Apparently." John's sentences cut to a single word when the time to end the discussion arrived. Perhaps Kevin could read his boyfriend after all. Maybe John used Eric's question as an opportunity to be civil and Kevin just didn't know the sign when he saw it.

"Well, not to be a bitch, but don't you think that as a member of the gay community, and being in a position to do something about the problems we face, that you might be a little concerned about this?" *Eric just had to go there, didn't he?* Kevin thought.

John pulled his napkin from his lap and stood up. "I'll be right back. I gotta use the bathroom."

Eric waited until John reached the bottom of the stairs and out of earshot. "Clearly, he just does not give a shit."

"And you do?" Whether Kevin agreed or not was irrelevant.

Eric glared back, as if Kevin had accused him of the unthinkable. "Yeah, actually I do. My life isn't all labels and liquor."

"It's not?" Funny how the two things that once endeared them to one another proved a point of contention. Kevin was not sure if Eric had outgrown his past or was uncomfortable naming the skin in which he walked.

"Whatever. Make excuses for your boyfriend like you always do, but you know as well as I do that John is just a bitter faggot and should be protecting us. It's queens like him that are the reason our community is in shambles." Eric sat back, flustered, while Kevin took up his drink and gazed down on the people who were seated below. He wondered what his table looked like from the outside.

What looked pretty on the plate weighed heavily in their stomachs, making room for dessert out of the question. When the server dropped off the check, she did so without needing to ask if the check would be split between John and Eric's credit cards equally. When they both fussed with their pens, Eric deliberately paused to survey John's tip, then shook his head as he compensated with his percentage. Now the night held the promise of two equally enjoyable comments: how cheap John was, and what an excessive bitch Eric enjoyed being.

Once they reconvened outside, Eric exclaimed quite emphatically how cold it was.

John's phone rang. "Thompson." Eric rolled his eyes as he leaned into Mike to get some warmth. Mike rested his chin on Eric's head, and that instant picture of tenderness must have been what Eric lived for, for it was genuine effort and effortless all at once. Instead of a warm shoulder in the intolerable cold, Kevin's hands kept his jacket company while the warm hum of the cell phone graced John's ear. The long silence on John's part meant Glenn was on the other end, for John would not tolerate anyone else taking up so much of his time. In another minute, John would hang up and only three from dinner would be at the bar enjoying a cocktail. Kevin buried his hands deeper into his long jacket, deeper than the stitching intended, and distracted himself with the dirty snow caked all over his new shoes. Why did everything that started as fun and beautiful have to turn out so dirty and annoying?

"That was Glenn. I have to go out on a call. Do you want to share a cab with me and I can drop you home or are you heading out with them?" John moved in close to Kevin. John settled into his apologetic tone, as if giving Kevin two wonderful options from which to choose.

"I think I'll go out with them. I just don't feel like going home yet." Kevin lifted his chin up. At least in front of John, he would put on a show for Eric and Mike. John leaned his head down and softly kissed Kevin.

"Okay, I'm gonna catch a cab." John held out his hand for a cab and one pulled right over. "Have fun tonight." He waved to Mike and Eric as he settled into the backseat before the car pulled away.

Kevin edged towards Eric and Mike, who stood wrapped around one another. Eric turned his head around on Mike's chest to look at Kevin. "You okay, girl?"

"Yeah, whatever." He would get over it. What choice did he have?

Eric's cure for everything: "Come on, let's go get a drink."

Perhaps the cold dampened his disdain for John, or perhaps he welcomed the clean exit. In either case, at least the evening would be a little smoother without the tension between those two, but Kevin wanted a better solution than keeping the two separate. Maybe he should just be thankful for the dinner and take what he could get. Kevin did not know which thought would bring more comfort, but he did know he wanted to get out of the snow and cold sooner, rather than later. He silently cursed John's luck, as the three wandered down the street, the distance to the bar not worthy of a cab's time. Plus, standing and waiting for a cab would be more trouble than it was worth, and John seemed to have snagged the only one in sight.

Chapter 8

The prospect of a deep huff of fresh air was not enough to appease Scott's annoyance as he wedged his way through the crowd to the exit. With his duffel bag clutched at his side, some fag in a hurry to get to the bar plowed right into him. As usual, the bitch shrieked a "Damn!" but more important things preoccupied Scott's mind than to tend to someone crying over a little body contact. Any real man would have done something about it, but every time Scott walked into one of these clubs he felt like the only man in the room; instances like this only confirmed his opinion.

"Eric, you okay?" Scott heard one of the other fags squeal as he moved away. Scott half wished he would hear an invite to discuss the matter further. If the little bitch didn't speak up, he deserved being pushed around.

"Yeah, Kevin. Thanks," Scott heard instead. As usual, the gays just let you walk right over them. Though this mentality tended to work in his favor, he could not help but feel completely disgusted being among people who operated under this mentality, which is perhaps the real reason he hated hanging out in the clubs. But on to a more important thing; Scott had a clock to beat—arriving past 11:00 made securing a room at the bathhouse difficult.

Scott turned to his right and walked down the block. When he rounded 18th Street, he slowed in front of a solid steel black door. Studying the crowd that was spilling out onto the sidewalk from the bar across the street, he tugged at the door handle when he felt like he could cross the threshold under that tattered purple awning without being noticed.

At the top of the stairs, Scott stepped toward the "cashier," more securely guarded by the thick Plexiglas than any bank Scott had come to to cash a check.

"Hi." Scott aroused more emotions out of the guy at the gas station.

Scott set down his duffel bag and reached for his wallet. He pulled out a worn membership card and slid it through the metal opening in the window. The cashier checked the number with his computer and smirked as he slid the card back through the window.

"Do you want a room or a locker?"

"Room."

"That'll be $27 for eight hours."

The guy pushed a key, a white towel and Scott's change through the window.

"Your room is on the top floor. Number 216."

As the buzzer sounded, the attendant waited as if the effort of holding the button to the secured door was more than he could stomach. Scott felt that the cashier should show some more respect, but found his mind shifting to other thoughts as he stripped off his boxers and wrapped a towel around himself in his room. Like a player on game day, the hunt was on. There was so much less work involved when you took away the banter and could just bring a guy up to your room. That ease made him more comfortable than being out at the bars, even though the courtship presented less of a contest. There was something to be said for mixing up a challenge with cruising in anonymity. Business ran more smoothly that way. Scott looked at the clock on the wall and wondered how much time he should devote to this night as he checked to make sure he had locked the door behind him on his way out.

The pungent sweat, humidity and steam gave the building an odor all its own. Scott could not decide if this distinct smell of man offended or aroused him. Down the hall, he cruised past the "gym," where the "weightlifters" used the wall-length mirror to watch themselves get blowjobs. Though a little disgusted, when Scott shifted his towel it seemed that both heads of his didn't agree. He moved on.

As he strolled on, he wondered about the god-knows-how-many-diseases brushed against his bare feet as he strolled along the worn carpet. Scott paused to take in the three men who were keeping each other company in the recessed Jacuzzi. They invited Scott to join with a nod of the head. Though the idea appealed for a moment, he figured he better make a full lap before courting anyone. Besides, three may be biting off a little too much.

Scott rounded the corner to the right, past the showers and steam room. The two doors were all fogged up and he thought he would continue on before checking in there. Next to that, he peered into the cramped sauna room through the small window to see three guys pretzeled around one another on the wooden benches. Though they clearly had other things on their minds than being watched, Scott was sure they would enjoy the attention. Moving on, he came to the bottom of the stairs. Some guys passed by, carrying their towels in their hands, and advertising their goods. Scott shifted himself under his towel. *Can't they at least have the fucking decency to keep their fucking cocks under wraps?*

At the top of the stairs he strolled past the various open doors, with guys lying on beds, doing to themselves what they hoped someone might care to do to them. He took at least a moment watching each one before walking on. He paused when he came to the maid service turning a room over. Scott leaned against the doorjamb.. Though having to wear latex gloves probably qualified as some form of hazard pay, the scowl on Matt's face as he ripped the soiled linens from the mattress dashed all hopes of him having some fun with the situation. *Oh, well, they could not all enjoy their part in the grand scheme.*

When Matt realized he had company, he motioned for Scott to keep moving, but when he looked up and saw that his efforts went unheeded, Scott's face did little to change his mood. He waved Scott inside and told him to close the door behind him. Scott wondered just how many guys tested the waters with Matt, questioning whether the same number walked away rejected. Having a mission conveniently trumped all declarations of one's sexuality, and Matt could play without the burden of a conscience if he wanted to. Scott embraced the freedom to speak his mind, to chide Matt a bit, for while on the job, what could Matt really say back to a customer? But Scott let the opportunity pass, for now.

"What room are you in?"

"216."

"Let me know when you leave. I'll clean up after you and give you a call later."

Perhaps forgetting the thought that had entered his conscience mere moments before, with his lips parted, Scott felt the urge to say something, to ask how things were coming along...

Matt must have known what would follow, but he let the semen oozing through his gloved hands speak for him. Scott admired his dedication. He wished everyone would work as hard, and without complaint. Scott left Matt to his chore.

Scott passed the lockers and looked into the smoking lounge. No prospects there and he would not tolerate smoke to find one. He backtracked and found a comfy spot along the wall in the back of the movie room. Six guys spread themselves out on one of four carpeted tiers of steps, one eye watching the porn flashing on the screen, the other watching the guy next to or in front of him have his way with himself. They seemed to have their own little games of feigning interest long enough to have their watcher look away. Any other man would have snatched what he was after, but these guys had to complicate things.

After a few more laps did not provide any sure bets, Scott caved to the slight ping of interest aroused from the clean-cut guy doing his duty of holding up the wall. Since he had been there for the last few laps, Scott knew he had found his mark. Besides, he was cute enough. Good looks proved to be somewhat of a badge of honor with Scott, though Matt could not care less and Isaac could not afford to be picky. Since William did not bother with the details, Scott would have to keep the pride to himself.

"Hey." Scott believed speaking first in a care-free, could-give-a-shit manner gave you control in any dialogue.

"Hey." He seemed nice enough.

"You got a room here?" Cutting to the chase simplified things for everyone involved.

"Nope. You?"

"Yeah, wanna come up?" For a moment, Scott felt the challenge of it all slipping away. He hesitated for a moment, wavering on whether to throw the fish back into the water for one more worthy of an actual contest, but his schedule ticked away in the back of his mind. He did not feel like forking over another $27 if he passed his 8-hour limit. They could be such sticklers on policy here. Scott led the way up the stairs.

Closing the door to his room, Scott turned on the television, feeling the sudden need for distraction. The guy made himself comfortable on the bed; moments later he worked on pulling Scott in close. As Scott turned his eyes from the guy's face, he wondered how long it took this guy to shave his entire body, but when he ran an obligatory hand down the guy's stomach, he appreciated the smooth feeling on his fingers, like running your hand across a freshly planed piece of wood.

Looking to try something new, Scott positioned himself behind the guy. Too much eye contact etched an unpleasant memory. Scott kissed the guy's back, adding his tongue to act like he was into it. As he moved his mouth all over the body in his arms, he began to enjoy the task at hand, applauding his increased ability to mask his contempt. Things rolled along faster when he pretended he enjoyed it, so Scott found himself going with the flow. He ran his hands along the guy's hips and over his perked nipples. Bored with working from behind, he came around and started on the front. The body contorted ever so slightly with Scott's affection, and as he leaned in, he could feel his affection reciprocated by what was poking into his towel. Scott ran his hand down the guy's thigh, then back up and into the towel.

"That feels good," the guy said.

Scott removed his hand immediately, the voice snapping him back into reality. Something always forced him out of his headspace. Like when he was in high school and the guy he jerked off, just to see what it was like, began telling everyone about it as if it were no big deal. If only Scott could find that guy now, grown into a man worthy of his bashing. Had he only been stronger as a kid he could have done something about it then. What could do about the past now? He had all the strength he needed now.

"Why did you stop?" The guy was as relaxed as a guy would be at a picnic.

"I just..." Scott's heartbeat galloped. The thought of this fucking fag being able to hear it mortified him. Scott reached back and turned off the light.

"Lights off, huh? S'okay. Either way."

Scott waited and waited for some resistance to make this worth his time. This ease made him resent this guy even more.

Using the bed for support, Scott propped himself up, allowing the guy to scoot further down. He yielded control as the guy worked overtime to bring their lips together. He resisted, but the guy won out. Scott's entire body tensed up as their lips met, but he eased a bit when the guy worked in his tongue and used his hands to pull Scott over him. He reached down and undid his towel, his erection tenting up through the threadbare cloth. Scott could feel the throbbing erection press against him and his towel, down his hip. He closed his eyes and concentrated on feeling the guy's lips pressed against his. The guy's skin vibrated with Scott's hand moving up and down his back. When the fingers gravitated towards his ass, Scott broke away from the lip lock and rested his head on the guy's chest. His heartbeat thumped like a soothing drumbeat. He could rest like that all night, calmed and comforted with every beat.

"If you're feeling a little awkward, I can split." He sounded a little annoyed. *So much for understanding. Where was the famous compassion gays were said to have?*

Scott pulled away and looked at the guy, the whites of his eyes eerily visible even in the dark. He pictured the soft brown eyes he had met on the stairs and the ones he had turned off the lights to avoid. *Such inviting eyes.* Eyes that should not have beckoned to him. Eyes that should not have brought him in here. Scott reached down into his bag and pulled out a needle.

"Searching for some toys? Whatever." The guy just had to keep talking. Scott thrust his hand over the mouth that had to keep flapping open and shoved the head into the pillow. As he rammed the needle into the chest, he dropped the plunger down with one firm stroke.

The body squirmed and he could feel the teeth digging into his palm, but they were not going to break skin. He wished he had a pair of Matthew's gloves. *Oh well, next time,* he thought. *Must find a way to get the gloves on for next time.*

Scott put his full weight on the body and leaned in with his shoulder as he fished for a vein to show a slowed pulse. When he pulled back, gazing down at the sedated form staring up at the ceiling, he couldn't help feeling a little envious. So at peace... Scott rested his head on the body's chest, searching to locate the beat that had been soaring only moments before. He ran his hand along the barely stubbled chest and circled one of the nipples with two fingers. He drew figure eights around the needle that was still protruding from the chest. He was somewhat proud that he had managed to pull it off by not only remaining nameless, but not bothering to find out the other fellow's name as well. It was better when they didn't have a name. They were easier to forget that way.

As he dressed, Scott lingered in his triumph about his ability to pile another body onto the cause without any snags. He did have to hurry, though. Matt needed ample time to escort the body out of the room unnoticed—though he couldn't see that being a problem—and over to the warehouse before this guy emerged from his stupor. Although Scott could not have asked for a better teammate in all of this, the ease of this outing left him feeling a bit cold. He needed to discover a way to take the level up a notch. He drifted back to the image of the three guys in the hot tub and wondered when he would muster the gumption to take on a whole team. That would be the true mark of success; but "everything in good time," as William always said, yet Scott also wondered if changing up the hours would yield a better product. They constantly moved around to avoid creating a pattern and every virgin voyage presented its anxieties. Oh well, he'd go back to the warehouse and wait for the call.

On his way out, Scott felt obliged to circle through again to see who he had spared. He could not help feeling a sense of pride in how his "criminal" past, something jail briefly dampened, came in handier everyday. Knowing that someone like William—though Scott started to feel like his boss needed to step things up—found his talents as just that—talents. He had learned how to channel his skills at stealing cars and entering houses into something more useful. Scott finally found a job in life that encouraged his talents instead of locking him up for them. So much the better that those same talents were helping him fight his sexual desires.

When he passed the sauna, he stopped to admire the face that was smiling back at him. He resisted the urge to enter when he remembered that the stench would linger in his clothes long after he left. *Oh well*, he thought, *as he smiled back at the anonymous face, you don't know what you are missing. Next time*, he thought, as he strode down the hall, silently thanking bathhouses for their existence. He could not have asked for a better venue in which to execute his plan, or William's, or whoever's plan it had become.

Chapter 9

Pulling away from the scene—carrying a fresh body—the ambulance kicked up dust around John and Glenn, its red lights disappearing into the night.

John lit a cigarette, speaking between puffs. "How many's that now?"

"Five." Glenn waved the smoke out of his face. John thought for a few seconds about apologizing, but he took another drag instead. How many times would he need to apologize for something for which he wasn't sorry?

"So, assuming this is another from our stack of missing persons, and given the same set of marks on his arm, there'll be the same dope in his system. Where does that leave us?"

"Thirsty?" Glenn avoided pushing further than he needed to when his job intruded on his personal time. "You're not planning on heading back to the office, are you? We can file this report in the morning." Since his night with Renee was shot the moment he got the call to come down to the crime scene, Glenn figured he might as well make something out of the evening.

"Yeah, I won't bother with it 'til tomorrow." John reached into his coat pocket and fished out his phone. The image of the recently deceased they had retrieved from the water kept flashing in his mind. Something about the soft brown eyes, close-cropped hair and obvious gay attire reminded him of Kevin and how his own evening had been cut short.

"Checkin' in?"

"Gonna try home, see if Kevin stayed out." Holding down the '1', he lowered his head into his collar to shelter his neck from the wind. On the third ring he looked at Glenn. "What'd you have in mind?"

"Grab a beer up in the northeast somewhere."

When the machine clicked on after the fourth ring, John closed his phone. No need to try the cell phone. Kevin would probably not answer anyway if he was out and about. Against the prospect of sitting home in an empty apartment waiting for Kevin to come home god-knows-when wearing a lingering smell of alcohol, he weighed traipsing up to the northeast to huddle with a bunch of people whose only knowledge of culture ended at the Martha Stewart aisle of K-mart. God, he was starting to sound like a judgmental bitch. "Yeah, a beer sounds good." He should have paid more thought to how he embraced any excuse to ditch his boyfriend for the evening, but that thought quickly faded to his growing need for a beverage. Some things, like his report, were better left for another day.

In a neighborhood bar close to Glenn's house about ten minutes outside of town, they snagged a table by one of the few windows in the place. Though he realized he would never go out of his way to frequent a place like this—with its outdated jukebox, neon-lit beer signs and drinks specials scrawled out on a cheesy "special' paper tacked to the side of the bar—he did feel at ease with its homeyness, the type of bar he never could find during his stint in San Diego. Sure, he may not have looked that hard, but some things should not be that hard to find. Yet here he had found one, even if he lived where it would be difficult to appreciate it again any time soon. Maybe he and Kevin could retreat from the city someday, get away from the pulse. He pictured Kevin's face reacting to the suggestion that they follow Glenn and Renee's lead and settle down, buy a place within their means. When he felt his mood dip at this image, John surveyed the bar, refreshed by the fact that he was able to walk into a place where heads did not turn to size up every new person. "Quaint," the place felt. When Glenn asked what John thought of the place, John told himself to leave "quaint" out of the opinion.

A waitress appeared as if out of nowhere, smacking her gum as she took their order. Perhaps if they had been somewhere else, somewhere downtown maybe, John would have found her gum annoying. Here, however, he found it endearing, much like when he sat across from Kevin for the first time, watching him fiddle with his knife and fork, commenting on how they should do a better job of running their silverware through the dishwasher. Who cares about silverware? But something in the way Kevin cared about standards, even in that little restaurant bar they decided on that night along the strip in Pacific Beach, endeared Kevin to him right away. He looked so cute, squirming in his hard wooden booth. Kevin never could sit still for too long. You could tell that he did not frequent bars in this part of town often for, as he would later discover, Kevin felt ill at ease without another gay guy in sight. "You seem a little jumpy," John remarked. Though partly genuine concern, he liked to bring dates here; it was part of his screening process. He needed someone who could live

103

a life outside the "community." Throughout their life in San Diego, they frequented that spot once every few weeks, though that seemed to be the only spot—the only "breeder bar"—Kevin entered. Apparently, the one he worked at was enough for him to want to avoid others on his downtime. At least they had that spot. As John scratched away the top layer of his coaster, he realized that they had yet to find a similar spot here in town. *Hmm...*

As the waitress dropped off their beers, Lynyrd Skynard kicked on the jukebox. *God, I can't remember the last time I was out and heard guitar chords cranking through the speakers instead of a droning bass line that only gave me a headache.* As he took up the frosted pint glass, he turned his attention to the crowd, finding a tinge of enjoyment while watching people talk to one another and with the bartender. *How nice it was to not have to notice the type of underwear he wore.* Why could this not be his life? He had been so buried in his job since coming back to the East Coast that he had not given himself time to unwind and do something he truly missed, like just relaxing and having a beer over a nice conversation.

Glenn watched the waitress walk away and John wondered how the ass assessment would come out. John chuckled at watching Glenn's obvious admiration. "Renee get pissed when you do that?" John took out his pack of cigarettes and placed them on the table.

"Are you kidding? She'd have my nuts if I did that in front of her. It's not like for you people; you just get to look and do whatever you want. Us straight married guys don't get to have fun." Glenn needed a new act with some new material.

"You've seen too many bad movies if you think I have it so good." John lit a cigarette.

"Yeah, yeah, all you guys say that it's so hard. Come on, two guys, what's so hard about that? Nothing to explain." Glenn shifted so his back was to the wall and threw his legs across the bench. For a moment John pictured this to be Glenn's relaxed mode, the same pose he slumped in for his Sunday football games: perched on the couch, a beer in one hand, the remote in the other.

"It's more work than you think. At least for us, anyway." John took a big sip and savored the flavor in his mouth before he allowed it to glide down his throat. He sat back, rolled up his sleeves and took a long drag from his cigarette. Uttering what had weighed on him for some many months sent his mind racing. *We are never supposed to be like this,* he thought, wondering, if asked how he would define "this."

Some two years earlier, they almost did not happen. John relented on trying out the Internet to meet people, but he would only let it work for him if he could control where he would meet whoever sat at the desk on the other end of the connection, assuming he owned a desk. John transferred to the SDPD office to experience the sunshine, but something never sat right with him on the left coast. He could not relate to the people who told him to relax at least once a day. Plus, you could not smoke in bars or restaurants, or any building, for that matter. Even walking down the street with a cigarette in his hand invited looks and mumbled comments that no one was bold enough to utter to his face. *Too much sunshine for these people,* he concluded.

Kevin eased John's discontent, at least for a while. His loneliness subsiding—though he did not realize how alone he was until he had settled in with Kevin—he started to enjoy his time in the sun. He soon chalked his bitter impression to the lack of physical contact, finding it easy to lose himself in the softness of Kevin's baby browns. But everyone else John ran into had some "painful" experience masquerading as a bunch of drama bullshit concocted to pass the time. Yet something in Kevin's eyes told John they had never seen too much pain, not *real* pain or hurt, anyway. John would see to it that those eyes never changed. Thus John had a project: someone in need of rescuing from the scene.

That need became apparent when they frequented their spot, watching Kevin fumble with the darts. Though John threw a few games to keep Kevin hopeful, Kevin improved on his own. That was Kevin; he just needed a little hope. He could pick up anything; he just had never been exposed to life outside the "community." So, maybe believing that, John felt like he had not given the San Diego scene a fair shake. With a few drinks, John felt more at ease when he trekked around with Kevin to the various bars and clubs where he seemed to know everybody. This popularity made John feel a bit awkward, questioning at what price this familiarity came his way. For the first six months he never questioned, not wanting to kill what they were building.

When the first year crept up on them, routine killed the spark they had been fanning. The walks on the beach and bonfires at night during those first summer months felt more like a vacation, with John yearning to get back to reality. He had spent enough time with the department, enough time to know that he wanted to return home, and with a few favors called in from his chief, he would be able to do that. Kevin was not enough of a reason to stay anymore, and that became more apparent with each passing day. Did they really have that much in common? John's work defined him— saving, helping people; Kevin worked to be able to afford a social life that allowed him to be the man he wanted to be. John needed someone who wanted more out of life. Feeling like he had happened upon the best San Diego had to offer, John told himself he would never find what he needed in a town distracted by its 300 days of sunshine.

What could not fit in his SUV, John sold off or donated even if he had not finished paying MasterCard for it. As long as it was gone, that was all that mattered. When it came time to head out, he went to say goodbye to Kevin, but Kevin refused to see him. Over the phone, Kevin "enlightened" John to the fact that he was running. Kevin didn't understand why he had to go, and John did not know how to explain it, not sure Kevin would even grasp his motives, since he had never had to leave his comfort zone except to have a drink. John left without seeing him one last time.

When three months had passed, Kevin sent an email; a few weeks after that, he was on a plane to visit; a couple months following, he was packing some belongings and selling off the rest of his stuff. "A fresh start," he would tell his friends. They all told him he was crazy for chasing John, but John did not care. All he cared about was seeing whether yanking Kevin out of la-la-land would help him shed all those bullshit tendencies he had. Here, he would not need the scene, John told himself, and for the most part, he was happy with the result. When Kevin adjusted better than expected, getting the feel of a neighborhood he did not need a car for, learning to appreciate corner stores and different seasons, John knew he had chosen a partner wisely. Sure, they had problems—Kevin still enjoyed leaving his shoes everywhere in the apartment to ensure John would trip all the time and he cluttered up every surface he could with his magazines—but it was nothing time wouldn't fix. But time dragged its feet and John wondered if what they needed was another level to reach for, though what level that was John did not know.

"You still with me, partner?"

"Huh?" John did not recognize the song playing. How long had he spaced out? "Sorry, dazed a bit. Lot on my mind."

"S'okay. So, as I was getting at, how hard could it be, you know, with two guys?" Glenn picked at his coaster's corner.

Rolling his eyes, wishing for the ease Glenn believed existed, John said, "Seriously, we go through the same shit you and Renee go through, I'm sure." John wished there was something to hold his stare through his beer besides the thin ring of foam and the dwindling bubbles, trying to convince himself, now that talking about this, even in vague terms, put him in touch with thoughts he never acknowledged were still there.

"I'm going to go out on a limb here, partner, and assume that Kevin doesn't let you not stick it to him cause he's bleeding like a fucking fish for a couple of days." Glenn sure knew how to paint a picture. For a minute, John debated whether to throw in that blood was not always the least of his worries, but skirted the obvious chance for "trophy for best example" of crudity.

"If that's your biggest complaint with your wife, you're pretty damn lucky." John sat back against the support of his bench and massaged the stubble on his chin. He thought he had shaved it all before they had left for dinner. He picked at some of the food in between his teeth and the quality of the meal returned to his tongue. Then he thought how good it felt to have Kevin lean into him before John had to take the call. For that brief moment he felt a little sorry that he had not chosen to meet back up with Kevin, Eric and Mike.

"Oh come on. You know I'm just shittin' you. We have our fights, but over all we're a pretty easy-goin' couple. Renee doesn't bitch too much and I get enough sex, so life's pretty good. Nice and simple—quiet time when I need it, nice brunch on Sundays and a couple beers in between." His sincerity glowed through his relaxed face. Maybe that was what leaving the station at a reasonable hour did for a person. "And how about you? You guys that happy?"

"What makes you think we wouldn't be?" John shifted in his seat. The wood caused him subtle discomfort with every passing moment. He gulped his beer and reached for his pack of cigarettes.

"Oh, you know, you spend all your time on the job and you always look a little haggard, like you haven't been getting a lot of sleep. Usually means something isn't sitting with you, that's all." Glenn studied John's face.

John could not get comfortable on the damned bench for the life of him. Perhaps the ebbing circles under his eyes appeared more visible in this setting. For the first moment in the evening, John wished for poorer lighting.

"We're fine, it's just...I don't know, sometimes I wonder how happy he is, but we'll see...he's still getting used to being here." Not even John bought the words trickling out of his mouth. Would Glenn understand the frustration Eric's presence added to their plate? Eric's mixture of amusement and temptation for Kevin left John questioning whether to write off his emotions to jealousy or caution. He resented having to feel either option, so he declined to venture into the topic with his partner. Some lines need not be crossed, but he could not deny the tolerance for Eric waning within his stomach, knowing—believing—that every night out,

Eric dropped endless yarns of advice into Kevin's ear, words designed to convince Kevin that his life would be better with someone else, that John was nothing more than a stick in the mud. Eric, left comfortable with his trust fund—no matter how "hard" he worked at his "job"—could never appreciate a job that warranted so much dedication, so much time away from the things you love. John had to believe that Kevin understood. But then, what was John doing sitting with Glenn, having a beer when he should be back out with his boyfriend?

John allowed the need to think pass out of his mind as he swallowed the last of his beer. Glenn flagged down the waitress and ordered another round without being asked. Maybe Glenn knew him better than he thought. John worried how much of his anxiety with Kevin spelled out across his face. Or maybe he merely over-analyzed everything. Maybe his exhaustion had caught up to him, or perhaps the particulars of this case added stress—perhaps the comment Eric made at dinner— maybe he *should* take more of an interest.

As he ran through the files in his head, John found himself returning to pictures of Kevin and their time together. Interspersed, he saw their drifting, he envisioned the tattering and unraveling of their relationship and what he would have to go through should they split, should he have a life, a future without Kevin. It wasn't a picture he was prepared for. In California it had been easy to pass off the failure of the relationship, but here, back home on the East Coast, there were no excuses. He could feel Kevin slipping away, even if he would only admit it to himself when he was trying to drift off to sleep. Even John could not ignore the signs. Maybe they just weren't meant for each other. Maybe he was failing as a boyfriend, not doing what he set out to do all those months ago, to protect Kevin so he could become the person he deserved to be.

Across the table, Glenn's eyes remained fixed on John, a note of concern there never before present. John needed to snap out of it. A good sleep would get him up to speed on everything, but for the remainder of the evening, he would suck down a few more beers and ask about the latest basketball game. If he could kill enough time, John hoped that when eventually he found his way home, whatever time it was, Kevin would already be in bed, signaling the change John felt he needed to see. If he wasn't, well, John would decide how to handle that situation then.

As the waitress brought over the second round of drinks, John's gaze fell on Glenn's gold wedding ring as his hand grabbed for a beer. John wondered if he would ever know the feeling of wearing one of those. *What comfort that commitment must bring.* For a fleeting instant, John wondered if a wedding ring was the answer to not only his problem, but also every other gay couple who was willing to work things out. When you have nothing to hope for, no future to work towards, why wouldn't you throw in the towel? When you reach as far as you are going to go, maybe you just do what you do when you cannot solve a case; you file it away and move on to another one.

Chapter 10

Although Kevin had lost track of exactly the number of drinks he had downed, he did remember that each one was emptied to drown out the minutes since John had chosen work over him. As Eric held court at the end of the bar, Kevin huddled close to the semi-circle, watching guys breeze in, gab for a while, then vanish to another part of the club, allowing room for more guests to pay their respects. A few looked his way, making eye contact, only to roll their eyes when Eric mentioned that Kevin had a boyfriend. Although once out of earshot, Eric would pull one aside—he had done it so many times—and impart that a rayon stretch shirt stood a better chance in a hot water cycle than their relationship. This night, however, Kevin could give a shit. Each drink brought him closer to wishing someone—anyone—would bend his ear and shower him, if only briefly, with a moment's happiness.

But a moment would be all he could tempt. He would be damned if he would cave and destroy the time he had put in with John. He had worked too hard to maintain the faithfulness he never understood before. Avoiding the impulse to cheat proved more important than the relationship. Kevin needed to know he could stay true to his relationship. Nothing would break his longest streak, yet every time John passed on going out or left him for a call, Kevin felt his will power wane. Even though he was unhappy, he felt responsible, his feet firmly on the ground; although a tad shaky, he was learning to stand in one place. He was experiencing the opposite of motion sickness. He needed another drink.

Moving East had provided a clean break, and he was going to see this relationship through. As he swirled the lonely ice in his glass, having sucked dry all that gave the ice purpose, he could not squelch the aching feeling that maybe the relationship had gone as far as possible. Maybe the time had come to move on; yet he did not want to acknowledge that maybe things just do not work, and some dramatic event does not need to be the catalyst. He tried to think of the saying that involved beating a dead horse, but he could not, for his head tingled and his hearing had dulled a bit.

Kevin thanked the bartender, who shoved a drink in front of him without being asked, apparently the benefits of having one of Eric's open tabs. With one strong sip, his sinuses perked up at the whiff of alcohol. *Damn!* He looked up to see not one person notice and share in the reaction. John would have noticed. He jabbed at the ice in his glass, trying to get them to melt a bit, to water down the drink a little, though, of course, he would have to work a touch harder. Ice did not cooperate on command. He felt John's kiss on his forehead from earlier. Perhaps he should appreciate having a life separate from his partner, enjoy the freedom that everyone who had a boyfriend said they missed so much. But those same people were the ones that could only tolerate being single for a day, resuming the finding-someone hunt whenever the sun rose. Damn queens could never make up their minds. One minute Martha Stewart was the shit, the next she was on their shit list, only to change again and say "I knew I still liked Martha when she strolled out of prison wearing a knitted poncho." He blinked a few times to focus out the blur in his eyes.

"Girl, stop thinking about him. We are out to have a good time." Eric's hand squeezed Kevin's shoulder and pulled him in closer. "Let's disco." Eric gulped down his drink and set the glass on the bar. When Eric started to groove to the dance floor's beat, Kevin could tell by some people's glares that they wished he would take his party elsewhere. Donnie, stacking glasses behind the bar, smiled. *Had he been the one who put a drink in front of me moments ago?* He held out two fingers to his forehead like a salute. Eric waved back, grooving to the music as he turned every which way.

"It's time. Finish that bitch up and let's hit the floor." Staring down at his drink, Kevin decided he had nothing better to do, so he downed it, stifling a burp as he set the glass down on the bar, then obediently followed Eric as they snaked through the crowd and created a space for themselves on the dance floor.

After a few good turns, Kevin fussed his way to the bathroom. The liquor numbed him in all the right places, but when he stumbled out of the stall and into a soft obstacle, he knew he might have had a little too much too fast.

"Need a little help?"

"Huh? No, I'm fine. Sorry, I..." Kevin's tongue failed him when his eyes met Josh's. The name came so quickly to his mind, as if they had been old friends.

"Don't mention it, Kevin."

Kevin felt himself falling forward and a little to the left, yet his body did not move, his arms rubber in Josh's grip. He could stay there all night, just staring up into those green eyes that pulsed and wiggled a little.

"You look a little soused."

Kevin could hear through the Southern Comfort an unspoken invitation for something. Remembering that John was not in the building, he felt a little better about spending another few moments in Josh's safe company. Why did this guy's name come right to him? They had only talked before, right?

Kevin felt a cool breeze on his neck. Through a little break in his mind's fog he felt a little firmness return to his arms, legs. "I'm fine. I didn't mean to bump into you; sorry about that." Looking down at Josh's firm fingers wrapped around his biceps, he felt a little heat course through his arms. Nice finger—nice, long fingers. *Water. I need some water.*

"I didn't want you to fall."

"I'll be all right." A weird sensation hit Kevin when Josh let go of him, like shuddering from the cold once you kill the shower's hot water.

"Well, what now?"

"Sorry?" Josh spoke with that air of familiarity that Kevin knew he should resent, but felt all right coasting with.

"Can I buy you a drink?"

Kevin's eyes evened out the dullness in the fringes of his vision. *Water, water,* he thought, *and then, perhaps, another drink.* As Josh turned to lead the way out of the bathroom, Kevin wished he had been the one to go first, stumbling once again to have Josh save him before he hit the floor. He was sure Josh would have caught him.

"Cheers." They clinked glasses. Josh stared down at Kevin from the rim of his glass and Kevin took a sip, looking absently out onto the dance floor. Were Eric and Mike in there somewhere? Did he want them to find him, offer some approving look? Or did he want to hide, afraid of what they might think of him for sharing a drink—it was just a drink, right? What's the harm in a drink—with Josh? Since Eric and Mike had probably already relocated to the couches upstairs, they would find Kevin when they were done with whomever they were entertaining.

"So, Kevin, still got that boyfriend who doesn't make you happy?"

The tone stung a bit, like a shot injected a bit abruptly without warning. "Yes...I mean, no. Wait." He paused, took another sip, and turned towards Josh. How much had they talked about? Or was he just testing the waters? Kevin's head cleared a bit. "What makes you think I am so unhappy?" That sounded far more defensive than he intended. "Yes, I still have a boyfriend, No, I am not unhappy." He felt like Josh read every signal he was giving off and would not pay attention to a word he said. *Damn! How could this guy read me so well without knowing a thing about me?*

"Okay, fine, you're happy, whatever. So, where is he?"

Kevin felt the cracks in his confidence crackle. "Working late." What time was it anyway? Was John still working?

"Ahh, working late. He seems to do a lot of that."

"His work calls for it." Kevin's tone softened and hollowed out. He took another sip from his drink and wished John would swoop in and save him from the interrogation. Then he would have an easy way out of this conversation without being rude. Of course he did not really want to leave it unless he was made to. That bothered him too, but not enough to do something about it.

"Does his work allow time for you?" Through the door Kevin had propped open, Josh waltzed right in.

"What about you? Why are you single?" Kevin didn't want to talk about John anymore. He had had enough of these chats with Eric and they were growing bothersome. He was tired of everyone telling him how he felt. What happened to his buzz?

"Maybe I like being single."

Yeah, so did everyone, Kevin thought. *Then they get a boyfriend and enjoy being tied down.* "Yeah, whatever. Nobody likes being single." Kevin felt like he was getting out from under Josh.

"Really? Maybe you should try it sometime."

"I like coming home to someone, thank you."

"But is he there when you come home, or just asleep?"

Kevin paused. He didn't have a response that Josh would understand. No one understood. He was tired of having to justify his relationship. Why did everyone make it his mission to tell him how unhappy he was all the time?

Josh kneaded his fingers into Kevin's shoulders. Kevin looked over and didn't remember telling Josh to touch him.

Josh took his hand away. "Sorry. I couldn't resist. I won't do it again."

"Okay." Kevin felt some color come into his face and his pulse quicken. There was his buzz again.

Josh put his hand back and rubbed some more. "You can tell me to stop, you know."

"Stop." Kevin felt obligated to tell him to stop, but he didn't want to.

Josh moved his hand away for a moment, then put it back and resumed massaging. "You didn't mean that."

"I didn't?" Kevin's morals conducted his mouth from autopilot.

"Nope." Josh moved a little closer to Kevin and rubbed harder.

The tension in Kevin's neck and shoulder muscles relaxed. His heart rate continued to escalate. *Why am I enjoying this?* He lifted his glass to his mouth, stared Josh in the eyes, then turned around and faced the dance floor. He hoped that no one was watching, feeling at any minute that John would walk through the door and see him, and he wasn't sure if that would be a good thing or a bad one. Maybe if John saw that he could receive some attention from another guy he would be more inclined to show him some affection. A little jealousy could go a long way.

Josh moved his hand to the other side and closed the gap between them. He rested his head on Kevin's left shoulder while his hand worked out the knots in his right. He whispered softly in his ear while Kevin tried to drain his drink slowly. "You know, we could go somewhere." Josh rubbed harder, sending the sweet pain coursing down Kevin's back, forcing Kevin to feel his wonderful hands, shutting his mouth before a reflex could spit out an answer.

Kevin finished his drink and held the empty glass down below his waist. He lowered his head, getting lost in the moment. He closed his eyes and hated himself for letting Josh touch him and despised himself for liking it. Josh moved his hand around Kevin's shoulder, then back across the nape of his neck and up the back of his skull, just below his hairline. Josh used two fingers to manipulate the skin and caress the small hairs in circles. Kevin's whole head tingled. He had never been touched like this before, and it felt damn good.

He turned his head to see who was watching them, and when he caught Donnie's eyes, he felt guilty, as if he had been caught. Kevin could see the disappointment in Donnie's eyes. When Donnie walked away to help another customer, Kevin felt like he had let someone down. Was Donnie passing judgment on Kevin for having a boyfriend and having a random guy caress him in this way? He had to distance himself so he could at least say he was only humoring this guy to be polite, to run up to Donnie and say that he wasn't doing anything wrong.

When Kevin's eyes roamed around the bar, he felt the weight of a thousand eyes judging him. Even though the eyes might be skipping right over him, their indifference spoke volumes. He had felt the same eyes in San Diego, but those eyes saw a much different picture. He and Josh would soon take the next step—steps out the door to somewhere private. Kevin knew the ending to that story, and he remembered in a breath of stale air the emotions that trailed far behind. The moment's euphoria crested into a sea of regret at not being able to fully enjoy the sex for what it was—for a relationship waited a phone call away—and he could not stay single enough to explore his libido fully. A catch-22 forever plagued his desires. Why could John not touch him this way?

Under Josh's confident hands, Kevin's whole body loosened. The alcohol whispered confidence, secrecy into Kevin's ears. This felt good. Too good. *Don't let yourself get excited over this.* Each thrust of thumbs brought Kevin closer to bachelorhood. Josh whispered, "Did you want to go somewhere more private?" He softly kissed Kevin's ear a few times. As Josh's soft lips caressed the tiny hairs on Kevin's ear lobe, something within him struggled, like a swimmer fighting to reach the surface. Like that swimmer, he felt a strong push and his surface was breached, letting his lungs expand, taking in a breath of sobriety for one important moment. Kevin yanked himself away from Josh, who looked perplexed. In one instant, Kevin longed to hear John's voice, and when Josh's traveled to his heart, he snapped to his senses.

Kevin stretched his neck out a little and rolled his shoulders. "I'm sorry, I really can't. I have to go." Kevin turned without waiting for a response and pushed his way through the crowd.

Eric stabilized Kevin at the door. Kevin avoided eye contact. He wanted to go home, and he mumbled so. Everything came in and out of focus.

"Girl, you okay?" Kevin could have sworn Eric's voice resonated with concern.

Kevin shook his head.

"You looked like you were having a good time to me." And then there came the obligatory sarcasm. Eric didn't understand; he would never understand.

"I just want to go home. That's all." With Kevin on the verge of tears, Eric released him. Whether to an empty apartment or a sleeping John, Kevin needed the predictability of those four walls.

"Okay, I'll come with you. You don't look like you should be going alone. I'll retrieve our coats and tell Mike I need to leave. You'll be fine for a few minutes."

Ten minutes later, they met back up at the door.

"Sorry to keep you waiting. Had to do some damage control. Some troll named Isaac was talking Mike's ear off. Now, let's catch a cab."

The cab pulled away from the curb with Eric and Kevin in the back. *Water. I need water, and fast*, Kevin thought

"So, what's the big deal?" Eric asked. "You looked like someone died back there."

"You wouldn't understand." Explaining the situation might force Kevin to examine the situation more closely, and he longed to put it as far behind him as the club. He didn't want to feel or think anymore that night. Besides, he wanted to avoid one of Eric's lectures on how you never pass up a potentially good thing.

"Wouldn't I? Christ, I would have let that man give me a massage any day." And as usual, the advice came served with a hint of jealousy.

Kevin sat silent, replaying the sensation of having Josh's hands on him and how good it felt.

"Guilt? You feel guilty over that?" The high pitch had left his voice.

Kevin stayed silent. He didn't know what he felt.

Eric took the hint and kept quiet during the rest of the ride home. When the cab pulled up outside of Kevin's door, Eric made no move to get out. "Oh no, honey, I'm going back to the bar. But seriously, you gonna be okay?"

Kevin had his leg outside the cab. "Yeah, sure."

"You really love that man of yours, don't you?"

Feeling his throat close up, he eked out, "Yes."

Eric could not take his eyes off Kevin's face. Perhaps he was testing Kevin's sincerity. The cab driver coughed. Kevin felt his night gurgling in his stomach. Water, he needed some water...and maybe a safe toilet to lean over. When Kevin didn't turn away, Eric rolled his eyes and shook his head while he smirked. "Well, all right then. Go take a cold shower. I'm off to have me some more cocktails."

Kevin felt like he had just passed some test, but more importantly, he cursed how slow the elevator sludged up to his floor, making him wait too long to get through the front door, in front of which he struggled with his keys, unable to find which key he needed, cursing every damn drink he had had in order. The second time through his key ring he found the one he needed and finally got it into the lock, which turned right over for him.

Chapter 11

Across the table, Barbara sat engrossed in her crossword puzzle. The aroma of her orange tea floated between them, compelling Dr. Riles to wonder whether a cup of his own might temper the slight scratchiness building in his throat, but with a mug resting in front of him already, he settled for his cold coffee, a film of cream floating on the top. He took a sip and glanced out the window. The weather report promised snow soon and the dense cloud cover did a lot to support that forecast. He made a mental note to take his overcoat. He thought of asking if Barbara had any pressing errands to run, checking to see if she might not put them off so as not to get caught out in the snow without those new snow tires he had seen advertised the other day. It seemed like only yesterday she had nagged him to replace all four of them on the car. He searched his memory. *No, it could not have been that long ago. A full year?* Maybe he should stop home on his break from classes and make sure the driveway was properly salted. *No, she would best be able to assess her own situation for the day.*

When the last drop of coffee finished irritating the sore spot in his throat, Dr. Riles folded his newspaper in half; a headline caught his eye: Pattern Emerging with

Missing Gays. He skimmed the first few paragraphs. Bodies found...Last seen...Details sketchy, but community...Police aren't sure... Dr. Riles could not find the details that drew his curiosity, so he deemed it best to examine the full article later, at the office. He tossed the paper down, harder than he intended to, compelling Barbara to glance up over her reading glasses, pencil in hand. He pushed his chair back from the table and slung his coat over his forearm. He walked over to Barbara, who leaned back in her chair. He put his arm around her and kissed her forehead, anticipating what was likely going through her head. "Don't worry, I haven't forgotten about tomorrow night." He pulled himself away and walked to the door. *Make yourself a note about tomorrow night,* he reinforced, as he ran through options about where he should stop and pick up an anniversary gift.

"And how old do you take him to be?" Dr. Riles asked his assistant. This young man, Chuck, had been of wonderful use to him, who could not help but take pride in helping fashion a fine addition to the future medical field.

"Early twenties? Maybe mid-twenties?"

Dr. Riles devised this guessing game of theirs to hone Chuck's observation skills. Chuck slightly bemoaned the game—like Tommy complaining of an early curfew when he had lived at home—but Chuck knew when to humor and when to challenge, showing off one of several qualities Dr. Riles admired in his assistant.

"Not bad, but of course the young ones are always easier to detect. But no matter." In the few months they had been working together, preparing for this important study, Dr. Riles solidified the bond with Chuck that had begun when Chuck first took his seminar last year. Even though Tommy and Dr. Riles had shared so much early on, his little boy took a left turn somewhere, and he questioned whether he should follow or not; for this reason, he sought out other people in which to invest his time. His son no longer needed him, he felt. How he wished everything in life could be so easily ascertained as accepting what his son needed in life. Returning his attention to the task at hand, he said, "Now, let's walk through this again. What are we after here?"

"We are going to sample a portion of the subject's hypothalamus tissue, measuring the levels of interstitial nuclei of the anterior hypothalamus."

Chuck sounded a touch annoyed at being made to recite on command, but repetition is the best way to learn something, Dr. Riles knew. "Excellent. And how are we validating this subject?" Dr. Riles made sure he paced his questions so as to allow Chuck to deliver the answers with confidence and ease.

"The brain is in healthy condition, and valuable, given that it is from a documented homosexual."

"And what will our findings point to?" Swing for the lobbed pitch, Dr. Riles coached.

Chuck laughed at this one. He knew the end of the warm-up drill lay just ahead. "To quote Levay, 'Gay men simply don't have the brain cells to be attracted to women.'"

"Good, good. Now, put on your goggles and let's get cutting."

Dr. Riles moved his tool tray closer to the cadaver. Chuck followed directions to a tee, fanning out Dr. Riles' chosen tools in the exact order instructed: a small rotary saw, some different gauged calipers, a scalpel, a pair of forceps, and a long shaving blade. Positioning himself at the head of the cadaver, Dr. Riles leaned over the body and pulled it back on the table, allowing the head to jut out just enough to promote a clean cut.

He looked around for a moment. "Would you bring me the metal bowl up in that cabinet over there?" Chuck obliged. Without being asked, Chuck went to the sink and filled it up part way with some hot water. "Good, good. Thank you." He had been well trained.

Dr. Riles rinsed his left hand and the straight razor in the bowl. He slicked back the hair on the head of the cadaver with his moist rubber-gloved hand, then proceeded to shave off the hair, guiding the razor along the scalp with his right hand. Thanks to his measured strokes, the hair fell to the ground in clumps. "This is much easier when you're not worrying about actually hurting someone. Funny how the absence of pain not only instills confidence, but provides license as well." At every other turn, Dr. Riles dipped the razor back into the bowl and moistened his hand.

"Yes, something like that, Dr. Riles," Chuck responded.

The head shone clean within a few minutes and Dr. Riles set the razor in the bowl as he stood up.

"Now, hand me my mask, if you would. Have you gotten used to the smell yet, Chuck?" The color seemed to have left Chuck's face for a moment. His tolerance would come with time. Perhaps his turn to work the saw had arrived. Some issues must be forced, for few will move forward of their own volition in sensitive matters.

Dr. Riles fixed his mask over his mouth, adjusted it for comfort, then set the goggles over his eyes. He tightened up the straps at the back of his neck and pulled on them a bit so they were not too tight, not too loose.

He took a black felt pen in his right hand, then leaned over the head, dabbing the pen along the forehead and down the temple, circling around the back of the skull, then back up to the other temple. "I'm doing this for your benefit, Chuck. Once you have done this enough times you will not need a guide, but you should always start out with one." Once he capped the pen, he holstered it in his coat pocket. He gave his sketch a once-over, then sat back down on the stool. He took up the saw in one hand and, caving to his superstition, gave the power button a few presses. He scooted his stool to one side of the head, then judged for the best angle. He pulled out a sliding tray from under the table to catch the stray fluid.

Like a spectator waiting for the pitcher to put the ball in play, Chuck watched. His time had come.

Changing the way the saw rested in his hand, Dr. Riles handed the butt end towards Chuck. "Here you are, Chuck. Time to take you to the next step."

After hesitating for a brief moment, Chuck snatched up the tool. He leaned into his uncertainty, clearly feeding off his adrenaline. Dr. Riles recalled his first cut, the first chance he had to dig for answers under his own discretion. Chuck assumed Dr. Riles' seat as Dr. Riles stepped to one side. Chuck made a few motions up and down with the saw, planning out his cut.

He had it almost right, so Dr. Riles placed his hand over Chuck's and corrected the angle. "You almost had it, but pull back slightly so as not to disturb the tissue, yet firm enough to penetrate the bone." Sometimes the skin proved a little tougher than imagined, so finding the right amount of pressure called for the right amount of experience to gauge.

As his hand guided Chuck's hand, an odd memory surfaced, a moment when Dr. Riles' hand rested atop

Tommy's, helping his son guide a wooden baseball bat through a swing. Of course Tommy, even at nine years old, possessed a better understanding of what the motion should look like, but he attempted as best he could, as any father would do. When Tommy had his first at-bat turn and hit nothing but air in the batter's box, he vowed to leave his son's athletic training to other, more qualified individuals. He was a better spectator in these things, unable to bring his joy for the game into practice. But that scene had nothing to do with his situation with Chuck. The two men sat in Dr. Riles' arena and Dr. Riles did not waver in his abilities here.

With that brief wavering passed, Dr. Riles offered his words of encouragement. "Make the cut, Chuck, just like I showed you."

Chuck set the saw to the side of the head and powered up the instrument. He ran the blade up along the temple and across the forehead. He stood to maneuver the tool down the other side and around the back of the head. A slow start gave way to an expert cut. A miniscule amount of fluid trickled down into the tray. Underneath his mask, Dr. Riles hummed softly as Chuck worked his way around the head. Dr. Riles felt that teacher rush—observing a student *get* it.

The distinct odor of burning bone, the scent of a mouthful of cavities being filled at one time in a dentist's chair, gave neither Dr. Riles nor Chuck pause. Both had smelled it so often it failed to move either man. During his first time cutting, Dr. Riles had had to give some extra torque to an especially problematic piece of bone. While he dug in and gritted his teeth, his teacher assured him that this was just like carving a turkey. Chuck stepped back to examine his handiwork.

Content with his cut, he set the saw down on the tray. He leaned over and placed both of his hands on the bald dome. He eased the top of the skull off, but stopped halfway through.

"Ah, that can be a little bit of a pain. Sometimes you have to twist it a little," Dr. Riles assured. With some effort, the casing pulled away and Chuck set the useless mold on the tray, in the bowl, with the water washing right over it.

Finding the thin plastic covering over the brain intact pleased Dr. Riles. Chuck provided just the right amount of force after all. "Don't be shy, Chuck. Lightly dig your nails into the membrane and pull it back to expose the brain fully.

Dr. Riles fielded criticism for replicating out-dated research, namely Simon Levay's, yet he understood the way no other researcher did that the answer rested in Levay's findings; someone just needed to dig a little deeper to give them more validity. Healthy brains, ones not infected with HIV or AIDS, provided that missing variable that hampered Levay's results. Dr. Riles knew that if he could duplicate the findings with healthy brains, then he could build on them. Finding *the* genes would still be a ways off, and recently, researchers in the field had speculated that perhaps the gene didn't exist. Yet these murmurs left Dr. Riles unfazed, for he had faith in Levay's work. The brain had to be the key in dictating a person's sexuality. If both Levay and Dr. Riles proved correct, then the future of medicine offered many possibilities, with Dr. Riles standing at the forefront of that discovery—for once.

"Now, Chuck, give me a hand with this, will you?" Dr. Riles took up his scalpel and began to trim away to what mattered to him. Chuck could have handled the task, but Dr. Riles needed to be sure he handled the important parts personally. Let failure fall on their shoulders—if they were incorrect—but success would land squarely at his feet alone. Teaching would have to be a secondary concern at some point.

Once Chuck finished the cleanup and departed for the day, Dr. Riles retreated to his office for some leisure time. Notes needed to be made and data needed to be compiled. Once the busy work set in, his mind drifted, traipsing through his thoughts to Chuck's future and whether he was doing a good job of molding Chuck. Still further, he drifted to what he might cover during the next morning's lecture—something he had covered so many times it almost did not warrant any brushing up at all; thank God he only had the one class to teach that term—then he came back to Chuck in the lab, as his pencil dashed out their cadaver's relevant numbers, triggering the image of helping Chuck with the saw. Then Thomas entered his mind, and his pencil stopped moving.

Was he the father he had always thought he had been? Was he good enough? He set the pencil down and turned his attention to the family photo on his desk. He pictured Thomas, now grown and making a man of himself in college, and then he pictured his wife, just like she had been that same morning, growing gracefully more luminous every year. There in her robe, with her crossword puzzle, she commanded his attention, him conjecturing how her mind worked as her eyes fluttered while reading those crossword clues she so loved, her requisite cup of tea right next to her, keeping her company. How much they had been through in their life together, for their...how many years had it been?

Wait, tomorrow, our anniversary...dinner, gift; must make a note, a note. He jerked his briefcase, throwing it onto the desk, and went to pull out his appointment book. Surely he would have the number of years written there, to remind him.

But instead of seeing his appointment book, his eyes met the folded morning's paper. With trepidation, he extracted the paper, suddenly overcome and more in tune with why it had caught his attention at the kitchen table. His eyes immediately raced to the article in question: "Pattern Emerging with Missing Gays."

As he combed through the details of the article, Dr. Riles felt no anxiety of this case being linked to his work in any way, shape, or form; however, it did occur to him that this might reflect negatively on his project. He was so close; to suffer some backlash, some setback would be devastating. Of course the public would probably never link his work to this case. By the time his results went public, this case would surely be solved. But something tugged at his conscience and he didn't know why. Perhaps the article's front-page location proved the most significant, for he could not recall any issue involving gays making the front page before, but maybe if the press got wind of his work they would condemn his work for promoting hatred to homosexuals. Maybe some young reporter, trying to make a name for himself would sacrifice his work just to achieve some notoriety within the field. Some people would do anything to climb the career ladder, no matter the cost to the individuals targeted.

Then he wondered what would transpire should members of his own family happen upon this article. Would they draw some meaningless connection to his study? Would they think he had a hand in it? Or if not a direct hand, would they think that his work perpetuated this kind of hatred and bigotry? And what if, under the most remote set of circumstances, one of his bodies just happened to be tied to these disappearances? What would that do to not only his life, but his career as well?

His head started to swell under the impractical inquiries coursing through his brain. He quickly realized that he had not received enough rest the night before and the exhaustion weighed heavily on his shoulders. He needed to put some distance between his work and the random acts carried out throughout society. Before he shut his thoughts down for the day, he wondered how he could get across to the public that he was only out to help people. Perhaps an essay-question prompt for his class? Then he reminded himself that morals did not fall within his discipline. He had to stop worrying so much. However, he made a mental note to keep one eye trained towards the news to see if anything else surfaced. In the meantime, important work called out for his attention. Before he got up from his chair, however, he could not, for the life of him, recall why exactly he had gone into his briefcase in the first place.

Chapter 12

"You seen this yet?"

"What?" From over his coffee mug, John scanned the paper in Glenn's hand.

"Pattern Emerging with Missing Gays."

"When'd you learn to read?" John had no interest in addressing the obvious.

"Well, you know, I have been listening to those cassettes."

"What does it say?"

"Oh, you know, gay this, gay that. Your people are all up in arms as to how we're not doing anything. Typical fun stuff that'll do wonders for the department's public perception."

If John did not know better, he could have sworn he saw a bit of concern on Glenn's face. "Chief seen it yet?" At the moment, that is what mattered most.

"Not sure yet, but when he does, he's going to want to know why you haven't come up with anything yet. Right or wrong, he put you on this case for a reason."

John got up and reached for his coat. "Yeah, I know. Put the paper on my desk when you're done with it. I'll read it when I get back." John checked his watch and ignored the part about him being responsible, completely overlooking Glenn's part in *their* case. "I gotta get going."

"Where you off to? I thought we were grabbing a late lunch." Although he was feeling a little catty that morning, John fought the urge to tell Glenn it looked like he should skip lunch for fear of adding to the gut hanging over his trousers.

"I got a bartender to talk to. Maybe by the time I get back, Chief will be gone for the day."

"Doubt it."

After a ten-minute wait which almost prompted John to come back later, an intercom crackled and the manager buzzed him in. A couple of people moved boxes around, while others were cleaning up the empty club. *This place looks shabbier in the daylight.* John did not think that possible, as he stepped over the worn, stained carpet, thinking that perhaps the dim lighting did more than make people more attractive. You would think they would invest some of the money they took in at the door on carpeting that held up better; a fresh coat of paint on the walls would not hurt either, as the light shown down on some subtle cracks in the finish. But maybe the things the crowd helped block out did not warrant any attention. John wondered if seeing the building in the light would change any of the guys' impressions of it. But then again, as far as John saw, "his people," especially the ones who flocked to bars to drink their weekends away, had little use for reality beyond walls like these.

John caught the attention of Donnie, who was behind the bar in a sweatshirt and jeans, cutting some fruit. With his knife in his hand, he waved John over to the bar. John set his notebook down and looked for a stool. Donnie set his knife down and handed an over-turned stool on the bar to John. Donnie reached back underneath the bar and lowered the volume of Barry White's greatest hits that were blaring from the speakers.

"They let you play your own music?" The absence of a redundant bass-line told John the disc did not belong to the DJ booth.

"Yeah, when we're opening up we can bring in whatever we want."

John looked at his watch, and even though he knew they had an appointment at 3:00, he was checking anyway. "You have to be here this early to open up?"

"No, not really. The cleaning crews are here and the management comes in and does some paperwork. I like to come in, set up at my leisure and then leave, maybe take my girl to a nice dinner. I like to start my day calm—nice and relaxed." Donnie motioned his hands to the length of the bar, pointing out the length of his domain. He punctuated the statement with a broad smile of perfectly white teeth.

John, wondering how much bleach it took to get those teeth that white, decided to come back to "the girlfriend" detail. Why would a straight guy work in a gay bar? Donnie was a salesman, all right, and John was not sure what he was trying to sell him, but he was sure this would be an entertaining interview at the very least. He flipped open his notebook and took a pen from the inside of his coat.

"So, what do you want to know, boss? You got questions for Don Brown about what's been going down?" He waved his knife in the air as he placed a new lemon on the cutting board.

137

John was a little taken aback. "Do you have something concrete for us?"

"No, I'm just saying, you know, what do you want to know?" Donnie flashed the smile again.

"Well, to start with, what do you know about any of the people who have disappeared?" John rattled off some names.

Donnie just shook his head. "Listen to me, I know a lot. I see couples get together. I see couples step out on each other. I see guys come in here whacked out of their minds." Donnie set the cutting board to the side and leaned on the bar with his elbow. "I see all kinds of crazy shit that a lot of people take for granted. But I am terrible with names. I remember drinks and I remember faces, but I don't do names." He stood up, set the knife down on the cutting board and adjusted his jeans at the waist. "Don Brown does not do names."

John watched Donnie adjust his sweater and turn to the mirror behind the bar, flashing himself a quick smile the way people check the mirror to psych themselves up before an important job interview. No wonder this guy worked here. "So I could show you some pictures, then?" John slid a folder out of his notebook and flipped it open. He took the photos that had been brought in from the families, and handed them to Donnie.

Donnie took the pictures and leaned back onto the bar, this time supported by both elbows. "Yeah, I know this guy. He used to come in here all the time on Wednesdays. Loved to cruise. Yeah, this one too. He was a big beer drinker—good tipper too. This one I don't think I've ever seen." He lifted his head ever so slightly and looked to his right, lost in thought for a moment, then returned to the pictures. "No, definitely don't know that guy." While he talked, John made notations on his notepad, assigning numbers to each picture. "This guy..." His voice trailed off as his mind probed his memories. He pointed to the picture. "I do remember this guy. He was in months ago and left with some guy. He was a pool player. He used to hole up in that corner over there and play all night. Never danced, just played pool all night."

John took that particular photo and flipped it over. He glanced at the name printed on the back, wrote down "Benny Jamieson," then underlined it on his pad.

"The last time he was here was, shit, some time ago, maybe last fall? Yeah, September, maybe October?" Donnie raised himself off the bar and folded his arms across his chest, his eyes staring off while he tried to rebuild that night the way a general surveys the battlefield before the fighting is to begin. "And he left with some guy...this guy was in here the other night too. That's where I recognized him from."

"You said you saw him in here? You sure?"

"Yeah, real sure. Couldn't place the face then, but looking at that picture... Yeah, it's him. Definitely."

John started scribbling notes, then, talking as he wrote, he asked, "Could you come down to the station and give a description of this guy so we could get a rendering?"

Donnie set his foot on one of the drink wells behind the bar and rested his hand on his knee. "No, listen, this is what it is." Donnie put both hands in the air and cupped them to form two halves of what he intended to be...well, John was not quite sure. "See, Don Brown does not think like that. You know, I go down there, I start describing something and then one of these artist types starts drawing and then they show it to me and I look, and it doesn't look anything like I said. I mean, come on, I look at this and I go, are you kidding me? That's not what I said. And you know, I'm sure these guys you got down there are very good at what they do, but I don't have what it takes to rattle off the right things. You know what I'm saying? I tend bar. I pour drinks for a living. Doesn't mean Don Brown is stupid, but I can't communicate with these artist types. I'd have to see the guy again and point him out."

John set his pen down, admiring something in Donnie that he could not quite place, at the same time feeling a bit exhausted from listening to him run off at the mouth. Donnie missed his calling in the theater…or maybe as a network political commentator.

Donnie smiled wide and went into a relaxed pose. "Listen, here's what I'll do." Donnie extended his hand across the bar and brushed John's hand. John watched him do it and wondered why he had been touched. "Give me your card." Donnie illustrated the shape of a card with his hands. "And when I see this guy again, which I will, because you know these guys are creatures of habit, I'll pick up the phone and I'll call you."

Normally, John would keep pushing a potential source, but something in Donnie's delivery and demeanor told him to save his breath. He reached into his pocket, pulled out a card and passed it across the bar. Donnie took it and held it up, winking at John in the process. *What an odd straight guy.* But John somehow knew he would come through for him.

"So let me ask you something, 'kay?" Donnie twirled the card between his fingers while John closed his notebook.

"Sure." This had to be interesting.

"How come I see your boyfriend all the time, but never you?" Donnie returned his foot to the liquor well.

John stared blankly at Donnie. How did he know Kevin and why did he know that he was his boyfriend?

"What makes you think I have a boyfriend?"

"Come on, you think Don Brown is some slouch? Some amateur? I can pick you out a mile away." Donnie's hand came across the bar. There was that touching thing again.

"Yeah, how so?" John watched Donnie retract his hand.

"Come on, you need me to spell it out for you? Besides, he's friends with that other fellow, the real animated one." John thought of calling Eric a lot of things, but animated was not one of the euphemisms. "It came up one night that his friend's boyfriend was a cop. How many gay cops can there be in this city and how many would end up on this case, huh?"

John felt he had finished what he had come to do and stood up. He smiled at Donnie, slightly annoyed at what he took to be an invasion of his privacy, but shrugged it off nonetheless. "Well, Donnie, thanks for your time. I hope to hear from you soon." John put out his hand and Donnie shook it lightly. He had real soft skin for a straight guy. John examined his hand at the end of the handshake. He felt a strange film on his palm and fingers.

"Lotion, these winters are horrible on the skin, you know what I mean?"

John chuckled, resisting, for the second time today, the urge to rattle off a comment. Perhaps having to bite his tongue over Eric was spilling over into his job. In any event, he turned and walked towards the door.

"It's a good kid you got there. Better than most of the ones that come in here." Donnie was giving unsolicited advice to someone whom he felt needed to be reminded.

Just who does this guy think he is? John paused and turned his head to the side. "Thanks." *How the hell did he know?* He stood for a minute, then turned back around. Donnie had not moved. "Let me ask you something else, something personal."

"Shoot."

"Why does a straight guy work in a gay bar?"

Donnie laughed and let his teeth show. Apparently the answer was obvious. "You kidding me? You know how much money these guys throw around?" He shook his head, either amused or annoyed at such an obvious question.

Back at the station, Glenn was hunched over some papers. "How was the bartender?"

"Bizarre. Your kinda guy."

"Is that a gay joke?"

"No, just a joke." John tossed open his notepad and fished out Benny's picture. He set it aside, tacking his case's hopes on a bartender who would hopefully come through with something. Yet, as he was busy placing his faith in a guy whose teeth were far too white for his own good, he could not shake the weird feeling of having some bartender know Kevin. Just one more confirmation that Kevin was out to entrench himself in the scene here. San Diego was coming back all over again. Was he ready for this battle?

"Hey, when you're done daydreaming, Chief wants us to stop by."

Great. John reached for his cigarettes before he stood. Better to get the inevitable ass chewing over with. Then he remembered that Chief refused to let anyone else smoke in his office, but John carried his cigarette with him anyway.

Chapter 13

As William edged open the dull brown interior set
of doors to the church, he could not help thinking about
how vibrant they had once been. A huge sense of
uneasiness over not knowing the reason Monsignor
Drollings summoned him in weighed on him. This lack
of knowledge put him at a disadvantage. But Carl was
his friend, one realized through working closely over
common purpose. Their means may have diverged
recently, yet their goals remained fixed, with Carl's
rooted in the past and William's planted in the future.
Should any accusation come his way today—and he
thought it might—he relied on his reputation to diffuse
such trivialities, at least until he was able wrap up their
work. Their results would dismiss any anxiety over the
methods used to achieve their inevitable success.
Besides, whereas he thrived with one-on-one
interaction, Carl wavered in face-to-face confrontation,
an unpleasant attribute honed by years of consoling and
lecturing from behind the safety of a dark screen.

When William reached the third row of pews,
Monsignor Drollings stepped out of the confessional,
the door creaking in the process. The wrinkles in Carl's
face hung from his cheeks and William had to wonder

about exactly the length of time since the last they had seen one another.

"And how are you today, William?" Carl seemed to croak out.

The years creased his face, his brittle hair swept over his forehead like decaying strands of grass. His eyes carried the exhaustion evident in his body, a burden bolstered by years of sorrow, weaned from his years as a man of the cloth. "You seem to be slowing down, Carl. Maybe you should be resting in this awful weather we are having."

"I have lasted through far worse than this. My bones, though, do not fare as well in the cold and I do slow down. But, with the spring coming in a few months, I shall be back to my full strength."

William's guard lowered as he watched with pity as Monsignor Drollings struggled to settle into the pew. The only man to extend a warm hand when William wandered into this very church so long ago—as a man stuck in a well of self-doubt and despair and in such dire need of guidance— now existed as a memory, paid tribute by a fragile set of bones that seemed on the brink of collapse at any moment. Something wrestled in Carl's face. William realized that Carl sought something in William's eyes, something that words over the telephone could not convey.

"It has been some time, my friend, but I did not call you here to catch up, nor did I ask you here to discuss my aging body." He coughed and used a handkerchief to wipe away the residue on his lips. "I have called you here today over less pleasant circumstances, I'm afraid."

"I'm listening." William worried that the Monsignor might pick up on the defensive tone that surged to the tip of his tongue as the words passed through his lips.

"Well, and this pains me to say, mind you, but lately I have been hearing things and reading things that have been quite troublesome." Monsignor Drollings avoided eye contact with William.

"I'm not sure what you are referring to."

"I've heard about some disappearances within the homosexual community and I've fielded people's concern over the recent behavior of some of the men in your group. I wonder if they might be veering off the guided path, requiring some other form of intervention." Catching himself for a moment, he continued, "I mean, beyond your capable leadership, that is."

William tried to shield his amusement at having someone under him be blamed for anything, when they were only following his directives, but that amusement quickly subsided to anger when it occurred to him that someone must have come to Monsignor Drollings with concerns. A short list of possible names scrolled through his mind.

"Anyway, William, no need to discuss it further. Think about it and decide if there is anything to be done. In the meantime, I have a young man here, someone whom I happened to come across on my visit to one of our churches, and I thought you might be able to help him. I wanted you to see what you could do for him before I extended an invitation to your new group. The one you left behind has not been having the same success of late, and it appears that you may be needed back here sometime soon."

"Yes, I'll speak with him. Whatever I can do to help, Carl." William did not want to be in a position to where he would "have to come back" to appease Monsignor Drollings.

"Thank you, William; I knew I could count on you. I realize you must be busy, but this seemed like a special case. I will go and fetch the boy."

Monsignor Drollings' labored departure left William alone with his concerns. He would have to deal with this leak, but he did not know who to accuse. It could only be Isaac, but how to deal with it—him? He needed to find a way to sure up Isaac's confidence without undermining their project. A big challenge indeed. And what if he could not succeed in doing this? He would cross that bridge when he came to it, but he knew that their work was bigger and more important than the individuals involved. Anyone who hindered their progress would simply have to go. He felt his heart pause for a moment, his chest swelling for a bit as his mind continued to turn over the phrase "have to go." Isaac's face seeped into his conscience, but before he could work out the moral dilemma gathering steam in his mind, Drollings returned, snapping William from his thoughts of the future and returning him to the present.

"Here you are, William. This young man is Anthony. Anthony, this is William. He can help you. Now, I will leave you two alone. William, I hope to hear from you soon. Good day, gentlemen."

Carl shuffled to the back of the church. William lowered his head and whispered a quick prayer for Carl's health, then he looked up into the pair of eyes he had forgotten about, the ones looking down on him, rather pathetically. "Hello, Anthony." The fingers on his hands hung limply, shaking slightly. "What can I do for you today? I must mention that I am not a man of the cloth, so I do not have the power to absolve you of your sins, but I can help you find your way out of them, if that is what you are after."

"Yes, yes, I am after that. I feel quite lost, sir. I do not know what direction to take my life in." His neck went soft, his head drooping, as if the words sadly leaving his lips sapped all the strength the young boy possessed.

The predictability of the confession took William out of the present and back to the past, back to another weak soul. When William saw himself years ago, counseling Isaac for the first time, the phrase "Have to go" echoed again in his ears as he searched with sadness through his convictions and dipped into his faith to put a finger on the strength he needed to do what he must. But he found nothing. No path illumined in front of him. He saw only indecision, a sign of weakness. If he could not pray for guidance, he would make the hard choice himself, regardless of his feelings towards Isaac. Not everyone would come through this to see the goal achieved, William realized from the beginning. Isaac would have to accept his fate in whatever form it came to him, but William would allow him some time.

An abrupt hand placed on William's knee shocked him to the present, and as William glared down at Anthony, crying his heart out to a distant audience, William realized, for the umpteenth time that he was not cut out for this counseling routine anymore. He had graduated to a higher purpose and needed to leave the Kleenex-waving to Drollings. One person at a time was useless to him, but William had to put on a good show.

"It will all be okay, son, someday." William put an obligatory hand on the quivering shoulder of the youth who was sobbing in front of him. Scott had never cried like this, but Isaac had. What had he done right with Scott that he could use with others? That was the real trick William would try and think about so other people could benefit from the advice.

While Anthony whimpered, William wondered if maybe he could help out this misguided individual in another way—a more permanent manner. After all, the good doctor would at some point need to have some volunteers for practical application of whatever his findings would be. William could feel the old salesman come out of him and he pretended to care. He had to make some of these people believe that he was acting in their own best interest in order to see his plan bear fruit.

"You know, Anthony, not everyone responds to therapy. Sometimes alternate routes need to be considered to find your way out of the darkness and into the light."

He looked up at William, understandably confused, but that often proved to be the most receptive. If you throw someone off-balance, they look to you first to set them right.

"I would do anything not to feel this way anymore." They were the words that sealed any deal, the ones William needed to hear before he proceeded.

"I'm going to give you my card so you can call me in a few months' time. At that time I will be able to discuss some other options, but not until then. In the meantime, two things: first, tell no one of this, for we are very careful in whom we are considering and do not want to have to wade through a deluge of bad candidates, of which you, of course, are not." Anthony swallowed hard and waited for the second condition, like a person lost in the desert for days without water encountering a passerby holding a full cantina just over his head. "Second, try going to Father Carmichael's groups and see how others measure out. If you think you see another who, like you, is not doing well, then I shall reward you by bringing in another strong candidate. Understood?"

Anthony shook his head, the hope in his heart keeping words from flowing from his mouth. William took out a business card and handed it to Anthony, who clutched it, marveling over every embossed letter. For a brief moment, William's confidence surged. Perhaps the hope he gave to Anthony opened a door for William, as if he saw another phase on the horizon, one he had not anticipated or had merely put off thinking about.

As his thoughts drifted back to Isaac, back to the moment he had bestowed upon Isaac a similar type of hope, William wondered, staring at Anthony's grateful eyes, if he instilled a false future. Then he wondered if the hope was, for him, merely a dream. William could not doubt himself at this hour. Things were progressing too quickly and just as he had foreseen. He merely wavered under undue jitters. Drollings' suspicions needed addressing, but how best to treat that situation?

Anthony remained transfixed by William's card. That scene caused William to consider if, in fact, Anthony would be more useful to him stretched out on a table in the back of the warehouse, waiting to have his blood drawn and sent off to a permanent sleep. Maybe it would be better to put him out of his misery sooner, rather than later.

Chapter 14

Why did people always turn up dead on days with bad weather? John took off his gloves so Kevin would not bitch about their tobacco smell when he got home. As the wind nipped at his skin, John felt a little like the barren branches reaching up to a sun that was not there all around him. He exhaled. Glenn was probably all bundled up on his couch with his wife, enjoying the comfort having your car "snowed in" could bring. Even though John bought the "snowplows haven't hit us yet" excuse, he hung up without calling in to question that experience—had he not lived here long enough?— should have equipped him with the ability to handle a couple of inches of snow on the ground. His fat ass could use the workout of shoveling out his tires enough to get them going. As he ditched his cigarette, something in him appreciated his ability to do this alone, without an audience. As he approached the hand coming out of the frozen river, ensnared by some branches, he eased his already slow pace. The thankfulness for some solitude gave way to a wish that someone—anyone— could have been called in to handle this frozen arm that was reaching up for something that would never be found. He turned away, closed his eyes, and told himself, "Not here, not now." Moments like these—as few and far between as they were, whether on the job or watching some random television show—whipped up a memory he felt he had long since put to bed. He opened his eyes again. Those damn knuckles grasping for one last chance at life. He could not take his eyes off that hand, crouching down, feeling his eyes well up to tears that the wind did an excellent job of holding back. He was a kid again, like that kid who, on the day the snow fell like a tornado on their neighborhood that day some twenty years ago, could not wait to go out and play. The wind cut through his clothing the way only boys without cares in the world could tolerate. What wreaked havoc on the adult's business schedule created a winter playground for John and his younger brother Danny.

"Danny, don't! Dad said it wasn't safe." John held out a hand, but he was his own audience. Stopping Danny was like trying to halt a charging lion, fresh from the confines of a cage on its way to the hunt. John stood up from his slouched position and took off after Danny.

Danny managed to grab hold of a side of the fragmented circle, trying in vain to clutch for some hope of safety. The cold ice took hold of Danny's red glove as his hand slipped free, surrendering into the rushing water that carried his body under the ice and off into nowhere. His glove lay fastened to the side of the ice. John dropped to his knees in disbelief, gazing at the motionless red glove. He remained on the surface of the ice, staring off, whimpering with a muffled, tear-soaked voice, "Help... help..."

"Detective Thompson?"

The officer, who remained a respectful few feet away, snapped him out of his daydream.

John turned his attention from the outstretched hand that had hypnotized him.

"The crew is here, Detective. We're ready to extract the body at your word."

"Yeah, send them in." John stepped back and let the crew go to work. Two men stretched into their wetsuits while two others waited with the safety harnesses. John turned away when he could not watch any more of the men running through the necessary safety steps. He kicked off a layer of snow from a nearby bench and tucked his jacket under himself to provide another layer of warmth for his thighs. Comfort took a moment to set in as the men passed their equipment amongst themselves.

The two suited men inched their way across the frozen surface; John winced as they crouched down, signaling for the torch to cut away some of the ice from the body. He turned his head away, just as most would right before the imminent departure of a supporting character in a horror film, and examined the impression his boots made in the snow at his feet. The bench and cold made for an uncomfortable surface, so he reached for his wallet in his back pocket to make things a little easier on himself.

As the wallet passed from one hand to another, he paused and unfolded it to tuck in some of the random pieces of paper sticking out. Through his gloves, the process became challenging, so out of frustration he let the wallet fall to his lap while he tugged one glove off. He arranged the papers in some semblance of order and held them ready to shove back in when a picture fell into his lap.

"Catch him, catch him! He's starting to shift." John looked as the officers secured the body and worked in a line to maneuver towards solid ground. He looked back to his lap and the picture resting in it. He shoved the wallet into his inner coat pocket, then reached down for the picture, a family portrait whose rough edges made clear that it had seen better days. John ran his hand along the border, boxing in the four occupants: his brother, with his gap-toothed grin, gumming away, supported by his mother's knee; John, wearing some coat they borrowed from one of their cousins, stood to her right, flanked by his father, looming over the clan with his imposing height, a height John would never reach. His father had always seemed so tall to him, much the same way all fathers do to their young sons, but John had not seen another 6'4" father when he was growing up.

John smiled as he remembered with utter clarity the day they went to sit for the picture and his father insisted, much to his mother's utter disapproval, that he wear that red scarf. He loved that scarf, looked forward to the winter so he could wear it, so proud that Danny had made it for him.

The winter. His brother. The two were forever linked in John's conscience. If only John had not promised to watch out for his little brother, he never would have had that accident. If only he had been more responsible as a brother, and more of an adult, they never would have gone into the woods that day. *Oh, Danny, I'm so sorry I let you down, let us all down.*

Kevin's face drifted into his mind. Was he there for Kevin as much as he should be? Was he letting Kevin down in some way? Kevin did, after all, move all this way for him. He would make it up to him. He wouldn't let his relationship end like his family's; he would not abandon the one he loved for any reason. Life was too fragile to not let the ones you love know how much of a priority they are.

"Detective."

John looked up as the officers called him over to tie things up. John tucked the picture into his coat without another look and refocused on the case that was being loaded into the ambulance. As he stepped away from the bench, putting his glove back on, he said, "Don't forget to get a Polaroid of his face before you cart him off."

A pair of John's old sweats hung low on Kevin's hips, the drawstrings pulled in as tight as the waist would allow. He plucked one of John's clean t-shirts from the top drawer of the dresser and wondered if reorganizing the storage closet would take up enough of his day of solitude.

In front of the cabinets in the hall, as he settled himself on the scratchy carpet, Kevin pulled one ankle over his knee to gauge how much flexibility he had lost. When his legs would not cooperate, he felt older than he had felt in some time, perhaps ever, more so than the last time he woke up with a slight headache after only four drinks. He would have called the dull annoyance in his head a hangover, but he refused to acknowledge that his tolerance had slipped so low. Oh well, on to the task at hand. As Abba's *Greatest Hits* bounced through the speakers in the living room, he took to the first box, rummaging through a number of books, setting the ones aside he was not quite sure why he owned in the first place, such as *Moby Dick* and *Tom Jones*, wondering if it would be worth his time to cart them down to the used book store to get a few bucks for them. Would that make him look desperate, as if he needed the money that bad? Into the trash they would go. Next came the two or three boxes full of John's stuff: old basketball jerseys, trophies, and other sports paraphernalia. Though John would say Kevin was going to all of this trouble just to annoy him, he hoped John would appreciate the better use of space in what little they had in this apartment. Kevin missed all the space San Diego apartments gave you. The people who designed those places appreciated the fact that people had "stuff" that needed space too. Perhaps that is why John always left so much unused space when he "packed." John would "pack" a box with a few things and wouldn't hear of the argument that shin guards rarely used could be stuffed tightly with his jerseys into one box. Perhaps because he kept so little, he saw no need to get them all in one box. *Well, tough!* Now Kevin needed room for all that he had, when, as he looked at all that he had strewn around the apartment, in piles on the dining room table, in stacks in front of the coffee table, seemed like a whole hell of a lot more than the boxes let on. *Damn, I am good at packing.* When he surveyed all his crap, he realized he had been carting around too much junk. Perhaps he should be thankful they only had so much room, for now he had to touch everything he owned and evaluate if he really needed all that he had trekked with him across the country.

Okay, he thought, as he tucked one box flag under the other to seal it up, *what is next?* Kevin opened the next cabinet and rummaged through the haphazard collection of pictures. The first batch brought back some good memories, some choice ones of him and Eric from college, back before Eric had cut his hair. God, he would die if he saw these. He would probably demand the negatives so they could be burned. *These go in the in-case-I see-Eric-later pile.* As he dug deeper, he came to a couple of envelopes of photos of him and John. As he

156

sifted through them, each picture brought a smile. Some showed John sitting in front of the TV, eating a burrito at some ungodly hour of the night, presumably after a night of drinking. How much fun they used to have when they went out. *God, that apartment!* John thought it looked like a bunch of college kids had lived there and trashed it. The remnants of the Christmas tree with only a few branches left, the ones that had not yet been used for firewood, did little to change that perception, looking so cute, still standing in the corner of the frame. Kevin thought it had an enormous amount of character. *So many memories in that apartment. Right in the gay area of town, near everything. Everything? My, how my perception of "everything" has changed.* Or had it? Had he just learned to accept something else, a substitute for what he really wanted? His fingers sweat onto the pictures in his hand. He really should get around to putting all of these in a photo album, but not today. Today he would just enjoy organizing them into the keepers and trash piles.

Just when he thought he had combed through them all, another pile sprang up. He hit a stack from his going away party from work. *That night.* Thank God there was a camera so he could remember that night. He missed all those people, especially the girls. He used to have so much fun swapping gossip with them and talking about guys. He really should call them and say hello, let them know that he was still alive. And then the summer at the beach photos. Then his favorite photo of him and John that he had forgotten he had even had tucked away. *Why isn't this up somewhere?* God, look at them. How long ago was that? A year and a half, maybe? *Look how happy we look there.* John had such a nice smile. He should smile more. *When did you lose that smile, baby?* He had not even thought about that lately. And look at his body. Had he put on that much weight? Kevin could not even picture his body; it had been so long since he had thought about it. It bothered him that he could not picture it. Oh, God, and those board shorts. John loved those hideously ugly shorts. But when was the last time he had even worn shorts? *Of course they do not really wear shorts out here in the winter,* Kevin thought, *but still.* Everything he wore was so...*stuffy* all the time. And that sunset...how he missed those California summer sunsets. *We were so happy that summer. Things were so easy for us. No arguments, no tension, no nothing, just us.*

This picture had to go up, for it erased any memory of John's disdain for the West Coast. Stuck out here, he would mutter under alcohol breath some nights. In that frame they were happy, and that was how they needed to remember their time there. He placed the picture in-between his teeth and set aside the stack of pictures weighing down his lap. He stood up, his legs a little asleep from being in the same position for that period of time, and walked to the entertainment center. He took down one of the picture frames with a photo they had taken soon after Kevin had moved there—some hopelessly boring function that required suits. He flipped the frame over and popped out the picture, replacing it with the more preferable image of them as a couple. His eyes stayed with the photo once he propped the frame up. There on the shelf, decked out in silver and gold, they were so happy. Why had it changed? When did the relationship go from fun to work? Why had it seemed that one day he just woke up and it was different? No fight, no argument, no reason, just different. Was this what he had to look forward to? Was it supposed to get better from here, or had they seen all their good times? Who was he supposed to talk to about it? Eric? He would prescribe a serious one-night stand to cure the cobwebs. And what would Eric always say? That he respected his boyfriend enough to wear a condom? He would always want to say to Eric that he should respect his boyfriend enough not to be in a position to have to use a condom at all. But that was his business, and Kevin had been just as guilty enough times in various relationships. Eric had his own way of living his life, and he seemed to be happy. They both did, he and Mike.

Why did Eric and Mike have it so easy? As Kevin surveyed the piles his life had amounted to all around him, he wondered if he could have seen how he would have ended up if he would have done things differently. Maybe he needed more friends, for he spent too much time alone. Or maybe something else stirred underneath his skin. He had trouble putting into words what collected in his stomach. More and more lately, as he pondered what his future might hold and whether that path would find John in tow, Kevin felt more and more like the person sitting at a restaurant table who picks at the entrée he ordered, not knowing whether to commit to eating it—even in the face of his dissatisfaction—or risk insult by sending it back to the kitchen. More and more this seemed to be the way he coasted through his relationship. He feared speaking up, worried, like the restaurant customer, that his dissatisfaction with the selection demonstrated an inability to effectively navigate the menu or that his disinterest in the dish spoke of an uncultured palate. But he had made neither decision, coping with each tasteless meal, leaving each restaurant hungry. He wondered what thinking in these terms said about him, beyond needing an occupation outside of waiting tables.

He turned to the window and watched the snow billow down from the sunless sky. So this is why everyone in Seattle needed light therapy. His increasing fist creased the picture he had replaced in the frame, and as he pondered at what moment he had woken up and noticed a change somewhere in his perception of his life, he felt that guy Josh's invisible touch on his shoulders. The firm, confident hands pressed into his knotted shoulders and he hated himself for allowing it to feel good. Temptation had come and gone, but never had a touch besides John's, in the course of their relationship, succeeded in producing the tiny shivers up and down Kevin's forearms. Did normal couples go through this? No doubt Eric had been there and far beyond, but was he the best barometer? Kevin did not think so. Eyes closed, he surrendered to the sensation of Josh's touch a little more. After a while, Kevin opened his eyes and turned towards the window. Outside, the snow coasted to the ground, drifting back and forth as the wind rocked it safely to the ground. He walked to the window to get a better view. Placing his hand on the window, still clutching the picture, he stared at the recent memory against the backdrop of a cold winter that made stepping outside miserable. He let the memory slip from his fingers. He watched as it settled face down on the carpet. Should he bend down and pick it up, perhaps tuck it away somewhere in one of these boxes to be discovered and gawked over another day, along with everything else he stored away safely in the boxes? Instead, Kevin turned away to the snow falling just outside their—his —window. He loved the snow, from as far back as he could remember, even when he knew nothing about waddling through it until he stepped off that plane not too long ago, yet no one out here understood his fascination with it. "It's just snow," they would say, "and it gets dirty really quick," they would add. "You will get over it quickly," they would prophesy. But he loved it, and nothing he had heard could convince him otherwise. Kevin loved that it fell when it wanted to, unchecked, just came down, falling with no pattern, no rhyme or reason; it just fell. Totally random. Why did everything in life demand a rational explanation? Thank God the holidays had come and gone already.

Chapter 15

Tommy finally felt comfortable to breathe once his roommate took off for his afternoon class. Tommy had been to the computer lab to see if Garrett's email had come through, but he had been too paranoid to open and read it for fear of someone he knew coming by and grabbing a peek at whatever might be on the screen. Tommy could only take so many chances, and he needed the security of his vacant room to delve into Garrett's words, which he hoped would be a breath of fresh air from the only gay people Tommy knew on campus. Thank God for the T1 line in the dorms so he did not have to wait long for his mailbox to open up so he could scroll through his junk mail—letters from his mom, stuff of that nature—until he found Garrett's message, tucked away near the bottom, waiting to be read for the past three and a half days:

Hey you. It was nice seein' u while you were home for x-mas break. How was the trip home? Did u have a good flight? At least you're lucky to be back in good weather, it's too damn cold here!! Anyway, just thought I would drop you a line and see what's up. Did you start checking out any of the chat rooms

*I told you about? Careful who you hook up with,
though. I don't know what's goin' on your way, but
there's a lot of talk here about people not coming
back from trickin', so be careful!!*
-Garrett
ps. Any progress with Pops?

With the groundwork for a strong friendship
forming, Tommy drew a certain security from knowing
someone like him was out there, encouraging him by
his presence. Tommy would not only have someone to
hang with when he went home, but also had someone
to bounce stuff off of, someone who had been around a
little. The gay club meetings on campus, ones Tommy
had paced around outside every Monday for a few
months before venturing in, offered nothing in the way
of social connections. Those guys were nice, sure, and
they were comfortable with who they were, but being
gay only served as part of the grounding Tommy knew
that he needed, even though he could not articulate this.
Being gay was *part* of who he was, not *who* he was. He
was not sure the uptight gay club members understood
that, not that Tommy did yet either, but they did not
seem to mind, finding stronger connections in *Buffy
the Vampire Slayer* than they did in the world around
them. That dinky little room the school "offered" to
them provided all the affirmation they needed in the
world, but Tommy needed something more than a place
to hang Ellen DeGeneres posters and a spot to store
Donna Summer's Greatest Hits cassettes. But he hung
around, briefly, clinging to the fear that those who sat
around Indian-style in cushioned chairs presented his
only options. When he met Garrett, hope sprang again,
unveiling a whole new world of opportunities. He felt a
responsibility to explore the world he knew had to exist

out there for him, as if now his efforts would somehow be rewarded. Garrett, even now in the infancy of their friendship, had become that dim light in a dank basement; it was okay to venture down there when you had someone to light the way. When Tommy passed on this feeling to Garrett, he typed back that Tommy should show a little more respect to the members of the gay community who made it possible for him to come along—regardless of how stereotypically they chose to live. "Please do not become one of those *too cool to hang out with fags* people," he said, punctuated with a happy face.

One day, he hoped, with all these words back and forth, he could convey his regret over the kid he used to be in high school towards Garrett. Perhaps this friction between his intended responses and his desire to cut into what had been eating at him all these months since they had met up was what sent his fingers over every other wrong key as he knocked out his response, having to stop every other word in order to let spell check do its job. He got through things such as "yeah, flight was fine, good to be back in the warmth," etc. This time, however, he wondered how best to convey the tremendous guilt that weighed on him like an impending final exam he knew he had not read anything for. How would he apologize for how he had acted towards Garrett in high school? And did he even have to? Clearly, the pit in his stomach suggested that he needed to say something, but he did not know how to put into words that his actions were not out of hate, but some subtle jealousy for being able to live a life he did not even know he wanted at the time. He had always felt like there was something missing in his life, but finding the clues only a few years earlier was about as useful as coming across the tools in his father's laboratory and trying to use them to work on his car. Why could school not teach you anything useful?

He capped the email by saying he would catch up with Garrett later, and as he sent it, he couldn't help feeling that what he was leaving out was more important than what he put in. Still, keeping the door open for a later date encouraged him that time would tell him when the time was right to get the weight off his shoulders, a burden he did not know was there until the past smacked him in the face, so to speak. This too provided Tommy with confidence, as if righting past wrongs would set him up to be a happier person in the future. He hoped this strength would translate into other areas of his life as he wondered how much time he would have to delve further into some chatrooms.

Of course he had cruised them before, but his profile hinted at a different person, suggesting someone Tommy wanted to be, or someone more appealing to the gay world. With Garrett's prodding, he logged on and reconfigured his stats to reflect himself a bit more accurately, wondering if this change would bring in more interest, but when no sentence sounded right, he logged off. He could not justify putting off his studies any longer. He did, after all, have his priorities.

The proper on-line etiquette Garrett spoke so highly of took a few days to employ, but Tommy found his way, huddled at the computer every free night his roommate went out on a late study session or some date. Ignoring the initial query, "Got a pic?" or "What are you into?" proved to be the easiest people to fend off first.

Eventually, the pin-pinging of the fresh opening windows that signaled a new interest saying "hi" made

Tommy think he was in an arcade. Whether he was fresh meat or merely someone who seemed interesting did not matter to him, as long as the attention came. He lowered the volume on his computer so his suitemates could not hear through the walls and wonder what he was doing. So this was what it was like to be the hot new thing. It was like seeing a swarm of sharks converge on a single stream of blood in the water, but he was not flinching; he rather enjoyed the nibbling. With each inquiry response, he found himself emboldened by dismissing people who were after sex right off the bat. He had so much more to offer someone than just his body, and he was determined to find love, not some cheap thrill.

So this is what puberty is supposed to feel like—that sensation of standing at a dance, unsure if you should ask a girl to dance, or marveling when you could take a girl's hand into yours and walk with her for a while. Now he understood what his friends bragged about, things that sounded like a foreign language to him for so long. For Tommy, hitting puberty was like watching everyone collect Pokemon cards and wondering what all the fuss was about. Now he felt that light tickle, that feeling of falling down an unexpected drop on a roller coaster, and he was curious to see what lay ahead on the tracks.

Yet even he got bored after awhile, but just before he was about to log off, his eye caught an interesting name: FratGuyNSD. Although Tommy generally held a high disdain for anyone in a fraternity, this association became endearing when he realized how cute he found most of these guys to be. When FratGuyNSD made the first move by saying "Hi," Tommy felt a pull in his throat as he commanded the hand clutching his mouse to move to retrieve the guy's profile. Clean-cut, brown eyes, brown hair, tallish... Of course Tommy did not buy that he liked to read one bit. Nobody actually liked to read these days. Tommy responded: "Hey."

"Name" came back. Tommy wrestled with a witty quip, but wondered if that might not be the best way to handle this fish. Be honest or bitchy? That all depended if a cute guy sat on the other end or a troll was taking up his time. What to do, what to do? What would Garrett do? Be honest. "Tommy," he wrote. What did he have to lose? A computer screen provided enough security to be himself. Tommy asked the same question, but got no response. Instead: "Pic for trade?" Tommy panicked a bit. He felt like the conversation was going well and didn't want to spoil it when he didn't have a pic to send. He cursed himself for not taking care of that sooner. "I don't have one in return," Tommy typed with trepidation, fearing the conversation's end approaching the moment he hit "send." But much to his surprise, his email chime sounded, and he opened it to find an embedded picture, waiting for his approval.

Cute, but is it him? No one used his actual picture, Garrett had warned him. "Cute" he typed back. He bit at his fingernail while he waited for a response. As he waited, a knock at the door turned his attention. The clock over the door told him that it was his study partner. *Fuck! Is it that time already?* He looked back at the computer screen. No response. *Shit, I have to go.* Besides, he had to log off so his friend did not get curious about his screen. If he saw it, he would ask what chatroom he was in and Tommy did not have a good lie handy. What would FratGuyNSD think? He typed fast, "I have to go. Hopefully we can catch up later." He logged off and flicked off the monitor before he went to the door.

"Hello. I almost left."

"Sorry, Roger. I was just finishing up some stuff."

"Anything important?"

"Nah. Come on in; let's head over to the library." They trekked through campus on their way to the library—the sun shining through a few clouds looming in the sky that Tommy had learned, all too quickly, to take for granted—to knock out some research. He was rather enjoying the California "winter," although he did admit that he missed the snow, for at least a moment or two, anyway. In his head, he ran through all the journals they would have to track down, and he attempted to gauge the amount of time they would have to spend indoors. With each passing step he could not help feeling like maybe they should put off studying and just go have some fun. As they entered the large open-air courtyard outside the library, Tommy thought of his mother, sitting by the window, watching the snowfall after she had just hung up with him earlier in the day. He smiled, looking up at the sun shining down from the crystal blue sky.

With the library door-handle in his hand, Tommy said, "What do you say we bag this and go sit in the coffee shop?" *So this is why no one gets anything done in California*, Tommy thought as they cruised over the grass down the hill.

They took up at a small table, sipping their hot chocolate. Roger set his wood stirrer to the side, carefully placing it on a napkin. He said, "You know, I've been meaning to ask you something. A medical journal I'm using for my psych paper has an article written by a Dr. Stephen Riles. You related to him?"

Tommy stopped stirring his hot chocolate and stared blankly at Roger. "Yeah, that's my dad. I didn't know he wrote an article, though. What was it about?" He felt kind of stupid, not knowing that his father had published something.

"Researching the genetic links to homosexuality."

"Oh." Tommy felt a sting in his gut. And his mother wondered why he did not want to "come out" to his dad? "Was it interesting?" Tommy wondered if his voice carried any detectable anxiety.

"Yeah, I guess. I just don't know why people bother. Some people just need to make a name for themselves, I guess." Was there a dig in there on his father?

"Yeah, I guess." As Tommy's stomach turned sour, a familiar girl strolled by. "Hey, isn't that your girlfriend over there?"

Roger looked over, and then bowed his head down until she had passed. "Yeah, she kinda was, if you could call her that. I haven't called her in a while and she's sorta pissed at me." Tommy chuckled. Straight people were so amusing. It also tickled him that he now felt comfortable enough to comment on straight people.

"So, how come you don't ever date anyone?" Tommy fell back into a hole of his own making. He was not sure what would be a better conversation—explaining why his father's apparent research caused his anxiety or why he did not date. Saying he had not met the right guy did not seem to be the easy answer most people would take it for.

He truthfully enjoyed talking to all different types of guys on the computer without having to narrow it down to one guy. Having a boyfriend would be too surreal. He would not know what to look for. It was like knowing that you wanted to go to college but not being quite sure what you wanted your major to be. So many factors, so many variables to consider. "I like being single."

This time Roger chuckled. Maybe he would think Tommy was a player of sorts, but Tommy's attention soon left the table and drifted. Out of the corner of his eye he could have sworn he recognized the guy that just ducked into the student-run bookstore on campus, right next to the vegetarian co-op.

"You know what, I'll be right back." Roger looked perplexed, but made no comment as Tommy got up from the table, leaving his book bag on the empty chair.

Tommy purposefully went the other way, out of the coffee shop, circling around and coming back along the other side, until he had to crouch down when he realized that Roger would still have a good shot at him. Although he probably looked like some kind of an idiot, he made a right into the bookstore. Once inside, he got up on his tiptoes to see if any heads were behind some of the shelves. The girl behind the counter gave him an odd look from over the top of her book. Ignoring the look, he hiked up the spiral staircase when he did not see anyone on the first floor. At the top of the stairs, he caught what he was looking for; both standing and leaning against the wall by the window thumbing through a book, wearing a loose fitting sweatshirt and faded, yet crisp jeans, Tommy discovered his future.

When the guy lifted his head and eased the book back onto the shelf, his face came into focus. Tommy placed in an instant FratGuyNSD. He looked cuter in person, which Garrett told him never to expect. Did he go to school here? He would have to, to be in this bookstore. For the most part, not even the people who went to school here shopped here. How should he approach him? Should he walk right up to him? Should he just casually "happen" to bump into him? He stepped to the side so he could think a moment and dry off his itchy palms. Well, what if it was not him? He would be mortified if he embarrassed himself like that. Maybe he should just leave and wait to see him online again. Maybe he should just wait for him to walk by and say "hi." Maybe he should just go back to his dorm room and turn on his computer and log on and delete his name from his buddy list so he did not ever have to talk to him again because he did not know if he should say "hi" or not. *God, this sucks!*

Tommy could hear him turning the pages of another book, and then he heard a thud. Soon, there were footsteps on the carpet, coming towards the stairs. Before Tommy had time to slide down the stairs, he came around the corner just as Tommy looked up into the softest brown eyes he had ever seen. The sound around him died out. The hairs on his head seemed to sway back and forth in slow motion. Tommy had no idea how long his feet stayed fixed in that spot, and at what point his mouth dropped right open, before a cough from the floor slapped him in the face. Through beautiful lips, the guy offered with all the sincerity in the world, "Sorry. Didn't see you there."

Feeling as if he had just been offered the first bouquet of flowers in his life, Tommy smiled, and before he could think, "You're FratGuyNSD, aren't you?" spilled out of his mouth, consequences be damned. In the nano-seconds after the words left his mouth, a funny feeling curdled in his stomach. In that moment, his confidence shattered, causing him to instantly long for the safety of his keyboard. You could hear it in the crackling of his voice over the last syllable.

Scrunching his eyebrows in the absolute cutest way possible, he sputtered, "Sorry?"

Feeling a surge of bravery, Tommy blurted out, "I'm CollegeBoi3469. We chatted earlier." He waited to see if the light would turn on and suddenly the tension would pass, paving the way for them to lock lips in no time. Clearly, fate caused them to cross paths like this. *I mean, really, what were the chances that not only would I blow off research at the library, but also "happen" to be sitting at the exact table and "happen" to look over and see...*

But Tommy's fantasy took a turn. "Yeah, listen, I didn't know..." Tommy wanted to just lean over and kiss him, to prevent his lips from saying another word, telling him through connected lips how hot he was. But, he got out, "I didn't know I was talking to someone who went...I didn't...Look...I'm not..." Tommy soaked up every insecurity as if they were his own. Then he said, "Listen, I gotta go." That was not to be how this meeting was to end.

Before Tommy could say anything, Tommy's perfect match was down the stairs with his book bag in hand, cutting through the quad area that was the old student center, and off into another part of campus. Tommy slumped against the wall and tried to massage out the knot in his stomach. What, exactly, was this feeling? His knees were buckling a bit as he could not wipe FratGuyNSD's face out of his mind. *This sucks*, he thought, questioning why it all went down the way it did; but his mind perked up when he realized he came away with something: now he knew where he went to school. At this realization a wide smile lit up his face. *There, that is something.*

Tommy made his way back to the coffee shop. Roger was relaxing and showed some concern. "Everything all right?"

"Yeah, fine. I thought I saw an old friend." Tommy stared off into the trees. How was he going to find him again if he did not run into him online? He did not want to come on too strong by emailing him. "Do not chase," he heard Garrett advise. Still, at that moment, Tommy felt a little exercise sounded like quite a good idea.

Chapter 16

In his living room, John itched from the silence all around him. The lights from the city filtered in through the room that had been Windexed clean, highlighting the order with which Kevin had set the apartment. John had not noticed how in need of a cleaning the place was until he saw it put right. Maybe it had been that clean for a while; maybe Kevin had done it today. John would have to wait to ask him because he was still out running errands, maybe not expecting John to be finished with his case for the day. John surprised himself when he decided his report could wait. Hell, everyone else did it. Why should he break his back getting the work cranked out? Besides—and maybe this was the real reason—Kevin's face would not leave his sight, making work impossible. Perhaps he needed the little break; after all, he needed to make some time for Kevin, something he avoided doing for what seemed a long time now. A whiff of Pledge caught his nose. *Definitely cleaned today*, he thought, as he turned to inspect all that Kevin had accomplished.

He opened drawers and peered into cabinets. *Order.* The dishes were cleaned and put away, the counter clutter-free. Everything where it should be, but probably not where it had been in a while. *Clean*. In the bedroom, the top sheet was folded back over the comforter; no loose ends hung out over the sides. In their chest of drawers, all his shirts were folded neatly, down the middle, just the way he liked them. His socks, folded in pairs, not pushed into themselves, an annoying habit that did nothing but stretch out the elastic. Not a stray piece of paper occupied their computer desk, not a single sheet of a bill stuck out of a file folder. In the bathroom, not a trace of the specs of food Kevin left everywhere when he flossed his teeth. The tub glistened. The rugs had been washed, brought back to life a little. *Immaculate*.

Back in the front room, John ran his fingers across the top of the entertainment center. Not a speck of dust. He perused the pictures, and when he saw the one of him and Kevin at the beach, the San Diego sun setting behind them, illuminating their smiles, he picked up the frame. John's arm was wrapped around Kevin, holding him in close, protecting him. It had been what John had always wanted to be for Kevin: his protector, to guard him from the atrocities of human nature that he saw every day as a cop, and to be for his boyfriend what he had failed to be for his young brother all those years ago. John had managed to pull Kevin out of his rut, from out of the "scene" and away from all the drugs that infested it, the ones that brought so many down, like the ones he was investigating. Such a shame. John had succeeded with Kevin, been able to help Kevin move forward with his life, but was Kevin really that happy? Did John have the right to protect Kevin, to force his will on him, to try and be his moral compass?

Maybe the case was getting to him, but he could see how maybe he was not being there for Kevin as much as he should be, not being as "fun" as they used to be.

What could he do to change that? John ran his finger against the glass of the frame. Kevin was smiling wider than John could remember. How long had it been since anything had brought him that much joy?

Keys jangled at the door. Kevin kicked open the front door and waddled in with three or four grocery bags in hand. Odd how it took that moment for John to register that Kevin took it upon himself to venture out into the snow to run errands. He was standing on his own two feet.

"Hi." John hoped his tone spoke for the words he could not find.

"Hi." Sounding more like a reflex, Kevin's flat response to John spoke volumes about what they had become: crisp, routine, dull around the edges.

John moved his hands up Kevin's body and wrapped his hands around his neck, then pulled him in close to him. He left one hand around his neck and moved his other hand down his back.

Kevin, tense at first, gradually eased up a bit. He turned his head so he could say something. "Is everything okay?" His voice carried a tentativeness and caution to prepare himself for whatever John would say in reply.

Holding Kevin's body felt so good, he almost didn't want to interrupt it with a response, but he did anyway. "Everything's fine." John moved his hand from Kevin's neck and stroked the back of his head and his closely cropped hair. He was getting a few grey hairs back there.

"You sure?"

"Yeah," John whispered, then embraced Kevin like he had just returned from an extended tour at sea.

"Okay, then, honey...can you let me go a bit? You're crushing my arm." John let out a mild chuckle as he pulled his arms off Kevin. Kevin stretched out his shoulder. John put a hand on Kevin and Kevin still looked at him skeptically. John moved to the backside of the couch. His momentary exuberance shifted.

"You okay? Looks like I lost you there for a moment."

"I'm fine, it's just...I don't know, maybe it's this case. I haven't talked to you about this, but..." John felt the details collect on his tongue and he stopped himself before his jaw could open. Gritting his teeth, he took a deep breath. "This case is seeping into me a little more than usual."

Kevin walked up and brushed John's hairs to the side on his forehead, offering an expression like he understood what John was going through. "That one in the papers?"

John paused, unsure of how to answer, then he looked into Kevin's patient eyes and felt like he was safe for once. "Yeah, that one."

"You can talk about it if you want. You know, I can listen." Kevin's brown eyes did not need the details. No one needed the details, they just clamored for the results John needed to get faster at providing if he was to continue to do his job competently. His mother would say he was being far too hard on himself, but no one knew what he—what any cop lived with. Kevin's eyes still waited for some small piece to take in.

John paused and thought for a moment. A change of subject was in order. He had been toying with the question ever since he had started on this case. John heard himself ask, "Would you change it? If you could go back and choose, make the decision yourself, would you change it?"

Kevin thought for a moment, furrowing his brows and biting at his lips the way he did the one time in San Diego they had gotten together for a Trivial Pursuit couples match and Kevin feigned a thought process to

178

mask his lack of knowledge in the given area. Why he could not just say he did not know proved to be cute to John's eye then. He had forgotten about that night. Strange, how a sense of bitterness flared up in him as he remembered losing that game, feeling like maybe Kevin should have been able to fill out some of the categorizes John lacked; but now, looking back, he realized he should focus mainly on how cute Kevin looked.

Eventually, Kevin uttered in a soft tone, "Honey, I have no idea what you're talking about."

"Never mind." John reached for his pack of cigarettes. "What do you say we go out tonight? Just you and me. Maybe have a nice dinner, go grab some beers or something."

"You sure nothing is the matter?" Kevin searched John's eyes for something.

"Yeah, I just...I don't know, what do ya say?"

"Yeah, okay, that sounds like fun." Kevin looked thoroughly confused. John was basking in his spontaneity.

"Okay, well, hit the shower if you want and I'll get us in somewhere." John ran through a few options in his head of where being a cop pulled some weight.

"Okay. I'll just put away the groceries..."

"I'll do that; just get a move on."

As Kevin scampered to the bathroom, John walked with an unlit cigarette in his mouth, back to the entertainment center, back to the San Diego memory in the frame. *God, how we have changed since then.* What would it take to find those two people again? John would investigate that dilemma with some diligence, he promised himself. He smiled as he set the picture frame back on the shelf and turned towards the window. Watching the snow dump down, John lit his cigarette and puffed out a stream of smoke. John hoped they could hail a cab in this weather. Although a pain in the ass to drive in, the snow also kept more people inside to avoid this inconvenience of nature. Maybe those people in Southern California did have something figured out by living out there: no snow. At least the city provided some detachment: no forests. It was good to not have to look at the trees. Concrete had a way of making the snow bearable. As he took another long drag, once the last billow of smoke passed out of his mouth he remembered how clean everything in the apartment smelled and he wished he could suck all that smoke back in. He ran to the sink and doused his cigarette. From under the sink, he grabbed some air freshener and sprayed it all over.

Once they were out on the dance floor, John tugged at Kevin's shirt, losing himself to the indifference about what scene they might be causing. The alcohol settling in their blood streams encouraged them. Kevin stared into John's eyes while he unbuttoned his shirt. He slinked out of the shirt and tucked it into his pants, just over his ass. John ran his hands all along Kevin's stubbled chest. He smiled, as he moved around, circling his erect nipples, then back over Kevin's neck, and pulled him close; their gyrations moved more forcefully than the music. John yearned for something more private to accommodate his escalating mood.

John held the door open, his house keys still in the lock, as Kevin grinned, stumbling past John with his mis-buttoned shirt clinging to his body at an awkward angle. Kevin stood in the darkness of the room, tugging at his shirt as John shut the door and came from behind him, wrapping an arm around his torso and digging his teeth, with some restraint, into Kevin's neck. Kevin tensed for a moment, then acquiesced to the dull stinging that brought as much pleasure as John intended it to. Kevin fumbled around with the buttons and succeeded in small victories every few moments. John continued nibbling on Kevin's neck and took advantage of the opening in the shirt to run his hand inside it.

They left their clothes trailing from the front room into the bedroom, where John and Kevin had already tossed the bedspread aside and made themselves comfortable among the sheets. John held Kevin's wrists over his head on the pillow as he leaned his body over Kevin's, draping him with kisses. The hum of liquor still throbbed through their heads and the sound of the club still rang in their ears.

Kevin and John exchanged tongues with a feverish pace, turning their bodies from side to side, with Kevin on top one minute, then John to follow soon after. With John on his back, Kevin went down on him and worked his hands into the task as much as he did his mouth and tongue. John arched his back to put himself further into Kevin's mouth, but that only caused Kevin to slow so he wouldn't gag.

Kevin dug his nails into John's forearm as John entered him, but he wasn't used to being opened up that wide, so John paused, waiting for Kevin to take a few deep breaths before he continued in further. Kevin winced with each subtle push, telling John that he

wished that he was not so out of practice. This used to
be so much easier, but it still felt good, even if it stung a
bit. Kevin knew the sting would pass; he just wished it
would hurry up. John pulled out a little, then came back
a little deeper the next time. He repeated his actions at
a slow pace, allowing Kevin to ease up. A couple more
times and he would be up for more. He nodded and
smiled as John loomed over him. John kissed Kevin's
ankle that hovered to the right of his face and ran his
hand down his calf. It felt good to be inside of him. He
did not care how slow he had to take it, but he knew it
would not take him long to finish.

John eased into sleep quickly, and before he knew
it, he was running through the woods, his hands chilling
from the cold, wearing nothing more than his jacket
and some jeans. He stumbled continually in the snow
as his brother's voice rose and fell through the cover of
the trees. The trees grew in numbers, preventing him
from moving any faster. They gathered around him
while he covered his face with his hands. When he took
a few breaths, he removed his hands and the trees were
gone. He stood on a lake, not feeling the cold anymore,
and he turned. His brother was sitting in the center of
the ice and looked up when he saw John walk towards
him. John walked faster, and Danny smiled. When they
reached each other, Danny threw his arms around
John's waist, his head just below his navel. Danny
released himself with a laugh that John couldn't hear,
then he danced off in a circle. He continued to do circles
on the ice as he moved farther and farther out of view.
His hands twirled in the air and a red glove protected
only one of them. John called out to Danny, who moved

unaware, then disappeared from sight. John stopped cold in his tracks when Danny vanished, and he looked down at his hand and saw himself holding a small red glove.

He twitched, as his eyes opened and he found himself in the comfort of his own bed, Kevin nuzzled just next to him. He drew in a breath to slow his heart rate and glanced at the clock next to him, trying to shake off his dream. He wondered if sleeping for that brief hour would prevent him from nodding off again. John shrugged off the slight buzz in his head from the night's drinking as he put his arm around Kevin, underneath the pillow he was clutching, and leaned over and whispered in Kevin's ear as he kissed it, "I love you."

Kevin stirred a bit, but made no sign of hearing it. As he pulled Kevin in close to him, a little cold shiver ran through John's body.

Chapter 17

Scott failed to see the beauty in the snow that got in his way all around him, trickling down onto every inch of where he needed to step, caking onto his shoes, and threatening to trip him up with every step were he not confident enough on his feet to keep himself steady. How could he have ever enjoyed this weather as a kid? All the bullshit that came with it proved to be mind numbing. Public transportation was a nightmare and forget about driving in it. How people who lived through the winter year in and year out could still be so ill-equipped to maneuver a vehicle in less than ideal conditions escaped him. Every step in this godforsaken weather made him appreciate the warmth he could not feel fast enough from the warehouse. However, William's grave tone on the phone told him to brace for some bad news, though whatever lay in wait could not be any worse than this damn cold that would not stop biting at his face.

In typical fashion, William kept his back turned, wasting time gazing out into a city unworthy of his attention, waiting for the moment to turn around, even though he knew Scott had entered the room.

"Have a seat and close the door behind you." Scott obliged and William spun around. Scott took his time settling in, making William wait while Scott slowly eased out of his jacket. His patience reaching its limit—though electing not to speak up, as usual—William slid a folded newspaper across the desk. Scott snatched it up and glanced over the highlighted article: "Pattern Emerging with Missing Gays." Looking proud, Scott was not sure what accounted for William's uneasy demeanor. Why should William be worried about the inevitable? Scott cast the paper aside.

"We have a problem." William desperately needed a good night's sleep. Perhaps the stress of day-to-day operations proved too taxing for the old man, necessitating a changing of the guard.

"And what would that be?" Scott sat back and folded his arms. "Isaac fuck something up?" Everything had been going fine, as he saw it. No one could pin a thing on them. For this he had been called out in the snow?

"Let's take a walk, shall we?" William rose, leaving the Isaac comment to linger in the room as they left.

On the stairs, William led the way down. "I had a meeting with Monsignor Drollings yesterday. He has been hearing things—rumors—and he is a little concerned. He didn't come right out and speak his mind, but I think someone is not as sure of himself as he used to be."

"Isaac?" Scott tried to sound shocked, but was waiting for this admission. Isaac's betrayal ranked high on the list of inevitables of which the newspaper article would prove to be only the beginning. However, this indicated that things were rolling along as planned, with Isaac being a necessary casualty. Scott understood this, accepting that the weasel would always be used as a set-up—a sheep in need of slaughter to prolong the group's activities. So why the concern and slight shock in William's voice?

"I couldn't say for sure, but, yes." William put his hands over his mouth. Though the conversation obviously proved painful for him, William clearly maintained the proper set of priorities. William was ever the master of masking his guilt by feigning surprise. William walked to the cordoned off portion of the warehouse, separated by a long white sheet. At the drawing of their curtain, William gave a start.

"Well, then, we'll take care of that," Scott said, hoping to address William's flushed face. Those drooping cheeks did not signal the approval Scott anticipated, expecting William to jump to praise when he saw how they had been able to expand their holding area, cordoned off here to allow them to work without the annoyance of these bodies in makeshift cots stacked three high. Scott was not one to turn away from the collection of these pathetic people who were dying to put their sad lives to some use. Surely William had stayed in the loop these past few months. They had gotten their satellite groups across the country up and running, with those places sending over the "clean" bodies. Scott took the initiative, realizing that William only looked to be hands-on up to a point. The less he knew, the more he could deny, should anything come to pass. This was, in fact, the level to which they aspired. Was William getting cold feet?

"Now, don't be too rash. I just want you to keep an eye on him, watch him when he goes out." William's voice quivered in a way Scott had only come to expect from Isaac's whine. Was William losing the stomach for this?

Watching William study the bodies, Scott waited for a compliment. "Something the matter?" His tone grew indignant, compelling William to produce a genuine reaction. Without taking any of the risk, the least he could do would be to say something positive.

"No, no, certainly not. It's just that I was not aware that we had amassed such a supply, that's all... How..." His voice trailed off as he moved closer to the cots. "How many are there?"

"Not sure. Maybe 46, between here and the back rooms. A few of our satellite groups have shipped some down to us. Riles has taken in 47 so far."

"I see." William's eyes dropped. He took a labored breath and rubbed the sleepiness out of his eyes. "We need to curtail our collection efforts. The dust needs to settle. We may have gotten ahead of ourselves, perhaps jeopardizing our operation out of zeal. It seems we have enough to keep the good doctor satisfied for a few months."

William smoothed his coat and adjusted his tie. He wiped his forehead and tucked in some of the hair that was getting far too long behind his ears. Watching him, Scott saw the shell of the man whom he had admired so much take a turn down a weaker path. This was not supposed to happen to him. Why now? Why at all? Perhaps the time had arrived when someone else needed to be the one to make the tough calls, to take up the torch of leadership. After all, not everyone who starts a race finishes it, as long as someone crosses the finish line. William's words of wisdom, were they not? Would his philosophy apply to himself as well? Scott felt no doubts about being able to execute any command, should the need arise. "All right, whatever you think is best, William." A sense of camaraderie ebbed from his voice, his lack of faith in William waning. "As far as Isaac?"

William could not take his eyes off the bodies. "If he is making any trips to the Church for some little conscience reprieve, let me know and we'll deal with it then." Scott nodded. He invited this job. Maybe William was just having an off-day. "With your free time, see if you get more out of the space we have in back so these bodies do not turn into a nightmare." William turned and breezed through the curtain.

Scott followed, but not too closely. "Anything else?"

William turned on a dime. Mustering his old authority, he said, "Curb your anger, Scott. A couple of months and all those people will be forgotten and we can start again."

"You couldn't have told me this on the phone?"

William glared at Scott. "I like to be safe." William was officially paranoid.

"And Isaac? Does he have to come in, or does he get a phone call?"

"You must understand, Scott, I put this into motion with the best intentions, and if Isaac has not been able to live up to his expectations, well, then, I must take the blame for him. It was I who failed, not he."

"Whatever you say. Do you need me for anything else?"

"Do as you like, as long as you do as I ask."

"Thanks." With that, Scott breezed past him on his way to the stairs and up to fetch his coat. Suddenly, the cold outside did not seem all that bad.

The moment the wind's sting pricked his cheek, Scott's resentment boiled over. Yet, a few steps further, his mind drifted to happy thoughts—the picture of the phone call to Isaac telling him to cool his feeble heels. From this, Scott drew the strength to forget the cold that swirled around him, strength he drew upon whenever he was forced to sit across from that twerp in group sessions. As the wind stung his exposed skin, Scott pictured the pitiful expression cross Isaac's face as the reality of sitting alone in his pathetic little apartment kept coming as the notion of his loneliness set in, for he lacked the backbone to step outside those white walls without a directive to do so. Scott pictured Isaac, checking and rechecking all those goddamn door locks he and the rest of the group had had to hear so much about countless times. How their mission was supposed to fix all that shameful anxiety escaped him, but picturing Isaac having to sit alone with his thoughts, perhaps sniffling his tears away, seemed to do him some good. Maybe he could reach down into that well of despair and pull out some resolve to do something about it. Scott paused for a moment at this thought, the wind punishing him with a gust for slowing against its push. *Now that was a "William thought" if I ever thought one. Isaac could draw strength from something? Never.* As this day had taught him—a day he could not see coming—thinking like William would get him nowhere except out into cold like this, for where was William now? Undoubtedly staring out into a city that could care less about him or what he was trying to do. Yes, the baton being hurled in his direction was begging to be snatched up. And, Scott told himself, once he could feel his fingers again, he would do just that. In the meantime, Scott would not be the one to sit home on a Saturday night.

Scott decided to grab a drink at a pub near his apartment. He settled onto a stool at the bar.

"How ya doin', guy?" The bartender was on his toes.

"Good. Could I get a Yuengling draft?" Scott couldn't remember the last time he was able to order a beer without shouting.

"Here ya go. Tab?" Right to the point, Scott's kind of guy. Yet, being a little rough around the edges, the guy's dark brown eyes encouraged a little stirring in his pants. For a moment, Scott almost wished he had been checked out a bit before he disappeared to another customer once Scott nodded a yes. Scott adjusted his crotch.

In the corner near the ceiling, a TV trumpeted the big game on the following day. Scott watched the commentator babble on about something for a moment, and then, not wanting to bother with reading subtitles while he drank his beer, took in some of the other people sitting around the place. Everyone was either enjoying his own company or carrying on a rather uneventful conversation, if their relaxed attitude had anything to say about it. In the patrons' eyes you could see their existence, the lack of energy in the room reflecting their concession to life. *How sad.* Before he knew it, he had downed most of his beer.

Scott had to resist the temptation to go up and talk to someone. Fighting his routine, he had to remind himself where he was. At that moment of realization, Scott felt a little too detached for his liking, as if he was a little lonelier than he cared to be. Walking up to another single guy would draw contempt.

The bartender put another drink in front of his almost empty one and walked away. He took a long sip from his beer and wiped the head from his lip. After a few minutes, he felt compelled to down his drink as fast as he could without looking like he was trying to get out of there. He pulled out a ten-dollar bill and set it under his empty pint. The bartender watched him from his leaning position against the other end of the bar. He held up a hand as Scott moved away from the bar. Scott stepped out into the cold air that he hoped in vain had let up. Was there not some more interesting place to spend his Saturday night? Someplace he had not yet discovered? But the cold air smacking him from every direction would not allow for any search tonight. He was off to his place alone.

Tommy stopped at the coffee shop next to the club that some of the straight people at school dismissively dubbed "the gay Mecca." Of course they were just jealous that they only had the good DJ to themselves on Thursday nights. This was just one of the things Tommy had realized in recent weeks. Turns out, Garrett was right about some of the guys in the gay group on campus. They had more in common than Tommy realized; some of them even became his friends. Instead of just being people with whom he could kill some time, Tommy actually enjoyed being able to hang with some, getting coffee before they hit the club, hoping the caffeine would counter the negative effects of the alcohol so they could stay buzzed longer. Besides, the coffee helped his nerves. He had sent an e-mail to FratGuyNSD, hoping that when he addressed it to Kyle instead of his screen name he would not be freaked out. It paid to have a friend of a friend who knew someone who had Kyle in psych class and knew exactly who Tommy was describing. Garrett never said that would be another benefit of cozying up to the gay group. He hoped he did not sound like he was using his new friends. He would find a way to pull his own weight somehow, when the time came. In any event, Tommy was so psyched that gays seemed to know everyone. He hoped for that slim possibility that Kyle would bite at the invitation to meet him out at the club. It was a slim chance, but just sending the e-mail in the first place was its own victory. Besides, Garrett had suggested it. Tommy also knew that if he came out to that part of town early, he would have a better chance to be by the club without being in it, in case Kyle happened to walk by. He would not miss any opportunity to catch him. But with his friend getting antsy, he agreed to vacate their perch by the window and head over to the club.

All the body heat from the shirtless bodies made for an annoyingly humid condition, not unlike the summers Tommy had grown up with back home. But every time someone opened the door to the patio portion to go smoke, he was reminded that it was a cool 50 degrees out, far too cold to be wearing short sleeves. Yet the energy generated by the dance floor—aided by the cocktails—made it warm enough inside for as little clothes as possible. Tommy had made a few laps around the club, stopping to talk to some acquaintances along the way while he searched in vain for a glimpse of Kyle.

"Tommy, seriously, why don't you just relax and have a good time? You're obsessing over this guy for nothing." Zack's patience was wearing thin; though why he did not just take off on his own if he would rather be doing something else sort of annoyed Tommy, which was more than he needed to weigh on him at the moment.

"I'm not obsessing. I just don't want him to show up and think that I wasn't here." Clearly, Zack just didn't understand. It was always the people who did not have anyone that became experts in the field of romance. Tommy knew that Kyle would be there; he had to be, Tommy could feel it. Besides, in his own defense,

Tommy and Kyle sounded like the perfect couple's names. They just went together.

"Don't you think he would have sent you a message back if he planned on meeting you?" Anyone who had ever been in the throes of the beginning of something awesome knew that logic had nothing to do with anything. Although Tommy was not on that list of people, he had seen enough movies to know that this is how things worked.

Tommy felt compelled to answer with his own rationale. "Not necessarily. What if he replied, but hadn't gotten to me yet? He'd think I was a flake if he couldn't find me." It's not like he had not thought this through a thousand different ways.

Zack rolled his eyes. *Ah, the ones without any faith.* Tommy knew what he was doing. As he looked to his left, then got on his tiptoes to check out the back area, he decided that they should double back to the dance floor. Kyle may have walked through, using the other side, allowing them to have let him slip by.

Without another moment lost in conversation, Tommy led the charge through the mass of men, with his drink held at his shoulders so that it would be more difficult to knock and spill all over the place. There was nothing like having to go to the bathroom to rinse off sticky liquor from your hand. Zack kept his hand on Tommy's back to preserve contact, as well as to force the procession.

"God dammit!" The drink poured down Tommy's hand and into the sleeve of his shirt. He grabbed the drink by the other hand and shook off the excess fluid as he looked up, waiting for an apology. He thought he had guarded against being bumped, but some people always find a way to mess things up, regardless of how prepared one tries to be.

"Sorry, man, I didn't mean..." When their eyes met, Tommy forgot that he was pissed at having his drink spilled. It took a moment to register that Kyle could bump into him anytime he wanted. Zack wanted to know what the hold up was, but Tommy could not say anything. He just stared at Kyle, concentrating, waiting for the image to crystallize, like staring at those goddamn pictures that look all a mess, like random colors, the ones you have to stare at long enough, until something pops up. Like that, except not as annoying and much more worth the effort. *He came.*

A few guys nudged their way through the traffic jam they created, shoving Kyle and Tommy to the side as a pair. Zack came up from the rear, passed, gave Kyle a once-over, then smiled his approval. He obviously understood now, and Tommy could not wait to rub it in.

But Tommy had more important things to concentrate on, so he turned dramatically back to Kyle, who held the glare for a moment, then smiled. Kyle had such a discreet smile, like one you would see in a luxury car ad.

"Maybe we should..." Kyle stuttered a bit, obviously wanting to find someplace a little more private, more discreet.

"Yeah, yeah, how about..." Kyle turned, without waiting for Tommy to finish, and melted into the crowd of the back area of the bar. *Cool! A guy who takes charge.* A man like Kyle could lead Tommy anywhere he would like, Tommy following without question.

"Do you need a..."

Tommy ate up the fact that Kyle noticed that Tommy had an empty glass. That showed Kyle was not selfish. *Wow! Beautiful and considerate.* "Yeah, actually. Stoli and cranberry, thanks." Tommy stood back, out of the way of the crowded line that had formed at the bar. He wanted to stand back and admire Kyle, so cute as he waited in line, unable to keep his hands still. Kyle walked back over in what seemed an instant with the drinks. "Thanks." *No guy has ever bought me a drink before.*

"No problem."

He looks so manly with a bottle of Budweiser in his hand.

"So, ah...how long have you been here?"

How should he answer? Should he make it seem like he just got there, or should he be honest? What if he lied, saying he just got there and Kyle had seen him earlier? Would he be pissed that he lied? "About an hour, I think..." Best to round his answer off. He really had no idea how long he had been at the club so far that night. He had no idea where to start with Kyle. What did he want to ask him? Should he thank him for coming? Did he show up to see him? He looked so cute and out-of- place in his little frat boy jeans and polo, capped off with his carefully manicured cropped hair. He looked so "butch," downing his beer. "When, ah, when did you get here...? I was cruising around here for a bit..." Shit, did that mean he had been stalking Kyle? Should he have said that?

"Not sure, a little while... I was outside having a few cigarettes."

Tommy kicked himself for not looking out on the patio. *Oh well, next time.* He sucked down the remnants of his cocktail and moved forward, towards the bar. Kyle stopped him with his big, wonderful hands.

"I'll get you one. The same?"

Tommy liked feeling Kyle's hands on him and forced himself to back off from him, even though he bent right over them. "That's okay, you don't have to..." He could not believe he was asking to buy him another drink. That must mean that he liked him.

"No, really, I'm going to get myself another one."

"Okay...thanks." Kyle took his empty glass and turned to the bar. Tommy reclaimed his spot on the wall, unable to wipe the smile from his face. *Thank God the lighting was shit back here.* Things could not have been going better. He could not wait to tell Garrett about his triumph.

Tommy had lost track of the number of cocktails they had had, but he did know that they had not moved from that same spot for a good two hours. But at one point, Kyle took Tommy's hand in his and leaned over and kissed him quickly on the lips, then took a long drink from his beer. Kyle looked a little nervous, as he turned in every direction, perhaps to see if anyone else had seen him kiss Tommy, but Tommy did not care how he got the kiss, as long as he got it, knowing what it meant.

Tommy studied Kyle's every move, the whole time reminding himself to breathe. *God, he looks so damn cute picking at his bottle label, tapping his fingers against his jeans, fussing with his hair, bobbing his head around to the wrong dance beat.* Tommy was not sure if he was quite as drunk as he wanted to be, but he was sure he was in love.

Chapter 18

Along the small walkway between the front door and his bedroom, Isaac paced. His feet had long since grown tired, so he took to dragging the tattered soles of his sneakers across the worn hardwood floors. The exhaustion he sought did little to quell the restlessness in his mind. Going to the various clubs and bars every other week had become his routine, his reason for leaving these walls for something purposeful, the only thing with any meaning these days. Now that they were supposed to lay low, or whatever else Scott dramatized it as, the anxiety brought on by these walls potentially closing in all around him seemed to suffocate him.

When his leg cramped, he slumped onto his futon and clipped away the stray skin that was calling out to him on his finger tips. As he reached the end of the last cuticle on his left ring finger, a soothing thought entered his mind: the support group. This group, once led by William, offered him the safety he had come to need every Friday night. Perhaps it could do so again. Of course it had been so long since he had seen any of the others in the group, before he split off from them to work with Scott and William—a day he was beginning to regret—but he assumed he would still be welcomed back with open arms. But what if he did not know anyone? What if, instead of a familiar, welcoming environment he found a fresh group of despairing individuals with whom he would be forced to acclimate? His neighbor slammed the door shut. Moments later, a television kicked on, blaring through the thin walls. There had to be something—anything—for him to do to escape, for having to listen to the laughter on that distant television program threatened to plunge him into a well of despair he was not anxious to revisit. *No, no! I have to get to my feet, cross over to the door, and venture out. I must summon the courage William repeatedly convinced me that I possessed. Strength! I need strength.*

On second thought, William had said to be patient, which meant avoid thinking for yourself. All along, he had said to be patient; in time it will come. *What to do, what to do?* How long had he been the person clutching a lottery ticket, waiting for his numbers to be called? Finding the group to which William welcomed him had been his winning ticket, his invitation to a better, more satisfying life, but his shallow confidence found no such elevation in William's hands. Sure, William countered every doubt with assurance that time would cure everything, that something brewing, coming together just ahead stood to change everything for so many. Isaac, with his inclusion in this group, would have a hand in his destiny, a stake in the happiness of perhaps millions. This opportunity would be the answer to the avalanche of unanswered prayers. Sweat gathered under the arch of his feet. If he were to venture out, he would have to change his socks. But then he would have to fuss with the double knot on his shoes. *Damn!*

How many times had he found himself waiting? As the plan unfolded, initially, he felt fulfilled for fleeting moments, but now the doubt resurfaced again, his conviction doubting his purpose. He could not bring this to William, who would only think him weak and not up to the task. Was he weak? Or did it take a strong man to question things? William's exact advice escaped him at that moment. *Perhaps I should just wait*, he thought, as he put his hand to his stomach to ease the rumbling that was building inside. He would make a nice meal for himself and enjoy the night at home, embrace the waiting. "Lean into the pain," his stepmother would tell him. As he stepped in the small kitchen, he opened the cupboard door only to find barren shelves. He sank his head. Was he allowed to leave to get food? He ran his hand along the shelves and brushed the few stray crumbs forward. *Decisions, decisions...*

As he put on his coat and checked for his wallet, he wondered if he should clear anything with William first, but then he buried that thought. William had been telling him to stand up for himself; he would make his own decision. William and Scott—if they had a problem with it—they would just have to deal with it.

A sense of empowerment surged through Isaac's scalp as he waited for the bus on the corner. He almost did not even notice the snow drifting down all around him. He secured a seat in the back of the bus, this action recalling a time when, as a child, his father rewarded him for a month's worth of successful chores' completion with a trip to the circus. Isaac welcomed a visit to a place where he could lose himself in a different reality, a place where the freaks served as the main attraction. How he marveled at the world that day as it whooshed along that large bus window, his eyes growing wide with each new discovery. But they never made the circus that day because a traffic accident stalled traffic for an hour causing them to miss the circus and his father felt there would be no point going at that point. "Another time, son," his father assured him. But another time never arrived. Though Isaac held his breath every time his father returned home from an errand, hoping to learn that today they would make it to the big top, he learned to live with that feeling of unrequited hope. He had practiced this routine so often that he learned to hold his breath from that point on, in any situation, without realizing that he was doing it.

When, by chance he wandered into that outreach group, stepped into that circle of empty chairs, his lungs exhaled for what seemed the first time. Running his hands over his chest, Isaac realized he needed to experience that again, to sit amongst people who would understand him the way William once did. This realization made him pleasantly jittery. He would not again retreat into his hole. Deciding to venture out, perhaps against William's wishes, was a strong statement for Isaac, one that spoke of confidence to come. So this was the confidence William had predicted. Just depositing his token in the slot by the bus driver existed as a noble gesture on his part and Isaac saw his journey to the group that night as revisiting the source of his rebirth. William was right.

His stop was approaching.

As he stepped onto the curb, across the street from the bus stop, Isaac felt his palms grow sweaty as he reached for the entrance to the church.

"Yes, can I help you?"

Isaac smiled at the calming words. Acceptance waited peacefully on the other side of these doors. He had made the right decision.

"Yes, how do you do? Is Father Carmichael here this evening?" His confidence asserted itself on its way off his tongue.

"No, I'm afraid not. Is there something I can help you with?" With that, the confidence trickled back and stepped over his shoulder on its way back into the street. Isaac peered over the priest's shoulders and counted a few men seated across from one another on folding chairs. *I can do this, I can do this.* Every step back is an incentive to take another step forward.

"Well, yes, well, sort of. I used to come to these groups, a while ago, and was wondering if I might not join in tonight." Was that too forward to assert to someone you did not know? Was Isaac supposed to reveal his prior membership to anyone?

The priest's face warmed to the sentence and Isaac could feel the entire room pause and stare up at him. "Well, I, uh, you said you have been here before? I don't remember ever seeing you, young man."

"Oh, I understand. It has been a while, about six months. I used to come when William Thompson ran the group."

The priest's expression deepened with joy at hearing William's name mentioned. William's work was legendary. "Oh, I see, then yes, of course, come in and I will introduce you." The priest stepped aside, allowing Isaac to step into the room.

"Gentlemen, this young man," he paused as he put his hand on Isaac's shoulder. Isaac knew the gesture meant for him to introduce himself.

"Isaac—my name is Isaac." When everyone smiled and nodded their hellos, the rumbling in his stomach ebbed for a few moments. He took an empty seat and waited for the talking to resume. The sooner everyone stopped looking at him the better. He wanted to be a part of the whole, not to be the focus of attention.

"Now, Nick, if you would, resume your story."

"Oh, yes, I...lately I have felt like I have wanted to go back to my old ways. I was turning on the television and I came across that gay program and found myself watching it, laughing along with the jokes, the whole time thinking that what I was watching was just disgusting and that I shouldn't find these gay characters funny. But I did, and I wondered what to do. That was just last night, and I had been so tempted to go out to a club and see if I could resist, but I didn't feel strong enough, as if I would get sucked back into it all again."

Isaac felt the guy's pain through the sniffling, but wondered if he should offer up his own advice for how to go out and conduct yourself in the tempting environment. Then he thought about how the one thing that had enabled him to bolster his confidence had been snatched away from him by Scott and William, the very people who had given it to him in the first place. Was this what he had to look forward to—to coming back to these meetings again? He had found a purpose and now he felt like sitting in that chair, sitting around these people was taking a big step backward.

One group member turned to console the man who had finished the story. "Take a deep breath and just let it all out," the one said to the other.

That will not do you any good, Isaac thought. If his experiences of late had taught him anything it was that you have two choices: let it all out and look pitiful or take matters into your own hands and be subject to the orders of someone with more power. Then Isaac quietly shut his mind off. Thinking such bold thoughts betrayed the faith he had placed in not only God, but William as well.

The priest started in with his counseling and Isaac felt a tinge in his spine, as if he could have recited the words that would come. "Now, Nick, you did the right thing by coming to us for support and not caving in to your longings. You know that God would not have any sympathy had you failed Him by resorting to your old habits. You need to find your strength from within, through Him. Only then, when you have truly renounced all those thoughts and desires, can you be healed and accepted in the eyes of the Lord."

It had been so long since Isaac had heard that speech, yet he could have recited it the moment he saw the priest draw in his breath, but this time the bitter pill that he had always seen as therapeutic, as mildly encouraging, stung his ears. He felt a sadness creep into his heart for this Nick, someone he had never encountered, yet whom he knew through and through. He wanted to tell him that there was another way, but as he thought about it, he did not know what that other way would be. Was there any hope to be had?

"Isaac, perhaps you could share your struggle with us." The priest looked at him and Isaac looked away. What would he share? And as he turned away and stared into the wall, he felt the priest's eyes bore into him. Then a new thought occurred to him. He had mentioned William's name to the priest, and what if that priest happened to run into William and say he had seen Isaac? What position would that place him in? Would William be angry with him? Would he have jeopardized anything by venturing out and returning to the meetings when William had strictly forbidden it?

"Well, now, Isaac, if you are feeling a bit uneasy, then you may just sit and listen." As the group moved on, Isaac sat and listened, the whole time his thoughts telling him that he failed again, that he had let everyone down. The pride he felt in exercising his own judgment and taking responsibility for his own decisions slipped into shame for letting everyone down, a feeling much more comfortable to field than Isaac had anticipated, as if his slight reprieve from disappointment erased the memory of all his collective past decisions. He had fucked things up again.

"Okay, then, perhaps, Ted, you could share tonight."

Ted took up the baton, dutifully confessing all that he had been trained to perceive as sin, his words following the same script as everyone else's. All around him, the other men nodded their heads, sharing what Isaac understood as a sick comfort in having everyone learn the same drill. Before he knew it, not able to even watch the eyes convey the sadness that found no words, tears flowed down his face because of a melancholy he could not articulate as all the hope vanished out of his life. Would his fate be the same as everyone around him, as well as the men he brushed up against in the bars and clubs? Maybe William did have the right idea; maybe their group provided the only hope this curse of a life offered: an easy way out. But was that truly what God had in store for them? Could he really be so cruel, so dead inside?

When the meeting ended an hour later, Isaac could not have told you one thing that had been said, one story that had been relayed, or why one tear had been shed. He did know that he was the last one to leave, but not before the priest walked over to him.

"Isaac, you look troubled, and when you refrained from speaking, especially since you have had experiences here before, I wondered if there isn't something I might be able to do for you."

Isaac looked into the priest's loving eyes, the same eyes William had once possessed. Isaac had fallen into the net once before. He would avoid the trap this time.

"No, Father, I don't think so. I think I will be able to handle it on my own." As Isaac eased out of the front door of the church, he looked down the road to see the taillights of his bus.

As he walked down the street, killing time while he waited for the next bus to arrive, Isaac played out his options in his head. All he could do at this point was continue on. He would wait until he was told it was okay to go back out, and whatever happened after that, well, that was not for him to decide. Watching that young man sob in front of everyone, just as Isaac had for William all those long months ago, Isaac saw himself; he saw the exact same pain; and as he watched him dry his eyes, Isaac surrendered to the pity in his heart, for the hope that lingered there for so long had dried up as the realization set in that he had stepped into a situation from which he could not escape. All he could do now was surrender to whatever lay ahead of him. As always, his life now rested in the hands of others.

Now the snow mattered to him, doing a fine job of hampering his walk. As he mopped through the sludge, he could not help notice how this thing, which started out so beautiful, did a wonderful job of coming down and hiding everything under its white blanket. Of course, by tomorrow, the beauty would fade and leave a mess for everyone else to clean up.

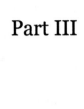

Part III

Chapter 19

Scott watched in amusement as the body-complimenting t-shirt-wearing worker replaced the "warning signs" above the urinals with cigarette ads. Leave it to the gay community to be unable to sustain interest in any one thing for too long. If Scott needed further proof that things had effectively cooled off, he had it in the tasteless ads touting cigarettes, compelling his attention as he took a leak. William was right; the time to take things up again stood before them, and Scott was all too eager to get things going. As Scott shook himself dry and zipped his jeans back up, he could not help but feel a bit sad over not seeing his work advertised on the bathroom walls, as if the ads were more about touting their accomplishments, rather than the cautionary pieces of paper the bar owners intended them to be. Perhaps "come and go with whom you know"—an interesting little campaign designed to discourage casual sex and one-night stands—could not quite reach its target audience, although Scott could not be sure the pun was intentional. Scott also missed the added challenge the warnings provided. Anyone could walk across an empty freeway, but doing it with cars zooming past, gunning for you, now that was a different matter.

Scott, however, moved on to a bigger and better challenge. The few months away had left him itchy for some action, which included finding a way to nudge Isaac out of the picture. He would fuck up. Scott just needed to make sure he was around when he dropped the ball. That should not be too difficult, and soon they would be rid of the little twerp.

Isaac poked his head in the doorway of the club not too long ago, without noticing Scott. *Figures.* Scott relaxed a little as he kept an eye on Isaac. *Strange that the first night I am back around all these fags feels so comfortable.*

"What can I get ya?" Scott found himself squinting from the bartender's bright white teeth.

"Lager, bottle." The bartender bobbed away to the new song that erupted into the front bar area. Someone brushed up against Scott. Prick could not even be bothered to say "sorry." Shoving the guy back did not seem like the right thing to do; Scott had learned some restraint. After all, Scott wanted to conserve his ire for another man.

"You should be out there dancing," the guy called out to the bartender.

"Yeah, shouldn't I? Boy, could I show these guys a thing or two," the bartender responded without raising his head from whatever took him too long to accomplish underneath the bar. How long did it take to fetch a bottle from the cooler? Finally, the guy handed Scott his beer, without making eye contact. *Rude. So hard to find good help these days.* Scott waited to see if he had to pay for the beer, but the asshole next to Scott commanded the bartender's attention.

"Hey, hey! If it ain't Serpico."

"How are you doin', Donnie?"

They knew each other. *Figures.* Something in this association proved more amusing than the alarm that should have sent Scott to the other side of the bar, far away from this pig. Just what this city needs: another gay cop.

"Is someone getting you a drink?"

"Yeah."

"Oh, I'm sorry, Hold on, John. Four for the beer." Scott handed a five and the bartender just held it in his hand when he should have been walking to the register to fetch Scott his change.

"So, you ever catch those guys that you talked to ol' Don Brown about?" Scott casually stepped a few steps away while he waited for his dollar, pretending he was not hanging on every word.

John shook his head and eased the drink placed in front of him closer.

"I got this one for him." The other bartender turned. "So things are good then?"

The cop sipped his drink. Leave it to a fag cop to not drink a beer. "Yeah, things are good."

"Your kid's out on the dance floor. He's with that other one—that kid Eric."

A new customer interrupted them and the bartender gave a two-finger salute to the cop as he walked away. Once the cop lost himself in the crowd, Scott slipped into a corner to lean against. He would let the bartender keep the charity donation; Scott suddenly had a bigger issue to address. A cop and a bartender talking. "Catch the guy." Did the bartender know about Isaac? Had he seen Isaac with one of their subjects? They had to be talking about Isaac. *This is too easy*, Scott thought. Now he had a clear reason to get Isaac out of the picture.

As if on cue, Isaac crossed the room, only a few feet in front of the bar. Scott kept one eye trained on him and another on the bartender to see if Scott had put the pieces of the puzzle together correctly. When the bartender zeroed in on Isaac and stopped what he was doing, Scott guessed that he was trying to put his own pieces together. Isaac had fucked up; someone had recognized him, and for whatever reason, it proved irrelevant. Maybe Isaac blew the guy. Maybe Isaac ordered a drink from the guy every time he came out, or maybe the bartender recognized Isaac as someone last seen with one of their victims. Whatever the reason that compelled the bartender to look like he was on his way out from behind the bar proved reason enough that Isaac was the idiot Scott always knew him to be. Scott had to move in on Isaac, and fast. The bartender would be after the cop for support and Scott had to plan their route out of there.

He bet that the bartender and cop would finish their sweep of the room before coming into the front room and possibly heading upstairs. He would have to cut around the dance floor and shove Isaac down to the coat check. They had not thought to look down there just yet. His eyes bounced off every face he saw pass him as he plowed through the sea of men. When he saw Isaac's shirt up ahead, just past the denim jacket walking slowly in front of him, he shoved through the human barricade and yanked Isaac by the arm.

All bent out of shape about having his arm tweaked, Isaac opened his mouth to say something before his eyes told him not to bother when he figured out Scott was maneuvering him through the passing lane next to the dance floor. At least he knew when not to question him. When Scott reached the top of the stairs that led down to the basement, he positioned Isaac in front of him and motioned for him to head down a few steps. Isaac obeyed. When Scott saw the bartender lead the way into the front room over the heads of the crowd, he stepped down and nudged Isaac into the hallway, past the empty coat-check room. Scott looked at his watch and thought back to the crowd they had just passed through. The concrete walls dulled the bass from the music and syncopated thuds echoed through the mostly deserted hallway, save for a few coupled-off men who were busy acquainting themselves with whomever they had just met. Everyone came to the basement for some privacy.

After the five minutes it would likely take for the bartender and cop to sweep through everyone on the first floor, Scott thought, they would most likely head upstairs to the lounge area or down the back stairs. Either way, they would not double back, which would allow for him and Isaac to go back up the front steps and head right out the front door. He put his watch down and bore his eyes deep into Isaac, who could not even mask the fear in his face. Scott felt the makings of sympathy build up in his chest: Looking at Isaac was like seeing a badly burned kitten in need of being put down, to put it out of its misery, but staying your hand for those brief moments of doubt, feeling like maybe there was a chance.

If anything, being in William's group had taught him that such hope was futile. Hard decisions yielded the best results. Scott needed to take charge. "In four minutes, we are going to move up those stairs and out the front door and you are never going to come here again. They know your face and they are looking for you." Making the directive sound as if Scott had Isaac's best interest at heart would make this all go down easier. Whatever it took.

They waited a few minutes, and when Scott had stomached all of Isaac's squirming he could, Scott felt the time was right to test the waters. He trotted to the top of the stairs, scanned the crowd and came up empty. He motioned for Isaac to hurry up the stairs, and when Isaac was on the same step as Scott, Scott caught the dynamic duo ascending the stairs in the back. Now he and Isaac would have their best shot at ducking out. As Scott brought Isaac ahead of him, he saw the bartender pause on the middle of the stairs and point. They had to move.

Scott clutched Isaac's arm and guided their direction, as well as dictated their pace.

They exited with little fanfare, as far be it for any staff to actually notice when commotion on the part of an employee—the bartender—might compel some form of intervention or effort. Getting free of the club took a few turns down different streets in only a few minutes' time. Scott eased their pace along the sidewalk, contemplating where to go and whether he should call someone in for a little assistance.

"Why are we walking this way? I live the other way." Scott kept a close hold on Isaac and hoped he did not plan on continuing to jabber. The high-pitched whine might force Scott to act sooner than his calm demeanor had intended to. Scott could cave in to his own impatience.

"Don't worry about it, just being safe." Scott mustered up his most sincere tone to placate Isaac until they could get to somewhere more private.

Occasionally, Scott looked behind them. Satisfied that no one was following them, he took a hard right down a dark alley and shoved Isaac against the wall.

"Why are we..."

"Shut up." Scott felt the need to reinforce his low tone by shoving Isaac against the wall even harder, planting his palm firmly against his chest so he would not bounce forward once his back hit the concrete. Confident that Isaac got the hint, Scott stepped back from Isaac and strode to the mouth of the alley to make sure they were alone. On the corner, a streetlight flickered, signaling the need to be changed. A couple of people off in the distance were giggling towards them. He cocked his head to the faint sounds of sirens. *Hurry.*

"Come on." Scott grabbed Isaac, whose elbow moved forward before the rest of his body could react.

"Where are we going?"

"To take care of the little mess you've managed to create. Did you even notice that they'd caught onto you?" Scott invited the conversation. *Get him talking to make this go down easier.*

"I did just as William asked every time." Isaac's voice dipped liked he had been punched in the stomach.

"Maybe William was not clear enough. Is that what you're suggesting?"

"No, no, I..."

Scott searched around for an open-hanging fire escape ladder that might lead to a rooftop, or at least up to a broken window that might let him into one of the buildings that shadowed the alley. They passed through the dumpsters, their footsteps sending rats scurrying along the cracked cement, while they trudged down towards the dead-end.

Scott found a good spot for Isaac, but he was at a loss for what to use; a gun would echo through the alley, and using a knife could be messy, although a couple stabs to the gut would do the trick, allowing Isaac to suffer a little, then bleed it all out until someone found him. Oh, he was thinking about it too much and Isaac was sniveling on about having to hide out in the alley. *Act quickly.*

"I have to go to the bathroom," Isaac whined. There was zero chance of him running, so why not let him drain it out?

"Sure, grab a wall. And make it quick." A strong sense of urgency collected in Scott's throat. The sirens collecting in the background created the need for haste. He needed to seize this opportunity, to ignore the doubt forming in his conscience. There would be no more saving. He needed to act to allow for the group and their all-important work to move forward.

Scott slipped his hand under his jacket and eased the long knife out of its holster. He would take Isaac from behind, but should he gut him with his dick out or wait until he had closed himself up? Scott was thinking too much. He needed to move quickly for the both of them. *Finish this and go about your evening,* he thought.

Isaac trembled a little when Scott came close to him and whispered, "You almost done?"

"Yeah." Isaac's voice quivered; Scott listened for the zipper. When the last tooth was firmly in place, Scott came around Isaac with his right hand, sliced into his stomach with the knife and covered the gaping mouth with his left. Two quick cuts and two stabs to the heart. Scott ripped his throat, just to be safe. He would endure a little pain, sure, but such was life. Scott left mercy to a higher power; he had to make sure the task got done.

Isaac slumped down on the ground; impassioned air passed through his windpipe while he cuddled up to the concrete. Scott stepped back as the blood flowed around his shoes, pulling them back just in time. He leaned down and cleaned the blade with Isaac's shirt and sheathed it. Scott glanced down the alley to see if Isaac's body could be easily seen from the street. When he figured he was in the clear, Scott knew he had time to get away, but running out of the alley, even casually, was not an option. He would be smart and take a ladder up to one of the rooftops and wait for the sirens to approach before he bolted. But Scott had to put Isaac out of his mind. He was just another hurdle along the way to their goal, Scott kept telling himself. Everyone had his purpose, and Isaac had fulfilled his. Still, it almost would have been amusing for Isaac to end up on a slab in the warehouse.

As Scott scaled the rickety ladder, he tried to piece together his speech to William. Scott would convince William that removing Isaac was necessary, something they had to do. Scott wondered if indeed he was the one that needed convincing. Whatever the case, he could not change the past. *What is done is done.* William would come around to see that it was necessary, or he would not. In either case, Scott had ultimately achieved his goal. Whether that goal stood differently than William's would be another matter for another day. All around him, the sirens grew louder until they finally stopped.

Chapter 20

"'Multiple stab wounds to the chest and stomach, deep laceration to the throat.' Whoever wanted this guy dead did the job right." As John breezed through the highlights of the report, he could not quiet the feeling that someone got to his man before he had a chance to bring him to justice. Clearly, the murder was an inside job, pointing to the existence of a deeper team or network of people, which only made the picture that much messier. For this reason, John felt a bit inadequate about the whole case, as if the clues came to him, instead of him trying to track down the culprits. Perhaps having Donnie be the one to provide the positive ID still rubbed him in a weird way.

"You sound sad. If he's our guy, he fucking got what he deserved."

John looked back down at the report. Although he could not agree with Glenn more, as he looked at the picture of the lifeless body on the slab, John thought that maybe this killer needed more than several knife wounds for what he had done. A prison cell was much more of a punishment than getting an express ticket away from his crimes.

"You think anyone deserves this?" John held up the morgue photo.

"Yeah. Hey, look on the bright side. Getting stabbed in one shot like that is better than getting stabbed every day of the rest of his life in jail, right?" Glenn was far too proud of his humor. Glenn used his pen to illustrate.

Glenn's voice thankfully trailed off as John's folder hit the desk and he took up the plastic bag that held the contents of Isaac's wallet. He rustled through the minimal contents and plucked out his ID.

"Here, write this down." Glenn needed a task and John needed to feel like he was moving forward with this case in a meaningful, controlling way.

"What you got?"

"The address from his license. Write it down." The city address meant they would not have to travel very far. It also meant that whoever was tied into this would be local as well, presumably.

John continued to thumb through the contents and paused when he hit a business card. *Now here is something interesting.* A glimmer of hope illuminated between his fingers. "Write this down too."

"What else?"

"A doctor's card with Taylor University's insignia on it. Write down Dr. Stephen Riles, Medical Department."

"What's so interesting about that?"

"Remind me to ask the good doctor when I talk to him. In the meantime, make the phone calls and get the warrant to turn the guy's apartment over. See if we can get this done today." John tucked Dr. Riles' card into his shirt pocket. His interest in the case bounced back from the prospect of the predictable tedium of rummaging through a suspect's apartment to find the typical nothing into a challenge. Why would a murder victim have a University professor's card on him—and a doctor at that?

"Okay, will there be anything else, Detective Thompson?"

John reclined in his chair. Glenn's tone carried just the right amount of indignation that signaled that he was in need of feeling like he was a little more involved in the case than just someone who hung around to do the dirty work. John welcomed the opportunity to throw in some humor of his own. "Actually, yeah. I could really use a blow job." Although John did feel in need of that particular job, he would not have allowed Glenn to handle it under any circumstances. Hopefully, Kevin would be around when John finally made it home. The comment, however, succeeded in shutting Glenn down, though briefly. Never to be taken seriously with the comment, John found the remark worth it, watching Glenn fidget with discomfort, shaking his head seconds apart, the way someone does after downing a stiff shot of Tequila.

Knowing it was a waste of time, they followed their procedure and pounded on the front door anyway. John, Glenn and the three officers waited a moment or two before they kicked in the door. The building manager mentioned that Townsend lived alone, but it could not hurt to give anyone who might be inside a chance to answer. John praised the makers of cheap door locks as the door gave way without much force.

They made a sweep of the one-bedroom apartment within moments to learn that they were safely alone. Though they sacked every cupboard and drawer, little turned up: A well-read Bible, modest wardrobe—

nothing but a fairly clean apartment. Little stuffy, though. It was interesting to see how single, heterosexual killers chose to decorate their apartments—or not, in this case. When asked, John never could give a solid generalization of what to expect in such an apartment. Television depicted killers with warped personalities, stacks of scribbled-in journals and clutter everywhere. Sure, John had seen those in his time, but the reverse usually proved closer to the true picture. Deviants acted out their perversions on their victims, not on their environments.

"Detective."

John walked to the bathroom to see what the officer turned up. "What'd you find? Black bag?" The officer pried it open to find a bunch of unmarked white pills collected in a plain plastic bag. *Doesn't look like Ecstasy; must be prescription pills of some kind.*

"Addict?"

"Who cares? Bag it and tag it." Instinct got you in the door, but analysis required a little more concentration—or should he say a *different* concentration—than being at a crime scene. Looking for clues and discerning their importance involved two different mindsets.

John walked over to the large window by the bed. Glenn was staring out intently at the street. "Not a bad view."

"Yeah, wonder how many people got to see it?"

"What'd you find in the bag?"

"Some pills, probably 'scrips of some kind. I'm sure the lab will tell us they are the same ones we found traces of in some of the bodies we recovered. At least that'll pin this guy to it. Beyond that, this place looks pretty useless. Hopefully, the doctor will have something to say. Maybe this Townsend used the doctor for supplies."

John felt the camera pull back to reveal the bigger picture, but the image was still a bit blurred at this point.

Glenn looked liked he had spied something. Probably peering into some girl's window. "Anything interesting?" John figured he would be a "guy" and take a peek.

"Check that out. Some guy across the way on the rooftop taking pictures."

"Some art student shooting the building?"

"Hard to say, but seems a bit odd to be perched on top of a building like that. Shit, the things people do for a picture. Can't he just buy a book like the rest of us?"

"Yeah, whatever. Let's go see what the doctor is up to this afternoon." John stepped away from the window, but Glenn did not budge. "What's up?"

"Oh, never mind. He scooted over and started snapping in another direction."

Dr. Riles wore guilt on his face the way most men wear bad cologne—all over the place. He clutched his briefcase and made an attempt to tidy up on his way out the door.

Day over at 2:30. Must be nice. Looked like John and Glenn had impeccable timing. "Dr. Stephen Riles?" John knocked on the door while he spoke, choosing to peek inside before announcing their presence.

"Yes?"

"I'm Detective John Thompson. This is my partner, Glenn Baker. We're conducting an investigation into a murder that took place a few days ago. We were wondering if we could borrow some of your time." The muscles in the doctor's face went taut and he eased his body into a rigid stance. *Guilty, but of what?*

"Ah...ye...yes, come in. And please, close the door behind you, detectives." John waited for the doctor to get comfortable before taking a seat. Glenn stood. John surveyed the walls of the office, impressed by the seemingly endless slew of degrees and awards.

"Nice office." John took the lead on talking.

"Thank you."

When John was satisfied enough silence seeped into Dr. Riles, "What kind of research do you do, Dr. Riles?"

He looked perplexed as he answered, "Brain functions and their determination in certain human behaviors."

"Sounds interesting."

"I'd like to think so."

"And you teach as well?"

"Yes, well, normally. I'm on a sabbatical this semester so I can devote my time to my current project. I'm working out of the school lab."

"You don't have another lab you work out of then?"

"No. Now, pardon me for asking, Detective, but what exactly can I help you with?"

The doctor's agitation grew. John waited, and then said, "Do you know an Isaac Townsend, Doctor?"

Dr. Riles' eyes looked to the right and his lips mumbled the name a few times. "Not off the top of my head. A student of mine, perhaps?"

"I don't know, Doctor. Was he?"

"I suppose I could check, but I believe you would have to go through the appropriate office to check that. You must understand, I have as many as 300 students in one of my lecture halls—and that is per class."

"Fair enough. But maybe you had a research assistant. Someone you worked with on a more personal or professional level?"

"No, not that I recall. I would remember an Isaac." He seemed to pause over the last syllable as it rolled off his tongue. Something formed in his mind.

"Well, Doctor, this particular Isaac turned up dead a few nights ago. That help with anything?" Glenn leaned forward to get closer to Dr. Riles' face. John was sure he had picked that move from some movie.

Dr. Riles leaned back in his chair as a response, staring intently at John. "No, I'm afraid not." His tone drooped. He was more confident of his lack of knowledge. That proved as much as anything that there was something there.

"Well, see, here is the interesting thing, Doctor. When we went through his wallet, we found your business card in it. Don't you think that it is kinda odd—for someone you have no recollection of to have your card in his wallet?"

He rocked back and forth in his chair, slowly. "Not really. Anyone could have my business card, Detective."

"Do you hand them out in class, Doctor?"

He laughed, "No, Detective. I don't hand them out in class."

"Well, you don't have them on your desk." John had looked for them while he waited for Dr. Riles to take his seat.

Dr. Riles scanned the surface of his desk, but said nothing in response.

"So you must have given it to him. Any idea where you might have met and given him the card, Doctor?"

"Not that I can recall. But maybe if you had a picture I could look at—something to jog my memory. I'd be happy to help any way I can." He was still rocking, his arrogance inviting John's loathing. The doctor was mocking him.

"I'll have to get back to you on that." He stood up and took out his wallet. "In the meantime, take *my* card. Let me know if anything comes loose in your head. Sound good, Doctor?" John extended his hand and Dr. Riles rose to meet it, circling the desk to walk them out.

John stood in the hall while Dr. Riles remained in the safety of his office. "What's down there?" John motioned to the double doors resembling a hospital operating room.

"That's my lab."

"Mind if I look around?"

"Yes. I have sensitive research I am conducting and I don't wish it to be disturbed." Dr. Riles must have known that only a warrant could force the issue.

"Yeah, sure." John studied his guilty face a moment longer. He would crack him soon enough. "Have a nice day, Doctor."

Once John and Glenn were back in their car, John asked, "What'd you think?"

"I would love to see what is in that lab." Dr. Riles was almost taunting John, and John hated being taunted.

Once the detectives disappeared from Dr. Riles' vision, he eased the door shut to block the incident out of his life once he achieved the satisfaction that no one had noticed the presence of police officers in his company. What would anyone think? What *was* there to think? Riles hoped the stiff cushions of his high-backed chair would offer some comfort. Over and over again, he ran the exchange in his mind. He attempted a few deep breaths, but could not inflate his lungs the whole way. He felt like he had been standing on a deserted set of railroad tracks for two hours, watching the train that should never have been on them rumble towards him, his legs not allowing him to step out of the way as it hurtled towards him. There, alone in his office, he could not fight the feeling that he had known the train was there all along, with the rumbling under his feet, as he planted himself on those tracks.

He remembered Isaac, all right. But why would he have ended up dead, and what did it have to do with what they were working on? Was it any of his business? And why did he feel reluctant about the detective seeing what was in the lab? Had he had some guilt written on his face? As he closed his eyes, images flooded his mind, his brain conjuring scenarios wherein those poor souls found their end towards him. *No, no, it could not be.* He must...*distance. I need distance.*

For the better part of an hour, he picked apart the past few months, searching for pieces that spelled out his situation, but his doubts and inquiries found no answers. Was there something criminal in what he had a part in? There was no need to sever the ties to the organization out of accusations; he was too close to his goals. But he did need to move into the next phase of research. Perhaps it was better if he knew nothing. He looked at his watch. Barbara would have expected him home hours ago; they were to enjoy his early days together, taking in the longer hours of sunshine in the crisp spring air.

But she would wait. He had more pressing matters to address. Dr. Riles could not squelch the murmurs in his head that uttered what his mind failed to recognize. He did not even know what compelled him to pick up the phone and dial a familiar number, yet an unfamiliar voice answered the call.

He had not expected Isaac's voice, but the shock of someone else still threw him. "He...hello. This is Dr..."

"Hello, Dr. Riles." The voice was too welcoming, as if he had expected his call.

"Hello, I'm sorry, I don't recogni..."

"My name is Scott, Dr. Riles. I'm sorry to have to inform you that an unfortunate accident befell Isaac and I have been asked to step up into his place. You'll be working with me from now on."

Dr. Riles had obviously no choice. "Well, all right then, ah, perhaps..." Was he sounding shocked enough over Isaac's death? Should he emote more? "Perhaps you and I should mee..."

"Sometime tomorrow would be preferable for us to meet one another and work out matters in person." The dark tone of the voice on the other end of the receiver gave Dr. Riles pause. He wanted to hang up the phone right then and there, but something in the inflection told him that he was somehow a part of whatever there was to be a part of, and it was not up for debate.

"Tomorrow, then. Here on campus. Around 11 in the morning?"

"That sounds fine, Doctor. I'm looking forward to finally meeting you." And then the line went dead.

The cold feeling inching up his legs did nothing to ease in the idea that Dr. Riles could feign ignorance. Was there anything *to* know? *Good Lord!* What if those that had been missing were somehow the ones that had turned up on his table? What if all those reports in the paper ended up on his doorsteps? Did they have official certificates with them? What if they were murdered? Was he then tied in with them? *No, no!* He could not let his mind run wild like that. He would not speculate without something concrete. Surely there was a clean answer to all of this. He refused to accept that he had entered into anything illegal, that he allowed his judgment to be so impaired by anything. He would calm down and think. *Think.* What would he ask this Scott when he saw him tomorrow? *Stay the course.* He needed to go forward with his research. If they were, in fact, legitimate, then he could request that Scott find volunteers, living ones to move on to the next phase. If Scott exhibited any oddity in the request, well...he would deal with that then. There was no need to involve the authorities at this point. That would make him look guilty of something to which he was wholly ignorant. All he knew at that moment was that a cold receiver remained clutched in his hand, the dead tone ringing through the speaker in his ear. Dr. Riles was not sure what had just transpired in the past two hours of his life, but he could feel something wicked on the horizon, descending in his direction, and he debated about whether he should go home at all, or just run.

Chapter 21

Kevin took pride in his ability to season and butterfly the marinated tenderloin exactly as the recipe dictated. Like a proud mother, he watched the heat settle into the meat through the tiny oven door window. From the living room, Madonna asked Argentina not to cry for her from the stereo speakers. It was truly a moment. Like Madonna, he felt like he needed to be recognized more often for his efforts and accomplishments.

The track changed just as the energy shifted in the room. John burst through the door and careened into the bedroom, draping clothes on the furniture along the way. He swallowed the reflex to ask why the hurry, for he knew whatever it was would likely not involve him. John never rushed unless an appointment slipped his mind or a case call beckoned him away with only the slightest hint that something useful might turn up, as if John would be the only one capable of finding it. Several of their early dates ended with an "I'm sorry" over John's desire to do what any officer under him held the credentials and experience for. Behind him, as Kevin smelled the steak's sizzle, resentment collected in his gut, causing his arms to tingle with anger.

Kevin's "Hey!" caught John's hand before it could finish turning the front door handle.

"Oh, hey, sorry Hon. I didn't see you there... I'm going to be late."

"Late? Late for what?"

"I have a basketball game tonight, remember?" His tone stopped short of irritated.

Oh yeah, that gay league he joined. Kevin breathed through his nose to ease the tension building in his neck. "You said that was tomorrow night." Kevin wanted John to think for a moment.

Slowly, a conversation between the two of them trickled into John's memory, but he pretended a different particular day found his ears. "No, I didn't, I said it was tonight. You just don't remember it correctly." His hand stayed on the doorknob.

"But I'm making dinner tonight, for just you and me." Kevin hoped his feel-sorry-for-me tone would sway John from going to his thing.

John scanned the mess on the kitchen counter, trying to figure out how much effort Kevin had put into it. "Oh. Well, Hon, I have to go. My team needs me...and... can't you put it off for a few hours? I'll be done by 9 or so, I promise. We'll have a late dinner."

The sincerity in John's voice almost passed as convincing; if only his hand had let go of the doorknob. *Believe him, believe him. This would not be the end of the world, would it? How long would one of his games really take? He can make it home in time. Just turn the oven down, keep it warm, it will be fine.* "All right. Go to your game." Kevin felt a swell of understanding sweep over him, as if some award were due him for his thoughts.

John's departure, without a word or a kiss, provided a canceling effect, like watching a bean bag chair slowly rise to reclaim the shape it was before someone dropped down into it. He dialed the heat way down on the oven.

The sizzling on the pan ceased. Kevin cut to the front room and flopped onto the couch, hoping to lose himself in the music, wishing he were *High-Flying Adored* right about then.

As the last song to *Evita* tolled to a close, Kevin found his mood relaxed. He took comfort in someone else's suffering—in this case, Madonna's. Suddenly, a phone call disrupted the beautiful closing lament.

"Hey, Hon."

Kevin glanced up at the clock at the sound of John's voice. Though the inter-workings of the game eluded him, Kevin felt confident that John should not have been able to steal away in the middle of the game for a phone call. "Hey!" Kevin could feel the apology coming. John rarely got so excited.

"You're gonna kill me. I mis-read the schedule. Our game is not until 10. I won't be home 'til late."

"Okay." Kevin said. His jaw hurt from grinding his teeth.

"You're pissed. I'm sorry. I'll make it up to you."

"Okay. Good luck in your game." He hoped John would pick up on the lack of sincerity.

"You're the best. Bye, Hon."

John just didn't get it. Kevin clicked off the phone, waited for a fresh dial tone, then called Eric. Kevin would not waste this evening.

"Girl, I don't know what you are so pissed off for, for Christ's sake. It's just dinner." Eric dabbed the olive on the edge of his second drink before he plucked it into his mouth. Kevin had not so much as sipped his first.

"That's not the point, and you know it." Eric's job was to agree with him. Why would Eric side with John? He hated John.

"You're right; you should have invited my ass over for a well-prepared tenderloin dinner."

Kevin did not bother trying to figure out which comment he meant seriously. *Both?* He was getting a headache; regret over having come out was collecting in his sinuses. Perhaps he would have been better off curling up under their new down comforter. Would John even notice that he had thrown out dinner? Would he understand why? Eric tried in vain to suggest that the point was not worth making, though he rolled his eyes as he picked up his drink and spoke at the same time, suggesting that he was only humoring Kevin. Kevin toyed with the idea of pointing out that Eric had not prepared a meal in some time—maybe never—and therefore could not appreciate all that went into it. Kevin pictured the steaks slowly browning in the oven before he snatched them out and trashed them. His stomach pulled a bit from hunger, as he watched them slide right into the week's trash. *Gone.*

After watching him closely for a moment or two, Eric thankfully recognized that his words weren't doing much good. "Fine, fine, be pissed, whatever, but at least be a decent human being and drink your drink before it gets warm." Eric hated drinking in public alone.

"Where'd you say Mike was tonight?" Though Kevin could care less, moving the conversation in some direction seemed the 'decent' thing to do.

"At home. It's not like we can go out every night." Eric made his aversion to constant nightlife sound obvious as he gulped the last half of his gin martini and ran the rim against his lips a few times.

Since when did they not go out every night? His head throbbed a bit, discouraging further thought. Maybe Kevin just needed to lose himself, stop thinking so much. So, he threw back his drink, wondering how long it would take to catch a buzz, and how long it would take to encourage some good old-fashioned poor decision making. If he got sloppy, he always had Eric to watch out for him.

Kevin misjudged the step that he knew should have been there as he scaled the back stairs, returning from an annoying long wait for the bathroom. Plus, by the time he got into a stall, his button fly would not cooperate, nor would the thumb that held down the waistband on his briefs, allowing his underwear to snap up right as he was finishing up, sprinkling his jeans a bit. He hoped no one would notice. *Why is this night working against me?* he wondered as he steadied himself against the wall, enjoying the nice burst of air coming at him from some direction. He needed another drink.

"Still in love, I see."

Something warm in the guy's tone told Kevin they knew each other. His grin slanted to the right, and through the slight blur in his brain, Kevin could not recall which television show he had picked that up from, but he knew it had to be from somewhere. *Josh.* Kevin raised a foot to the tiny ledge at the bottom of the bar to steady himself.

"Why so down all of a sudden?" Josh followed Kevin's eyes wherever they tried to hide.

Kevin did not respond.

"You know I am going to follow you around until you smile at least once tonight."

Kevin could not prevent a smile from surfacing. Kevin wished he could garner as much attention from his own boyfriend. He silenced the whisper that told him to stop indulging Josh's advances.

"There, that's better." Josh caressed Kevin's cheek with the backside of his hand, reminding Kevin's skin that it was still intact. After a few strokes, something drew him away. A reflex, perhaps? Feeling a bit hollow, like climbing up after a huge roller coaster dip, he needed a drink. Hopefully Josh would reach out and touch him again.

Something cleared in his head, the clarity that comes with a few deep breaths, like in that brief relief that follows that first drunken vomit. Kevin lifted his head from his drink slowly. "You don't take hints, do you?" Kevin meant his tone to be a little more indignant than it came out. However, it arrived far too playful, which would likely only goad Josh on. Maybe that was what he wanted. Something in those green eyes, watching them narrow a bit, sent his mind adrift, floating away somewhere that caused him to not even notice Eric nudge him a bit.

"Oh, sorry. Eric this is Josh. Josh, Eric." They shook hands while Eric sized up every square inch of Josh's body. Josh chuckled, obviously amused.

"We've met before. Nice to see you again, Josh. Well, I think I see somebody I haven't seen in a while, so I'm going to do a lap. You two boys have fun." Something in the way his voice trailed off reminded Kevin of being warned to get back to sleep when he and some friends were up too late on a sleepover. By telling them to have fun, Eric really meant *cut it out*. Kevin was not enjoying this respectable side of Eric.

"Now, where were we? Oh yes, the hint. What hint was I supposed to pick up on?"

Kevin had lost his place in their conversation. What did the words matter at this point? The alcohol nipped at the back of his brain. Autopilot. "So, what do you do?"

Josh looked amused, like a dog being teased with a ball. "What do you want to know?"

Kevin wanted to know how green the grass was. "Well, what do you do for a living?" *Water—I need some water.*

"You don't really care about that, do you?"

No. "Sure."

Josh chuckled. "Well, I design plastic mockups of products that go to the manufactures as a template."

Whatever he had just said, it sounded important. "So a nice nine-to-fiver?" Whatever did not involve a badge and a gun sounded wonderful. Somewhere, he thought he heard John's laugh. He looked around into the people that seemed to all run together.

"Sometimes. I make my own schedule and can work out of my house if I need to. I like having a flexible schedule."

"Keep your options open?" Kevin could feel himself getting back on the proverbial bike and the seat felt comfortable. A little of the fog in his head lifted.

"Yeah, something like that." Josh zeroed right in on him, caressing Kevin with those eyes—those deep, soft, wonderful green eyes. "So, where's your man tonight?"

Kevin tried to count his drinks in his head, like doing pushups or something to keep his mind sharp. He could not get past three, his mind forgetting what followed every time Josh's eyes pulsed. Kevin pushed the tip of his tongue against his teeth to see if it still worked. He could not control saying, "Does it matter?" as if those words were the most natural words he had ever spoken.

"No, not really." Josh's amusement stretched across his face, punctuated by his delicate dimples.

Josh's tender face carried not an ounce of the stress or burden that John wore like a badge of honor. When Kevin turned to dispel the unspoken accusation that he was checking out Josh too deeply, his eyes fell to Josh's empty hands.

"No drink?"

"Don't think I'll need one tonight. Besides, you seem thirsty enough for the two of us."

With that, Kevin finished his drink and ordered another one.

At some point, a voice came into focus somewhere.

"Kevin, Kevin..." Eric was waving his hands in Kevin's face.

"What? What? I see you, bitch. Can't you see I'm talking?" Eric was probably trying to move in on Josh, whose firm arm cradled Kevin's shoulders.

"Please, you're a mess."

Then Josh, like a perfect gentleman, said, "I think he's okay."

"Sure. Give us a moment, won't you?" Eric was up to something. "Girl, do you know what you're doing?" Kevin wasn't exactly sure what Eric was referring to, but he was sure, whatever it was, it was worth continuing to do. "Yes, girl. Now, go play." Kevin secured Josh's attention and wasn't going to let Eric squelch his fun. Kevin returned his attention to Josh. "Now, where were we?" Eric disappeared.

"I think you were telling me how many friends you have lying around."

"Whatever, anyway... " Kevin was feeling rather bold, as if their deep conversation was going to be interrupted all night. And he was having fun, or so he said, "Where can we go where people will stop bothering us?"

The taxi ride to Josh's blurred by, as did the elevator ride. He remembered some red numbers flashing and a door parting for them, but not moving up or down, whichever way they were headed. Somewhere, he could make out some classical music. Josh's voice sounded like he was speaking through a thin wall. If his words proved important, he would undoubtedly repeat them for Kevin's benefit.

"You've got a nice...that's a nice...I mean, I think I've seen that picture...can I sit?" Kevin made himself comfortable, without the official okay, on something that felt soft. Outside the window, lights sparkled all around. Was that the city out there? The lights pulsed with a dull hue. Something told Kevin that they were high up. His lips had gone numb. A chill spread out, down his neck and up the back of his head, and when Josh moved the glass into his hand, Kevin was half sorry that Josh hadn't held it there a little longer.

"I hope you don't mind. I brought you a beer." Josh made himself comfortable right next to Kevin.

Kevin was sure that there were too many lights on, although he couldn't tell where the nearest lamp was so he could dim it. "I didn't... No, I wasn't saying... I was going to say that you have a nice, a nice, uh..." Could Josh tell he was rambling? What an idiot he must look like.

"That I have a nice apartment?" Josh tickled the top of Kevin's skin with the tips of his fingernails.

"Yeah, you do." Kevin clutched the glass with both hands. He was sure it would slip out of his hands if he brought it up to his mouth. But he was thirsty, and he did not want to spill on Josh's carpet, which he was sure was nice.

"Do you really care?" Josh's fingers found Kevin's ears and worked around his earlobe. Kevin's toes curled under and his lips parted.

"No...I just...what did you say you did for a living? It's such a nice apartment..." Why he was making small talk?

Josh passed a bottle of poppers over Kevin's back. Kevin took the small brown vial to his nose, inhaling its magical odor without a second thought. It had been so long he had almost forgotten how much fun they were, and with each snort he drifted further and further into the fog that collected in his brain. He just went with it. It was like sitting in a steam bath, and Kevin closed his eyes and felt the sweat drip down his body. He almost could not feel Josh moving in and out of him from behind, and he almost did not care. He wanted to lay his head down and just let go, just release all that seemed to be binding him. How many drinks had he had? Maybe he was going to throw up... *No, no, do not think like that.* That next round of poppers needed to clear and he would be fine. The firm hand on his back smoothed out his muscles and he arched his back to let the fingers caress his spine. As he heard Josh's breathing get more erratic, Kevin clinched up out of habit, and then it was all over a moment later. The sensation was gone and he did not know whether he should turn on his side or go down and curl up on the carpet that looked so comfortable from where he was sitting, or standing, or whatever you called the position he was in. Then he felt a smack on his ass and Josh was walking into the room with a light that quickly went out. Kevin turned to a light coming from the window, while the edges of what he saw closed in. He felt himself fall back, burying his nose into something soft that smelled like pretty flowers.

Harsh nudging yanked Kevin from his slumber. *Where...?* Memories kicked in. What a strange dream he had been having. He sat upright. When the cool air hit his skin, he wondered what had happened to his shirt, and when he took a deep breath, the oxygen gave way to a pounding in his skull that called into question whether the flashes in his mind had actually transpired. And in another breath, he opened his eyes to find Josh staring at him with all the patience of a priest trying to get an unwilling boy to take communion.

A slight chill crossed his naked body when the whole picture collected in his consciousness. *This is not my bed.* He yanked the covers up. *Where are my clothes?* Each breath encouraged the rumbling in his head—the subtle stir that you feel when you know the full headache is still on its way. He glanced around, unable to find the words that might possibly be appropriate, given the circumstances. Josh just watched, a smirch painted across his face. *What time is it? 1:30. Fucking 1:30... Josh's apartment... how long had they been...?* Then Kevin felt the sting and tightness, and he knew instantly that he had given Josh more than a blowjob. *Fuck, fuck, fuck!*

"Hey, man. I hate to be a dick, but if you want a shower or anything, be my guest, but I really got to crash. I figured I'd let you snooze for a bit, but I really do kinda need you to leave."

Kevin waited for some more fresh air to clear his head as he listened to Josh ramble on. Kevin was not interested in staying. He waited for the window of opportunity for him to be able to lean down and gather his clothes that were sure to be on the floor. As he watched Josh help the process along, he tried to piece together the last few hours, but his brain was useless. *John.* He would be home already. *Fuck!* Kevin could not go home. John would smell the lube on him, and he could not go home showered. John would want to know why he did not smell like the bar. *What the fuck am I going to do?* By this point, Josh had helped with Kevin's socks and was lacing his shoes. Damn, that bitch was in a fucking hurry. *Eric.* He would have to call Eric on the way home. *No, wait.* He could not go home. Eric would...he would have to stay at Eric's and have him call John and say he was crashing there.

Josh successfully herded Kevin to the door and Kevin had his phone in hand by the time the dead bolt clicked behind him. He hit the speed dial for Eric's number and begged him to answer. *Fuck. Eric better not still be out and he better have his phone nearby.* Kevin looked up and down the lonely hallway. He trotted to the window and peered outside. First he would have to figure out where he was.

Thoughts of Kevin were far from John's mind earlier that night. "Hey, John." John felt stupid, being the only one from his team seated in the bleachers to watch the early game. Thank God, one of his teammates showed up to keep him company.

"How's it goin', Harvey?"

"Good. Hey, this is my friend, Chuck. He's in the med program at Taylor with my boyfriend. He's going to be filling in for Sid. Sid came down with a wicked cold."

"Sounds good. Nice to meet you, Chuck." They shook hands. John hoped Chuck would not let them down from the perimeter. Sid was their best shooter from outside.

"Hey, Harvey, you know this team coming in?" John studied the matching gym suits coming through the doors on the opposite end of the gym. He admired that they not only coordinated their outfits, but also managed to arrive at the same time. He wrote off their abilities the moment he figured they spent too much time on their appearance.

"Yeah, they're a pretty aggressive team, known for beating up the other team under the boards and in the lane."

John ignored the rumbling in his stomach, squelching the notion that he should have stayed in for a nice dinner instead of dealing with his teammates, who clearly did not have their heads in the game. Glancing at the scoreboard, John wondered how the other team's ten-point lead jumped to 18. The game had been total bullshit, and the ref could not be bothered to notice any of the contact going on under the boards every time he came down with a rebound and had the ball stripped away from him by having these queens paw at him. Yet, if he so much as stuck an arm in the wrong way, he got a whistle and the bitches on the other team got some time at the line. One of them was taking advantage of that time at the moment, and when the first ball coasted through the hoop, he wondered why the members of the other team did not have a set of pompoms to toss about every time they managed to score a point. *For this I skipped out on Kevin's dinner?*

When, by luck, they made the second toss-up, the ball bounced down to the ref and John's team in-bounded the ball. His teammate moved the ball up the court and John circled around the guy, guarding him so he could free himself up to take control of the ball, but the ball never made it into his hands. It got turned over, and John cussed as he helplessly watched the other team score with an easy lay-up. John's team captain called a time out so they could collect themselves. Hopefully, they would be able to rally against these guys in the second half.

"Fuck!" John stumbled out of bounds and waited for the whistle blow that never came. The ref missed yet another call and John massaged the side of his ribs that smarted from a well-delivered—and deliberate—elbow. *Fuck playing nice with these guys anymore.* John needed to step it up a notch and give them the physical game they were inviting. John would match them, blow for blow, if that was the way they wanted it.

They had twelve seconds to make a play happen. Down by two, they needed a three-point shot to seal the deal. The team agreed that the best option consisted of running a screen for John, getting him the ball and creating room for him to drill one from behind the line. The other team obviously had run out of steam. They must have forgotten to take their protein shake before the game, because they were starting to drag ass up and down the court. John felt a renewed faith in his boys' ability to outlast the competition.

The ref blew the whistle. His teammates passed the ball around. John freed himself from his guard, who was a little too slow on his toes, but the moment John clasped the ball, his man was all over him. Seconds ticked off on the clock. *Make something happen.* Out of his peripheral vision he saw a teammate open up, but John wanted to be the one to bring it home. John swerved his arms out in both directions, trying to draw out his defender's hands. The moment he leaned in too far, John would drive right past and take the shot. Seconds peeled away, and still no opening for him... 9...8...7...6...5...4...3...2...

John jerked to the left, his weak side. When the guy committed, John rolled out to his right. He dribbled once and lined up his shot just as the one became a zero on the clock and the horn sounded. John stayed in motion, spun around, posted up, and shot the ball. It rolled off his fingertips. As the ball fell through the net, the winning team had already turned from the court, cheering their success.

If only John's teammate had gotten the ball to him a second sooner, he could have beaten the clock. John felt it. Or maybe if he had faked to his right and gone to the left... Maybe that would have been the split second he needed. At the end of the day, they lost, and that's all that mattered—to his teammates, anyway. But to John, how they lost proved more significant than the loss itself. He had left Kevin home alone for nothing.

247

Chapter 22

"Girl, you're a fucking mess." Kevin finished the phrase in his head as Eric offered up the obvious, but the tone was a little off. Maybe the cappuccino had not quite worked its morning magic on Eric or Kevin's head simply hurt too much to hear anything properly. That undeniable, slightly condescending tone penetrated Kevin's hangover, preventing him from ignoring the hypocrisy carried with it. Wherever Eric discovered this newfound respectability, Kevin was sure he should take it back; the shirt did not fit right.

"Look who's talking." Kevin wished his coffee would hurry up and cool off so he could drink it. Blowing on it required more energy than he could muster.

"At least I would have the decency to put on some concealer before I left the house."

All of a sudden Eric became his press agent. Where had he been the night before, when Kevin needed some good advice? "You think I care what anyone else thinks of me?"

"I guess not, seeing as how you were acting like a little whore and giving it up to that hunk of a man last night. No, I don't think you do."

The way "whore" dropped out of Eric's mouth made Kevin wince a little and question whether he should tell Eric to go fuck himself with his criticism. "No more of a whore than you were." The night before had put him in a league with Eric and he felt ashamed to have finally fallen into a category to which he prided himself out of some time ago.

"Oh really? How do you figure?" Eric actually sounded like someone had accused him of shopping at an outlet store.

"The way you carry on with guys, you have the nerve to call me a whore?"

Kevin saw his hope of a morning consisting of a nice warm cup of coffee and a few hours for the aspirin to do their job dashed as the conversation slipped into a cat fight, the effort causing throbbing in his head. This proved to be about as exciting as pretending the dull pain in his ass was not really there.

"I'd say there's a major difference between what I do and what you do."

Without even thinking, Kevin rattled off, "Yeah, I have morals." His stomach turned at the last syllable. He was sure he had some food on its way up.

"Apparently." Eric cocked his eyes at Kevin. Kevin felt uncomfortable under the gaze that he never dreamed he would see. Eric was actually debating sexual morals. "One mistake doesn't compare to a hundred partners in a year." If Eric wanted to avoid the obvious, Kevin was more than prepared to feed it to him.

"Well, I wouldn't say there have been a hundred, although..." Eric sat back, allowing his eyes to drift. His lips formed a succession of numbers as he assigned numerals to faces to whose names he had never bothered to find out. But when he got bored, he returned with, "whatever the number is, there happens to be one major difference."

"This should be interesting."

"I don't have to lie about it."

Kevin quickly lost the gumption to press the matter any further; whether Eric was right or wrong was irrelevant.

"All quiet?" Eric reveled in the apparent success his comment produced. "You see, I have no misconceptions about what my relationship is about, nor does Mike. Now, you may think we are whores, or sluts, whatever, but the fact of the matter is that we have the relationship we want. And it works."

Kevin questioned if the relationship existed merely as a figment of Eric's imagination. "I don't want what you have, Eric, if that's what you're getting at."

"You don't even know what I have, Kevin dear." He was becoming quite an indignant bitch.

"Yeah? What's that?"

"Honesty. It fills in the holes when love gets old. You should try it sometime."

Kevin wished for the life of him that he could place the TV show or movie that Eric got that from, but he racked his brain in vain. He would let Eric pretend that it was his and just let it sit. "John and I are honest with each other." Even Kevin doubted the level of confidence in his own voice.

Eric just rolled his eyes. "Sure you are. Going to tell him how you got plowed last night?"

Kevin glared at Eric, then looked away when the room started to tilt. He closed his eyes and took a few deep breaths. God, he wished he could just get up and walk out. He had not been on a nice long walk in a while and a brisk stroll might clear his head a little. Eric was making him think too much, and he was not up to a deep conversation. Besides, Eric did not understand what he was going through. How could he expect him to?

"You just don't get it yet, do you, Kevin?"

"Get what?"

"It's not just about being honest with each other; it's about being honest with ourselves. Until you can do that, you'll never be happy in any relationship."

"How inspiring."

"Fine, be a bitch. If you don't want to know what I think, don't sit across from a bitch when she's drinking her morning cappuccino."

"What talk show did you get that from?" Kevin could feel a smile coming on as the tension left the table. Eric could never stay too serious for too long. It creased his forehead and he planned to put off a peal for at least another three or four years.

"Oh, shit, I don't know. I'm sure I heard it somewhere." He took up his mug and sipped.

Kevin was sure he was checking to see if they put the right amount of Bailey's in it by the way he savored the residue on his lips. "Do you really believe that?"

"Girl, sure, whatever, but I'm done giving you advice that you'll never listen to anyway. It's almost as much fun to watch you stumble as it is sad. You'll get there, I'm sure." As Eric turned to see who had passed on the street, Kevin could have sworn that he had muttered "hopefully soon" under his breath, but he didn't feel like asking.

"By the way, you missed a nice little gathering on 12th's roof deck last night. Rusty and Stevie came into the city—which they never do—so everyone came out. Brian and Frank were out—derailed, naturally; as were Brian and Tedd, who were on their best behavior; Tony and Mike were being their typical love-y dove-y selves; while Kurt—you know, the hair stylist—and John Paul—who was just back from some study abroad in Germany—were chatting away with Brad and Joshua at the bar with Sandy; Jessica was talking about a new art show she has coming up and how she was helping Daniel get his house together; as well as Ben, who was going on about some horrible root canal he had to perform earlier in the day, and his friend Ken; Kirsten was talking up some new drink she had come up with, which, incidentally, sounded fabulous; then everyone was heading back to Jim and Steve's in South Philly for an after party. I was gonna go, but you know, I was on trash pick-up thanks to you." He stopped to take a moment's breath. "Hey, are you even paying attention to me?"

Kevin looked up. "Huh?"

"So, anyway, on to more important things."

"Like what?"

"Like, I don't know. Did your man last night have a big dick or what? Don't keep details from your sister."

Kevin sat and thought for a moment and let the night before unspool in his head as long as he could. "I don't know." Kevin suppressed a sad feeling, although whether he was sad that he was reminded of his own indiscretion or the fact that he could not remember it escaped him. As his mind tackled this emotion, another tickled his conscience: although he could not say whether or not he really enjoyed the night—divorced from the moral implication—he could not deny that he felt more alive than he had felt in some time. This was something he would not utter or even attempt to accept.

Perhaps sensing the wheels turning in Kevin's mind, Eric rolled his eyes once again. "Messy, messy bitch. Goes to all the trouble to cheat on her man and doesn't even have the decency to recall the important stuff. Have I taught you nothing?"

Kevin let that comment roll right over him, right over the question he felt forming for Eric on his tongue. "Why are you with him?" The question just came out of Kevin's mouth and he seemed to register it the same time Eric did, although Eric looked confused.

"Why am I what?"

"With Mike? Why are you with him?"

"Girl, did you get your brain fucked out of you last night?"

"What do you mean?"

"You're being a simple bitch, that's what I mean. Why would you ask me that?" And Eric rolled his eyes again, like he always did to everything that was obvious to him, but not to the rest of the world.

"Well?"

With an exaggerated sigh that signaled he was putting forth more effort than he deemed necessary, "Because I love him. Why do you think?"

Obvious or not, that "fact" never occurred to Kevin. How could a relationship like the one Eric and Mike had have been built on love? He sat there and swirled his coffee, trying to see how high he could bring what was left to collect the streaks on the side back into the fold. They sat without another word passing between them for a while.

Scott found William exactly where he predicted he would: perched by the window, gazing off into nothing. Scott didn't knock, nor could he be bothered to ask what preoccupation "weighed" on William. As long as it did not interfere with business...

"William?" Scott was a little annoyed that he had to announce himself, but it did the trick. He chose to stand, as William took his seat.

"Were you able to clean up the apartment?" William's voice rang hollow, his trademark confidence noticeably absent. Maybe he needed a vacation.

"Yeah, but I couldn't get everything. Not before some friends stopped by." Scott dropped the manila folder on the desk and William snatched it up with reticence. "I managed to snap a few shots of the cops that dug through the place. Figure we could use these to track them down and send a message to the pigs on the case. Little distraction would throw them off long enough so we could finish up and cover the tracks all the way, just like we planned."

William squinted. "What exactly are you proposing?" Months before, he would not have needed to ask.

"If we find a way to take one of them out, that will buy us the time we need."

William rapped his fingers on the opened envelope flap. Scott challenged William's intent stare, William's eyes judging Scott as if his remarks proposed a hostile takeover of the nation's capitol. The cops were just another two bodies for the pile, the way Scott saw it. *Where is the hesitation coming from?*

"Scott, we are not out to kill people just to kill people. We need to stay focused on what our goals are. These police are only doing their job. While they do pose a possible threat, killing one of them would only make matters worse. We will just go about our business. The end is coming soon and we will be out of the woods. Do not, and I repeat, do not, take any..." William took the photos out and turned them over. His eyes fixed on something and his mouth slacked. Before Scott could ask what he saw, the phone rang and William paused, waiting for the second ring. William must have had too much on his mind to think clearly.

255

"Yes, this is..." William's face went pale and his eyes glided shut. Whatever news from the other end found his ears, he could not mask the severity. His grip on the photo tightened. His eyes opened; a glaze replacing the intent stare. Before Scott could ask what had happened, William had hung up the receiver and was collecting his jacket from the coat rack.

Without asking, William volunteered, "I must go to the hospital. It's Monsignor Drollings. We will pick up this conversation when I return, although I don't know how long I will be." William whisked down the stairs. Scott listened for the ping of the side door.

With William away for a while, Scott would be expected to watch over things, using his own judgment. Wouldn't he? Taking some initiative? A little joy collected in his cheeks. "My turn," he whispered, as if someone else might be around to hear him. He needed to get some balls rolling. Tomorrow he would visit with the doctor, and then he would be off to use some contacts at the police station to find out where the cops lived. Maybe he would pay their places a visit in the afternoon as well. Just as William stated, the end was near.

Scott made himself comfortable in William's chair and thumbed through the pictures, without paying too much attention to any of them. *Hmm.* There were five here. *What happened to the fifth?* William must have taken one with him by mistake in his haste.

Although Dr. Riles suggested that they take a walk, Scott insisted they stay inside, mumbling something about allergies, knowing their conversation must be contained within safe walls to prevent eavesdropping.

He would not be swayed by Riles' assertion that they should go outdoors to enjoy the "pleasant" afternoon. Besides, the flowering leaves were a distraction, almost a source of sadness for Scott, for they would die soon anyway, so what was the use in admiring them? When Riles would not relent, Scott needed to compromise so as to seem gracious. Besides, the more he thought about it, if the conversation turned unpleasant, Scott could always start sniffling and excuse himself. The two settled on a bench under a tree in what Riles maintained was a lightly traveled part of campus.

The tentativeness Riles had in his voice at the mention of Isaac over the phone warned Scott to tread lightly through this progress report. Scott had enough problems with William acting a little jittery; but for the doctor to get all mixed up could prove more of a problem than Scott wanted to deal with at the time. Why was it that every time he was teamed with people he was the only person who had the ability to see things through with the same energy with which he had started?

"I hate to start things on such a bad note, but I'm afraid I have had this on my mind. What did you say happened to Isaac?"

Scott studied Dr. Riles' face and ran through the appropriate stories. When he stumbled on the best one, he said, "They're not sure. They say it was a mugging and that they were only after money. It really is a shame." Scott wondered how convincing he sounded.

"Yes, you can imagine my shock when I came across the story in the paper. The article said that he was a suspect in some disappearances, but that there was nothing concrete put together on him. Had you heard any of that?"

"Yes, we heard it, but they are always trying to pin something on someone."

Dr. Riles had too many thoughts running through his head. "You do understand my concern that when they mentioned gay people in particular, I was a little taken aback? I could not ignore the coincidence." Doctors never could settle for what you told them was the truth. They always had to question everything. Scott recalled his numerous useless counseling sessions in jail and his agitation at having to humor those "doctors" so they would leave him alone. He learned how to give them the answers they wanted to hear to make their report writing smooth and convincing. No one ever had a use for the truth. Scott made sure he would be just as delicate with this doctor.

"Well, you see, Doctor, when you run a group like we do, through the Church, we are not exactly the most popular organization with the gay community. Surely you can appreciate that. And when they learned who Isaac worked with, they took the easiest scapegoat to place blame on a few crimes they could not solve. Though tragic, we can do nothing about it." Scott took amusement at the tone his voice achieved. Somewhere along the line, he had picked up that politician delivery, his success signaled by Dr. Riles' easing shoulders.

"I guess I never thought of it that way. However, you do offer an interesting point of view." Dr. Riles took a deep breath.

"Now, what we wanted to know from you, Doctor, is, how far along are you?"

Dr. Riles startled. Scott cursed himself for moving too fast, but he would make it up. The door was opened; there was no reason not to walk through it now. But, what had he said that was so wrong?

"Yes, I guess it seems only natural to move on to talk of business. Well, as far as my progress, I am happy to tell you that I have almost completed the first phase. I will require only a small batch more of cadavers."

So they were out of the woods sooner than William predicted. What about their inventory? Scott saw their luck turning, all their uneasiness now without merit, and for the first time in a while, Scott felt the light from the sun warm his neck. Perhaps sitting outside had been a good idea after all.

"However, there is the next phase of my project that we need to discuss. To truly do something with what I have found, I need you to orchestrate the volunteer control group William promised me would not be a problem."

Scott's neck bristled. William said nothing of a "volunteer control group." Did not the doctor just say he was done with bodies?

"You look confused." Dr. Riles' voice cracked with the same annoyance that Isaac brought to any conversation.

"Forgive me, Doctor, but I don't understand. Volunteers?" Scott could not hold back the question that his instincts told him to reserve for William.

"Well, yes, naturally I will need to ascertain the extent to which what I have found will affect the brain. Now that I know what I am working with, I'm ready to move into the clinical trial phase. I have zeroed in on the proper hormone I will use to target the appropriate brain site. William mentioned that members of your support group would be eager to volunteer so they can have their lives changed in a way that only science can make possible. Their days of therapy and group gatherings will come to an end." A light had entered Dr. Riles' eyes, something Scott wanted to turn from.

As he processed Dr. Riles' request, which must have been logical and easy on the surface, Scott wondered why William had said nothing of this before. What should he do? Their corps of volunteers would surely not come as easily as William had boasted. Of this Scott was sure. Those weak minds gathered all their gumption just to attend meetings. Dr. Riles waited for a response, and Scott knew that the longer he waited, the less confidence he would be able to carry off. In those moments, feeling left out of the big picture, Scott could see everything for which they had worked so hard peel away, like wood shavings from a lave, dropping onto the floor, waiting to be swept away.

"Is anything the matter, Mr. Everett? You look rather pale." Dr. Riles went to put his hand to Scott's forehead and Scott recoiled. Dr. Riles flinched, his expression changing from concern to confusion.

"I'm sorry, I'm...just...I don't know why, but, perhaps the trees. You don't mind if we pick this up another day? I really should get going and lie down, maybe." Scott stood up quickly, perhaps more quickly than someone who was complaining of feeling badly, but he didn't care. What had started as such an easy day, with so many possibilities, quickly faded as the sun climbed to the center of the sky. First William seemed to be drifting, and now the doctor would no longer be of use to them. What would the doctor do when they could not provide anyone for them? Scott found it impossible to believe that William planned this. He surely would have shared the information. Scott was important enough to know every detail of their organization.

But what to do with the doctor? Would he involve the authorities and draw a line to the group? Would he quietly vanish away? Not likely. He had had that same hunger in his eyes early on, and he would definitely want some validation for his work. But what if they could pin everything on the doctor and walk away from it?

Then he—they—would have wasted all their time, preventing them—him—from seeing the vision, the promise, materialize. Maybe it would be best to scrap the doctor altogether and relocate and start over. They had to make something of this. There was nothing else for Scott to go back to. He had finally found something that he was good at, something he was *very* good at. Above all else, he could not lose that, and he would do anything to preserve what he had worked so hard for. If they had to start fresh, so be it. He had learned enough to be able to move faster next time, to be able to branch out and pull from different areas at the same time, quicker, and next time they would know they would have to find some people to line up for the tail end. Scott tallied a list of mistakes they would not make again. It started with Isaac, and ended with the doctor.

As he trekked through campus, thinking about all his possibilities, he knew that he would put off letting William know any of the details about the doctor. He would not be of any use anyway. Scott would tie up all the loose ends himself. Somebody would have to pay for all his hard work going to waste, and he would start with some cops.

Chapter 23

Barbara let Tommy's friend pick him up from the airport. A monster of a headache held her head hostage and her body followed; driving to the airport would only exacerbate matters, though seeing her son a moment sooner might dissipate the fog in her head. Damn her migraine shots for not doing their trick. Thankfully, whatever occupied Stephen in his study kept him quiet, creating a tranquil environment that brought only a subtle easement to Barbara's condition, but under the circumstances, she would take what she could get. No matter how bad her headaches were, they could always be worse. Hopefully, Tommy would find some amusement with his friend, whose name she had forgotten, even after hearing it ten times over, for she was not up for entertaining.

When she got tired of lying in bed, she would will herself into the tub, praying the hot water and some flickering candles would do wonders for the circus in her cranium. If that failed, she would resort to calling on her husband to find something stronger for her to take. Though as a doctor he should be able to get something for her, the possibility that he might not come through held her tongue. She avoided the potential for disappointment with every turn. She would try her own remedies first. Besides, with everything Stephen seemed to have on his mind, the last thing he needed was her bothering him.

Before she had managed to sit upright and not vomit from the sudden feeling that smothered both her head and her stomach, Stephen appeared in the doorway and rushed to her side. He eased her back down, pulling his hand gently away from behind her head once it sank into the pillow.

"Can I get you anything?" He ran his hand over her forehead and brushed the hair away from her face. If it were not for the jackhammer in her head, she would have enjoyed the attention.

"No, I just...this headache... I was thinking a bath might do me some good." The mere thought of movement wrenched her stomach, daring her to move, as if it had other ideas. Perhaps the bed might be her best option for the time being.

"The water might, if you think you're up for it. Isn't the shot working?"

"No, not yet." Why did the medicine have to pick today to stop working?

"Well, wait a couple hours or so and I'll give you another one. Maybe a second dose will help."

"God willing." As she tried to comfort herself with anything, she felt Stephen's gaze upon her. Even through the fog in her head she saw the weight of something in his eyes. Whatever he had brought home the day before still sat with him. Even she could not pretend that he was just tired. "Is there something you want to talk about, Stephen? You look like you have something on your mind."

His eyes drooped the way they did when one of his projects had lost funding. She wanted to sit up and wrap her arms around him, but the thought of even moving her arms nauseated her.

"I...no, you rest. It can wait. Nothing too urgent." She must have been exaggerating his expression in her agony that no amount of dramatic description could possibly describe.

"What time was Thomas supposed to get in?"

She paused and took a breath. She wanted to still her body's movements while she thought. "His friend was to pick him up an hour ago, but he said yesterday that they were going to go out and run some errands in the city. He didn't know what time he would be home, but he said he'd be here in time to get something to eat." She was happy that he was paying attention to Tommy's schedule.

"Okay then, I'll just be in the study doing some reading. Did you want to try the bath?"

"Yes...well, maybe. I think I'd like to try anything at this point." Trying to avoid all thought, she wanted someone else to take over and rid her of this vice on her brain.

"Okay, I'll run the water." She watched him get up from the bed and walk into the bathroom. She heard her bath salts hit the basin as the faucet kicked on. *He remembered.*

When the grandfather clock in the hall chimed nine times, Stephen rose from his seat in the study to stretch, believing the hour could not possibly be that late. When he checked his wristwatch, he could not believe that his thoughts had melted away the time so unchecked. He returned to his seat just as a car pulled into the driveway. Within moments, Thomas eased through the front door, probably mindful of the lack of lights and the hour, and bounded up the stairs, his shoes thudding against the carpet. He must have needed to drop his things in his room and check with Barbara. He always checked with Barbara first. *Did he not see the light on in the study as he passed by? Did he assume I was not home?*

To the sound of his bedroom door opening, Stephen debated whether or not he should rise up and alert Thomas about his mother's state, but he knew that whatever her condition, Barbara would want to see their boy. Stephen put off his own inclination towards saying "hi," opting instead to let Thomas settle in before he came to say hello and ask him how his flight had been. Maybe when Thomas came down he would suggest that they go...well, he was not exactly sure what he should suggest. He would wait until Thomas came down to make any other suggestions.

Every other minute for half an hour Stephen checked and rechecked the minute hand on his watch. Reading a book did nothing to dissipate the anxiety in his throat. What was this feeling? Why did it not pass? It was not like Thomas was coming home for the last time or anything, and in fact he would be home for the whole summer, presumably, in a few months. Thinking about Thomas provided a welcome distraction to his state of mind.

Stephen had just finished the first paragraph for what seemed like the tenth time when Thomas knocked on the door. Setting his book on the desk, Stephen devoted his full attention to his son, but Thomas' troubled look gave him pause. Perhaps Thomas was having trouble in school or had run rather short on money. Such an independent spirit, Thomas rarely asked for assistance; for this, Stephen respected his son.

"Are you all right, Thomas?"

He waded into the room, reluctant to relinquish the door, as if expecting to be expelled at any minute. "Can I talk to you for a minute? I know you're busy and all, but I was hoping now would be an all right time."

Why did Thomas proceed with such trepidation? Surely he realized that he was no imposition. "Have a seat. Do you want something to drink? You look pale."

"Thanks, Dad." Thomas smiled. Whatever it was had not consumed him completely. "But I don't need anything to drink." His voice dropped in a way that reminded Stephen of the time he had had his bike stolen, feeling like he was in trouble for a mistake he could not prevent. "Some things just happen that are beyond our control," Stephen had consoled his son. *My, how grown up Thomas now looked.*

"All right. You have my attention." Thomas squirmed in his seat, as if awaiting a cross-examination. Perhaps Stephen should help the conversation along. "Your mother did mention that you needed to speak to me about something, although she would not divulge what it was about. I can assure you, whatever it is, it's not that bad, and you needn't feel intimidated. Whatever grade you got or how much money you need, you shouldn't feel in the least bit apprehensive. After all, what's a grade in the grand scheme of things? And as far as money goes, well, I'm sure it's not that bad, and it's not as if you have come to us..." Letting himself ramble seemed like the best thing to do, although he had not intended on running off at the mouth quite as long as he did.

Before he could find a natural stopping point, Thomas interjected with, "It's not about school and it's not about money, Dad; all those things are fine." He continued to fidget. Thomas' infectious nervous energy encouraged Stephen to jump up from his seat, as if ants were overtaking his legs. He fought the impulse, though the notion grew in appeal, but before Stephen could rise and pace, Thomas rose from his seat and buried his hands in his pockets. He examined the framed things on the wall as if seeing them for the first time. *Where was all this headed?*

"It's been so long since I've even been in here. I'd almost forgotten that you had all these pictures all over the place." Thomas glanced over the family photos, perhaps revisiting a more intimate time for the family. Thomas held his head high, his shoulders square. He looked a bit taller than Stephen remembered. His little boy was growing into more of a man with every visit. Stephen made a note to make time in the near future for a family vacation, to find that time again that had passed through his fingers.

Stephen's wishes surrendered to the fears in the recesses in his own mind; he briefly allowed himself to wonder if maybe he would not be in a position to have any time with his family in the near future. As he watched Thomas' eyes take on a hint of despair, Stephen ignored his own situation as he watched his son attempt to gather whatever he needed to get off his chest. Perhaps he should go to his son, rest a hand on his shoulder, tell him that everything would be all right, regardless of what the "everything" might consist of. Stephen had practiced his speech about Thomas not troubling himself with grades or money so much so that when the issues did not involve either of those things, he could do nothing more than wait for the matter to unfold. This proved both nerve-racking and somewhat enticing.

When he paused before one of Stephen's awards, Thomas seemed to eye the plaque with pride, but when the tears trickled down his cheek, Stephen effectively gave up his desire to speculate as to Thomas' predicament.

Stephen went to his son, but he felt awkward, as if an embrace would be more than Thomas could want— or need. When he put his hand on his son's shoulder, Thomas turned his head into Stephen's chest and sobbed. Stephen patted his son's back, like patting the back of the baby Thomas had been, the same one who needed help in the shower late at night when the steam from the hot water could not do all the work to get the phlegm out of his young lungs. Thankfully, he had grown out of that constant congestion as an adolescent. Strange, how those long nights made him and Barbara feel helpless, as if they were failing as parents because they stood helpless to their son's condition, yet now he regarded those moments with a certain level of fondness.

"I'm sorry, Dad. I'm so sorry." His breathing became regulated and his sniffling ceased. He pulled his head back and Stephen could do nothing more than stare down, rather confused at his son, who needed the answer to a question yet to be asked.

"What are you sorry for, Thomas? You haven't done anything." Stephen did not know why his own throat constricted.

"I just wanted you to always be proud of me, that's all."

Stephen reached back to his desk and offered Thomas a tissue. It seemed like an odd day to ask for assurance on how proud he and his wife had always been of their son's accomplishments, both as a person and in school. "What makes you think for a moment that both your mother and I are not proud of you?" He flirted with going to wake Barbara, to enlist her support, for moments like these were her department. If only he could offer her a better method with which to cope with her headaches. Stephen wished for just a moment that he possessed his wife's communication talents. *How best can I express what I always believed to be indisputably understood: my love for my family? How could my son ever doubt that?*

"Dad, you...you don't understand...it's...Dad...I will never be able to be the son you have always wanted me to be."

Stephen's heart sank under the strain of emotion that was controlling Thomas' voice. "Thomas...I..." Stephen lacked the proper response. Thomas had to know how his father felt towards him.

"Dad, I'm gay."

For moments, Stephen heard nothing. He blinked and blinked, then told himself to breathe. He squeezed his son to remind himself that he was still standing. Stephen wondered why those words came out as they did. The sweater muffling Thomas' mouth had obviously caused the wrong words to escape. As he waited for Thomas to repeat himself to clear up the mystery, all he heard was, "I'm so sorry, Dad." Thomas sobbed like Stephen never thought him capable of doing, the way Barbara had sobbed the day she learned her mother passed away. Still, Stephen struggled to make sense of the words Thomas had uttered. How could that phrase have come from his son's mouth? And then the truth of the words settled on him, pricking his skin like the feeling of raw skin under a freshly removed blister. He felt like he had just stepped into a hot bath, realizing the extent of the water's heat only when he was fully in. When the burning started, he had yet to decide if his body could take the heat, or it was in fact more reasonable to step out completely.

When his reasoning mind failed to trigger a response, his instincts instructed his mouth to utter something, but his lips parted to pass only a faint breath of air, followed by no words. Stephen was not in a place to be able to digest what had just been imparted to him. Tears raced down his cheeks and onto Tommy's shirt, making a small puddle over his shoulder. What exactly was life trying to tell him? He hugged his son as if for the last time, hoping his action would speak louder than the words he could not find. What had he done? Suddenly, his own situation came to his mind, front and center.

Scott figured the cop would be working in the afternoon, so he waited for his roommate to leave before he trekked up to the apartment. He did not know what he hoped to find, but he knew taking pictures from a distance would not be enough. Perhaps he would find something to hold against the cop and get him that way, or maybe he just wanted to get the lay of the apartment in case they had to work in there. Pausing before the door, he knocked just to be on the safe side. When listening up against the door offered silence, he slipped out his kit and went to work on the lock that should have been more difficult, given that a cop lived there. It must be his lucky day.

The well-kept basic furniture looked much like Scott anticipated, although he did not expect to step into an apartment that looked like Ikea had thrown up all over the place. And what was with that flowery smell? He could not picture a cop with potpourri. Scott kept his distance from the windows to avoid being seen by any random person who might look up.

When nothing in the kitchen cabinets proved interesting, he moved into the bedroom. Everything was fairly well kept. The cop must have had a maid. As he turned to look for a second bedroom, he did not find it. He ducked into the bathroom, rifled through the cabinets and found nothing. As he stepped back into the hallway, he went back into the bedroom and stared at the queen-sized bed. *Wait.* Where would the roommate sleep? He ruffled through the clothes in the closet, mildly messing up the carefully aligned hangers. *Hmm.* The front room gave him something else to focus on. All the pictures lined up along the entertainment center were more along the lines of what Scott was looking for. *Finally, something useful.* Getting the cop's address through a connection at the DMV only went so far.

The cop seemed to enjoy the company of his roommate an awful lot. When he noticed the apparent affection in the picture, absent of any other guys, something came together in his head. *This fucking cop is a fag.* Praising his own luck again, he took one picture frame in his hand and shook his head in disgust. *The cop is a fucking fag.* He popped the picture out from the back. He shoved the photo in his pocket, and then set the frame back in place. He had what he needed.

As he turned to walk out the door, the rustling of keys stopped him dead in his tracks. The door swung open.

"Oh! Sorry." It was the roommate—or fag, or whatever—from the photo. Scott clenched his teeth, cursing his decision to not bring a gun. Scott knew he could take him, but the struggle might be loud, and with the door open...

"Did you fix it?" He looked rather calm.

"Sorry?"

"The leak in the shower, did you manage to fix it?"

"Oh, ah, no, actually, I was just leaving..." Scott would not have to react after all. Besides, if he were going to take things over, he needed to leave messy details to someone else, to be able to delegate effectively.

Before he could think any further, the phone rang and the guy answered it on the first ring. Scott had to move, fast. As he moved to the door, the fag called out, "Does that mean you'll be back later?"

"Yeah, later. There's a part missing that I have to order. Not sure how long it will take." *This idiot did not even notice that I don't have tools. This was going to be easy.*

The tension in Scott's neck eased. He even got some amusement at the guy when he rolled his eyes in disgust. That shower must really have bothered him. Scott smiled on his way out the door. *Lucky twice in the same day.* He thanked God that fags seemed to ignore every warning sign in the book, even when it was right in front of their face. But who was he to look a gift horse in the mouth?

Chapter 24

The sun waged its battle along the morning horizon, tinting the sky a wonderful blue, the likes of which Stephen had never seen, or at least never noticed. Through the office window, Stephen wondered if the chill in the air turned with the sun's effort. He wondered what his family dreamed about as they lay sleeping in the home he had fled from late in the night. What brought him to his office, he did not know, though he felt an understanding arrive with the rising sun. Perhaps the guaranteed privacy of having the building all to himself at that early hour promised the isolation he needed to make sense of the chaos in his head. But his head did not carry the only burden; pockets of stiffness throughout his body kept the hollow ringing in his temples company.

To have Thomas think that he would love him any less for being gay stung. He lacked the words his wife undoubtedly articulated when she found out, but she should have spoken for both of them to their son. Surely, his own wife had known about their son for some time...that seemed a betrayal to which he could ascribe no words. He felt like he had been lecturing for an hour and all of sudden he looked up to realize that the class had left the room. In those moments of Thomas' confession he felt at once admiration for his son's ability to admit who he was, and sadness for his own position that he no longer knew his family.

The early light streamed into the dark room, shades of soft yellow landing on his papers, his charts, the records of his work. Everything that fueled his life would now amount to nothing. The future looked bleak for him, so much so that he dare not even think about what may lay ahead on the road built by his ambition. What would come to light of these people he had ties to? How many questions should he have asked, and what answers should he have doubted? Should he have more pointedly questioned someone's intentions? When was having faith in someone's motives a crime? But that chance, that opportunity to make a name for himself, to make a name for his family, he could not say that he would have done anything differently, even if he would like to think otherwise. Ironic, that Thomas had been so worried of making him proud. How he wished he could tell Thomas that the same weight rested around both of their necks. But did he really deserve his son's— or wife's, for that matter—sympathy?

His thoughts stayed with his family. How could they ever think that he would not understand? That he would not accept Thomas? And when he acknowledged the obvious for all of its glaring properties, he allowed the anger slowly simmering under his skin to guide his actions, to take up what his conscience whispered to his head. He did not know at whom to point the finger, but to have his family not understand that all his research on homosexuals stemmed not from a contempt for how they lived their lives. Surely his own family knew him well enough to comprehend that his work stemmed from a love of science, from a search for answers.

He paused to glare down at some of his charts. By this they judged him; by this they questioned him. How did they not understand that for them he had worked, had sacrificed? Never had these implications found their way into his head, or his heart.

He tried to cry for a while, but the tears only reached the surface of his eyes, never gathering enough to fall. The sun's rays grew in their brilliance, refracted in places by the dust on the outside of the window. Their light opened up, no longer highlighting the papers stacked on the desk, but rather moving on to the stacks of boxed documents that sat huddled in the corner.

Stephen snatched off the lids of a few boxes, thumbing through the contents. How much of his life lay catalogued here, collected with no eyes to view it? *Six boxes. Is that all?*

His family drifted from his thoughts. He allowed himself to dream that his work was received in the manner he deemed appropriate—embraced by the medical community. He imagined receiving recognition at every turn, his colleagues congratulating him in the halls, stopping conversations to voice their praise. He saw himself teaching his findings to his students, stopping every few ideas to allow their pens time to catch up. Then he saw their faces, their eyes, and he wondered what message they might interpret from all of this. What if some of his students were gay and he were lecturing on homosexuality as if it were some disease in need of curing? What would some do with his findings? Would they try and change people, unwillingly? Would that affect his son in some way? Was he contributing to his son's potential harm?

Then, for the first time, he questioned the people who had knocked on his door all those months ago. Who were these people with whom he had so foolishly aligned himself? Was it too late to sever their ties? He knew, moments after meeting with Scott that something off-color rotted under his skin, behind his eyes. More and more, as his thoughts delved further, he recognized that this observation resembled a gross understatement. How would people describe him, in light of his actions, were they to gaze upon him? *How could I have been so completely oblivious?*

*Give us a call if anything comes to mind...*The detective! Could that officer really help him? What help could Stephen offer in return? And what would that do to him? He really knew nothing, if in fact there was some malice tied in with these people. But was not asking enough questions grounds to implicate him? His mind sprinted too far down the road. His lack of sufficient sleep caused him to think irrationally. He would get through the morning and then move on. Best not to think too hard, though the more he dwelt on the past, the more apparent his lack of thinking became to him. Details—he could do nothing about them now. But he could do something.

Mustering his strength, propelled by a determination to take some action, he made his way to his lab down the hall. Once there, he yanked out the long drawer where a body lay, somewhat preserved. He cast aside the sheet, and then stood over the body. *Students took such messy care of their subjects.* Had he been the same way in medical school? Should he have cared for the body more once he took what he needed—the brain? Raising the eyelids, he felt a pain when he studied the eyes gapping blankly back at him. That could have been his son. His son could have thought he did not love him and taken his own life, if indeed these bodies came by way of suicide. No, he had to believe that. His conscience rejected what his brain made impossible to ignore.

Falling away from the slab, he hunched over the sink. The past 24 hours tortured him with one gut-wrenching revelation after another. How could any man be asked to process it all? What had he done in life to deserve all of this at once? Perhaps he had better sit down, have some juice, and rest his head.

The stool he chose offered no comfort, for as he buried his weary head into his hands, his closed eyes saw only all that lay behind and before him. His road offered no favorable exits. When he could ponder no more, he decided that his only recourse involved rectifying things as best as he could so as to affect the things that might still happen. He scowled as he surveyed his lab, as if to blame the room and all the promise it once held for making him follow the path he had chosen.

His life. In these walls he had sacrificed his family. Within these walls he knowingly had masked his own ambition by saying it was all for his family. He felt defeated, as if he had failed in every aspect of his life. What could he do? There was nothing for him to do. His life now amounted to nothing. Then he thought of his wife, and how she had looked up at him just the night before, with so much forgiveness in her eyes, yet he knew not why. Did she know without knowing? But maybe she saw that there was a chance for him—a blanket forgiveness for not having been there for their son.

His mind drifted to the boxes of documents in his office, those reams of paper designed to uncover a practical application for a twenty-year-old theory. But who would benefit? What were they going to do with this information? Would the medical community even listen? Perhaps he should have heeded the fact that no one would accept his papers? Would it send out a message that the condition could be corrected and that people should try? Stephen had never accounted for the final phase of that. What, then, was his obligation? The sunlight filled the windows. Within an hour or so the halls would be congested with staff and students.

With a hand truck in tow, he stalked to his office. On two trips, he stacked the six boxes, carted them into the lab, and placed them into the cement-based floor, right over the large drain. He located some alcohol and doused the cartons, careful to remove all the lids, and drenched the papers therein. He stood for a moment and took in all that the mound represented. If he struck the match, everything would be done with. The facts would reside strictly in his memory, safe from harmful use. Everything else dealing with the acquisition of the bodies was all stored elsewhere on campus. They would still be there to vindicate him of any legal wrongdoing. After all, he had not gotten around to getting the work into his computer.

Taking a deep breath, he tried to steady his hands while he held the match to the side of the box. *My hand cannot move.* The faces of his wife and son ran through his head. Laughing, playing, spending time together in front of the television like they used to do on Sunday nights. The match seemed to swipe itself across the board, then flew willingly to its charges. The boxes united in flame, kindling at first, crackling with a subtle intensity. The flames leapt over one another, joining in small teams to create larger, more effective arms of destruction across the boxes, spewing forth a funnel of smoke over singed paper and cardboard. Dr. Riles acted quickly, swinging open the skylights. The small brilliant flames rose, prompting him to pluck the nearby fire extinguisher from the wall. Every time the flame danced too high he sprinkled it with spray.

After fifteen minutes, carefully curbing the fire where necessary, the boxes collapsed on themselves, the ashes coughing to the floor. He doused the flames with the extinguisher until it slowly died down. He glared down at the ash heap, his decision sealed. *All gone. It is all gone,* his mind whispered.

He retreated to his office and rifled through his top drawer until he found the detective's card. With the card in hand, he took up the receiver; but before he could dial he looked at the clock and deemed 6:45 too early in the morning to make the call. Instead, he dialed for the janitor and asked for some assistance in hauling off some damaged documents. As he held the phone in his hand, he wondered how he would explain the burning of the boxes, as he dialed the appropriate extension. He rationalized that pleasing the janitor's curiosity stood as the least of his worries.

Chapter 25

So this was what it is like to lead, Scott thought, as he rocked back in William's chair, taking in what would be Matthew's eagerness. If he had sat here sooner, perhaps the group would be farther along, better off. Oh well, you can't dwell on the past.

"Right in the city, huh?" Matt studied one of the pictures Scott snapped while the cops were at Isaac's apartment.

"Yeah, right by the square. Must be nice, living on a cop's salary."

Matt's eagerness, though, took a little coaxing. Not everyone shared the same outlook on the bigger picture. "And one's a fag? You're sure?"

Scott tossed the picture he'd taken from the cop's apartment across the table. Matt held them side by side. "No shit." Scott enjoyed the irony of it all as well. "What about the other one?"

"Don't worry about him. One'll do. Plus it will be that much more rewarding, knowing we were able to go for the gay one."

"You really think this will make a difference?"

"Absolutely."

"And William wants this done? I can't see him getting behind this."

"Yes, he asked to have it taken care of while he tends to some personal matters over the next few days." Scott held back the announcement that things would run a little differently from here on out. Too much information at once only called for more questions, something Scott wanted to avoid for the time being. Perhaps William had operated with some knowledge of this all along. Scott would never know for sure, though he could not convince himself that he much cared.

"Doesn't matter to me. Just wasn't sure we had officially dropped the act, so to speak."

Scott rewarded Matthew with a confused look.

Matt continued: "I thought we were doing all this under the guise of helping the queers in the long run. That must have changed. You can't possibly think that William thinks this will have any impact."

"I try not to ask too many questions."

"Whatever. I'll get it done. You know I could care less." Matt dropped the pictures and made himself comfortable in the chair.

Scott tucked the material into a folder and set it aside.

"So what else is William planning on?" An air of disbelief in his tone factored too heavily in the delivery.

"I'm not sure I follow you." Scott hoped his own tone squelched any further doubts as to who made the decisions, ones not to be questioned.

"Look, don't bullshit me, Scott. I'm not here to rain on your fucking parade, but at least let me know what direction we're headed in. William disappears and all of a sudden you're signing death orders like a mob head. Now don't get me wrong, I got no problem with knocking off a fag or two. I'd rather be up front about it, but this really does go against everything you've been riding on for the past nine months. I could give two shits about whatever you did with Isaac. He was a fucking weasel. But don't snow me. Keep me in the loop." Matt let his excitement get the best of him. His pacing about the room caused Scott to be less than a little at ease.

"William is tending to an old friend at the hospital. You can reach him if you like. And as for necessary arrangements, they will fall into place. They'll buy us some time to tidy up and maybe relocate. Our doctor is not cooperating and may prove troublesome." Scott could feel the slight tinge of a headache coming on. He wondered if this was what William had to deal with when he was in control of things.

"Right. Knock him off too?" Matt was being annoyingly combative and Scott wondered what it took to have someone just shut up and listen to what he said.

"We'll cross that bridge when we come to it."

"Right, bridge. Whatever, Brando. Personally I think you've gone off the deep end, my friend. But in an amusing way. At least for now." He sat with his smug look and waited for a response of some kind. When only silence remained, Matt said, "Look, I got to line some stuff up. Let me know when you need me." A thought crossed his mind, but he held whatever it was in reserve as he offered, "I'll take care of this project. Let me know when William surfaces, won't you?" And he excused himself.

Scott had faith in Matthew's ability to take care of the cop business, but beyond that, he wondered how much loyalty Matt had left, but that was another bridge to cross when he came to it. In the meantime, he had phone calls to make.

✦ ✦ ✦

Stephen stared blankly at the ringing phone. Should he take up the ringer in the police officer's company?

"You gonna answer that, Doc?" What did the detective mean by that comment? The condescending tone spoke of accusations, but it could have been a polite permission.

Regardless of his interpretation of the inference, Stephen plucked up the receiver on the third ring.

"Hello?" The voice stirred up more emotions than he would have liked. "Yes, this is he." Suddenly, Stephen regretted having the police sit in front of him for this phone call, to watch him assume the position of the most unfortunate individual in the world. When the detective sitting across from him rose and took his pack of cigarettes with him, he knew the other one in the lab would give him his moment of privacy.

"Yes, of course." As if he could forget to whom he spoke. How he wished he could forget.

"Oh, really?" He had prepared himself to hear a number of things, even to not hear from them again, but to hear that something had come through in the way of subjects...perhaps he had rashly misjudged...at the moment, the incident in the morning with the matches seemed like the biggest mistake of his life, piling on to all the others. He cleared his throat until he found his voice again.

"Yes, I'm still here. Three, you say? Yes, that will do to begin with." What was he supposed to do, admit that he had turned his back on the project? Or could he rely on his memory to move forward? After all, what had been in those boxes was just background work. What he could prove in the future would be the significant part. But then he remembered Thomas and why he had burned those boxes in the first place. He needed some water.

"Tomorrow? It should be. Yes, but I will have to check my schedule. Can I get back to you?" Waiting for tomorrow—both too soon and too far off—was like knowing you had to go under the knife, wishing you didn't have to and wishing you had already come through it. What good would showing up be?

"Oh, at your facility? Well, I don't...I don't see why not...Oh, they would be more comfortable...well I think that will do. I would have to give them a preliminary screening by means of an interview, but that should be fine. If you could just... Oh, pick me up. Well I don't... Oh, easier, I see, hard to find... Well, let me just get back to you then...oh, your number changed. I see, I see...then try me back later in the day... Yes, yes." The line went dead before he had a chance to move it from his ear. How he wished he could be set down to rest as quietly as the phone, as he laid it inertly on its cradle, now undisturbed, its task complete.

The detective returned, punishing Stephen with the offensive smoke stench that preceded him into the room. The other walked in from the lab. The one whose presence necessitated opening a window to alleviate the smell spoke first. "So, Doctor, you say you have no means of getting a hold of this organization?"

"That was actually one of them on the phone, the one named Scott."

"How fortunate." The two officers exchanged skeptical glances with one another. "What'd he have to say? Stopping by to say hi?"

"He wants to meet with me tomorrow. Says he has some willing subjects for me to speak with."

They exchanged glances again. Whatever their eyes told one another, Dr. Riles wished he had been in on the conversation.

"To which you said..."

"I told him I would check my schedule and I asked him to get back to me later in the day."

"And you don't have a number to reach them?"

"No, their number changed."

"I thought you said you never had it in the first place."

"I...I" He had forgotten what he had said.

"Let us be blunt, Doctor. Not only do we not know what you may or may not be mixed up in, but also the moment you start spinning a yard of bullshit, the faster your ass goes in with these people, whoever these people are. Now, tell you what, when this person calls you back, meet with him, and we will be around and see what turns up."

"In the meantime, if you don't mind, we'll be back with a warrant to go through your files in the record's office or whatever you call the office that holds the info on your 'donated' bodies." The one standing up flipped his notepad closed while the other one rose out of his seat. "Don't worry, we'll show ourselves out, and Doctor, don't do anything stupid."

When Stephen again found himself within the solitude that brought more anxiety than reprieve, he could not help caving under the weight that he had not only done something stupid, but several other things. At least the school kept thorough records. The campus bureaucracy was good for something; he just questioned why he had not volunteered the information when he had the chance. Maybe something would come out of this after all and he had concocted a wild tale in his head for nothing.

+ + +

Once outside, John asked, "You think he's full of shit?" Glenn led the way to their parked car.

"How could he not be?" John slouched down to light his cigarette in the mild wind.

"Yeah, I guess. Seems like too much of a stooge to orchestrate anything. I mean, why blow everything on getting tied up with something like this?"

"Yeah, so what do we figure? Some group approaches him, knows he does this kind of research, promises a steady supply of bodies, but says they come from suicides. Only they don't happen to be suicides, just unlucky bastards picked off from gay hangouts. Yet how does the doctor not question anything?" John put the keys in the ignition, but he did not immediately crank the engine. He sat with his hand out the window so the smoke would not bother Glenn. "I mean, really, who could be that fucking stupid?"

"You think he's too much of a science geek to think they would be killing people?"

"I guess...church group, huh? You think he's telling the truth?"

"I don't think he could come up with that on his own. Plus, he did call us."

"Yeah, I guess. Must have had some crisis of the conscience."

"Back to the office and line up the search warrant?"

"Yeah, and while we're at it, tail him all day. I bet he doesn't call so looks like we'll be doing some driving tomorrow." John turned the key and got the engine revving. "Fucking Bible thumpers."

✦ ✦ ✦

As Scott hung up the phone, a sense of pride surged through his limbs. So that was what true accomplishment felt like. Oh, if only his dead parents could see him now, the ones who felt he would amount to nothing. This was all falling into place. Although he could not deny that things had become unnecessarily messy, he congratulated himself for finding the means to tidy it back up again. Matt would make a statement with the cop's boyfriend, while Scott would nullify the doctor. He smiled at the future, acknowledging his ability to learn from his mistakes. They would find another doctor, do a better job of anticipating his needs, but for the time being he would have to remember to get back to the doctor that afternoon and set up the meeting for tomorrow. Picking up Riles would prevent any extra cars from being near the warehouse, so when Scott got him secluded he would handle him, and then wait until nightfall to dump the body, just like all the others. *Life could be easy when you allowed it to be.* William's approval did not factor here, for eventually he would both appreciate the initiative and learn to see the bigger picture, or he would find a new cause. Scott's new role felt rather snug on his shoulders. Later, as he spun around and admired the view from William's window, he thought it might be a good night to go out on the town—one last hurrah, one for the road.

The doctor offered no comforting predictions as to Monsignor Drollings' condition. The unconscious body lying in the bed beside William's chair bore a sad resemblance to the man that at one time inspired William with such hope. That same body had failed to stir since William arrived at the hospital the night before. The chair hindered a comfortable sleep, but William forsook his own comfort for the chance of being there, by his friend, should he awake. He felt it not only his duty, but also his desire to be there when someone would be needed. The fresh cup of coffee he retrieved from the cafeteria did little to warm his chest and the cheerful nurse checking Carl's chart did little to ease his mind.

"Anything?" William knew the answer to his own question, but inquired on the off chance his instincts proved wrong.

"No, sir, I'm afraid there has been no change, but the doctor will be making his rounds shortly. Perhaps he will have something new to share with you then. In the meantime, are you sure there is not something I can do to make you a little more comfortable? Perhaps you should even think about going home, resting, and then returning later. There will be plenty of other visitors, and there really is nothing you can do for him here." William envied the sincerity she possessed, in light of all she undoubtedly encountered on a daily basis, but William trusted his faith that he needed to stay.

"Thank you, but no. You are very kind, but I think I will stay." Without pushing the matter any further, she gracefully departed. He set his coffee down on the floor and sought comfort in the window's view.

Staring out over the city from the ninth floor, William wondered why things had become so complicated. What had made so much sense all those months ago had begun with the absolute best intentions, but spiraled so disastrously out of hand, even costing him a person who had been like a son, but William had divorced emotion from the decision. Circumstances dictated that all this be handled like a business, but the reality gradually seeped into his soul, certain aspects of their work clarifying into focus while other components' intentions became obscured under the scrutiny of his conscience. *How different the future looks once you reach it.* There had been no one thing to place the marker on; he had merely woken up one day to find that his perspective had shifted. Maybe Scott's sudden change acted as the catalyst. He had become almost like a rabid dog that William no longer knew how to control, but that would be something to consider when his duty at the hospital reached an end. He had nothing to say to Carl, yet so many thoughts drifted in and out of his mind, none of which would be served justice by finding words to express them. Yet in the absence of words, William wanted to be by his friend's side, to support him, to give back to the man responsible for setting him on the right path in life. Where would he be if Carl had not been there for him all those years ago? Completely lost, no doubt.

As he reflected on his past experiences with the man who now lay catatonic in the bed next to him, he fished through his pockets for a handkerchief to clear his nose. Instead of a carefully folded piece of cloth, William's hand produced the folded picture he had been looking at the day before. William's haste to arrive at his friend's side had pushed aside the discovery that shook him unnoticeably to the trained eye the day before. As he unfolded it and gazed at the men in the picture, he could not help but wonder how exactly he had so easily discarded the knowledge the picture provided. That face! Even after all these years, it only took him moments to recognize his own son, all grown up.

His mind offered no enticing options about what to think. That past life echoed somewhere in the recesses of his mind, in images so vague they almost existed as someone else's past, as if they had been told to him second-hand, but when William gazed upon the almost imperceptible eyes in the photo, he felt his cheeks suck in as all those emotions, so long ago buried, found him again. So much love, and then so much sorrow—so much failure from which he felt drowned. He had succeeded in climbing to shore, but his direction ran opposite the life he knew: his family. He made the right decision, listened to the voice that compelled him in the direction that led him to his present position. Yet if he had made the right decision, why would all these feelings return to him in this manner? Why would God have deceived him into making the wrong choice? The rhythmic beeps on the heart monitor annoyed him.

Perhaps these questions had been the reason for his tentativeness, his newfound desire to peel things back, to know that his son was somehow involved... Maybe this was a way of protecting him and at the same time coming to—dare he say it—his senses? But what havoc had he wrecked in his life? He had destroyed his own family and now he was directly responsible for so much other pain. He had seen it in that light now. What had made sense to him as nothing more than a series of sacrifices for the greater good now looked like life. They now seemed human to him, and he did not understand why.

Maybe seeing his son's image, all grown into a man, sparked a need to question what his son would think of him now. Would he be proud of his father? Did that matter now, after all these years? A complete loss enveloped him, as if all sensation left his body simultaneously. Could he disappear again, like he had done all those years ago? Just slip away and act like the past was behind him and start again, somewhere else? Maybe that had been what he had been putting together while sitting vigilantly at the hospital, putting together his options. Scott would willingly assume his position and do with it what he willed. Soon this project would implode, and William did not plan on being around to see it fall. To remain in the city, knowing that the end of the project approached, an unsuccessful end was more than he could stand. He could not admit defeat, acknowledge that he made a horrible mistake and end it on his own. That would mean that he had failed again, had wasted the time he had built into it. To return to counseling would be a step backward and he could never take a step backwards. Making amends was never in the picture. His path had always been to accept the situation and move on, create new options somewhere else. Seeing his son's face only reinforced his need to flee. This sign, his past returning to him, reminded him that his failure had come full circle, but the last loose end lay unconscious in the bed.

Maybe that was what he was waiting for, to say goodbye to the friend who had helped him all those years ago. In that moment he realized what he had to do—to leave and start again, but this time he would start fresh, not make the same mistakes he had made in the city. He would learn from his errors.

Then he heard labored breathing. Monsignor Drollings' eyes fluttered. William crammed the photo into a pocket and stood over the bed.

As he clung to the hope of seeing his friend regain consciousness and once again impart the ability to remove all doubt from his mind, William recalled one of the earliest meetings with Drollings, at a time in his life when he needed the same level of guidance and wisdom. William again heard what Drollings' offered. "Whatever you have done before you entered this house, Mr. Thompson, God does not care. It is what you do with your future that is important. It is never too late to repair the past by doing right by God in your present and future. Only regret the things you leave unfinished." How William longed to hear those words spoken again from his friend's lips.

Carl's breathing became erratic, like one having a nightmare. William's heart jumped, unsure as to whether or not he should try and wake Carl, but William found the decision made for him, as his lungs calmed and descended for the last time. The heart monitor sirened and moments later brought a flurry of attention to the room. The doctor and nurse tried to revive their patient, but their efforts encountered no success, for modern medicine could only accomplish so much. Some things rested in God's hands, and his hands had taken Carl.

Later, William asked and received permission to say goodbye to his friend in private. He tried to cry, but he found his eyes dry. He took up his friend and mentor's limp hand in his and spoke the only words his energy could muster. "I will do you proud, Carl, whatever that means."

William placed the hand again at the body's side, stood for a while, taking in a final image of his friend, then gathered his things and walked to the elevator. William took a long drive to determine the move that lay ahead for him in his life.

Chapter 26

"So you finally did it, huh? Came out to your old man? Cheers to you, Miss Thing." Witnessing Garrett slip briefly into the stereotype provided Tommy with a brief respite from his personal drama, though just being around the friend who was as comfortable shopping at the mall as he was throwing back beers almost mitigated his broken heart—almost. The drink the bartender had just given him was not going down fast enough.

"Yeah."

"You look depressed." Garrett threw an encouraging arm around Tommy. Kyle's would have been better.

"I guess I should be happy, the hard part is over, but, I don't know."

"Well, yes and no. The hard part is living life, my friend."

"I thought you said life would be so much easier once I came out to him."

"Yeah, I did say that, but if I told you life didn't get any easier you probably wouldn't have done it. Coming out is one thing, but living life as a fag is something all together different."

Tommy watched Garrett's eyes, then noticed the new tint of Garrett's hair. Tommy thought the old blond was better than the new brown. "How's that?"

"There's more to being gay than sucking dick."

Tommy's mood made any interest in a deep philosophical discussion slim, but what he wanted to avoid even more was a lecture. Yet Tommy could only accomplish so much in one night, evident by Garrett's "You're thinking about him, aren't you?"

"Who?" Tommy played it off as best he could.

"You know who, Kyle. Your little frat brat back home."

"No... Yes... I don't know...it's just." Pretending the answer to be no, knowing it was yes, Tommy tried to be strong in front of Garrett. He did not want anyone to know that he really cared. The more he thought about it—him—the more his emotion turned from sadness to anger.

"Uh-oh."

"What?"

"You're getting that look."

"Which look?"

"That 'I'm going to show him' look."

"I don't know what you're talking about." Tommy lifted the corners of the label on his beer bottle using the chewed ends of his fingernails. Was it too much to ask for consolation in place of a lecture?

"Whatever. Don't think I don't know it when I see it. I've had it. Hell, everyone in this place has had it. And it's understandable. You think that just because some mess of a confused straight boy is not paying enough attention to you, you think that if you go out and hook up with somebody it will mean that you are worth something to somebody and that somehow frat boy'll feel it? Let me tell you something. First of all, that's stupid; secondly, he'll never know, unless you tell him, and he'll never care, at least he'll never admit it to your face. Don't ever make the mistake of thinking that your own self-worth needs to be validated by having a set of nuts across your nose."

Garrett should have his own talk show, but Tommy was not up for being a member of the audience. What came out of Garrett's mouth probably made sense; however, Garrett just did not understand this particular situation. Hearing him talk was like listening to an ex-smoker blather on about the dangers of smoking. Tommy knew what he was doing and he was entitled to have a little fun. He was old enough to make his own decisions.

Before he could deliberate on the matter any further, Garrett said, "And speaking of messes... If you ever wanted a shining example of what not to aspire to..." A pair of guys walked up; one looked rather excited to lay eyes on Garrett. The other one was annoyed to have stopped and could not take his eyes off the floor. While Garrett and the happy one exchanged cheeks, Tommy wondered why the sad one did not just go home. The happy one was literally shrieking with delight, illustrating what Garrett must have disdained in that one.

"Hey there, little Garrett." He tried to get the other one's attention. "Hey! Stop moping and pay attention. Garrett, this is Kevin. Kevin, this one reminds me of us when we were younger." While they shook hands, Tommy could see the effort in Garrett's strained smile. Though somewhat amused, hearing how he would probably blossom into one of these two obviously pained him.

"And who's your friend?" Garrett made the introductions all around. Eric assured Tommy, "Stick with Garrett, honey; he'll take care of you. Most of these bitches ain't got a head on their shoulders, but this one does." He reeked of alcohol as he came in close to deliver his declaration. Tommy could not help thinking that just because some designer made the shirt in that color, it did not justify wearing it in public.

"Anyway, boys, have a good night. I've got to continue trying to cheer this one up. He's got man troubles, if you can imagine that." He seemed to be rather free with offering up personal information. Tommy did feel an instant sympathy, knowing that he was not the only one with "man troubles."

Once they were alone again, Tommy turned to Garrett. "How'd you meet him?" There had to be a story there, and Tommy was looking for anything to shift the subject.

"Oh, back in the day, when I used to hang out at the coffee shop in high school, I ran into him. Thank God I had the sense not to sleep with him. He was such a mess back then, back before he became a trust fund baby."

"Trust fund baby?" Tommy knew what a trust fund was, but the context eluded him.

"His family died or something and left him a shit load of money. Now he just lives off of it, working when he feels like it, travels around the rest of the time, lives in different cities." Tommy thought he detected a note of jealousy, but he did not call him on it. "Besides, there's more to life than hiding under too much foundation."

Tommy did not know any guys that used makeup, but he took Garrett's word for it that that Eric guy was using it, but what really interested him was, "But why didn't you sleep with him? I think he's kinda cute." Tommy thought he would take that if it came his way.

"Because an old drag queen told me what I'm going to tell you, that you should get used to being gay before you start tagging everything in sight. Not only will you get a reputation, but you won't be able to see the forest for the trees."

Tommy never did understand that whole forest saying, but he did not question it now, for fear of another lecture on what he should or should not know, though his expression betrayed him. Garrett rolled his eyes. "You can't have a perspective on life when you spend every weekend with your face planted in a mattress. You did say you go to college, right?" Garrett laughed before taking a swig. Tommy made an uncomfortable laugh and determined that Garrett could conduct himself as he pleased. Tommy, however, deserved a little fun. If he was able to get back at Kyle in the process, even better. On the other hand, maybe all Kyle needed was some time, and Tommy was willing to give it to him. He just needed a distraction while Kyle was figuring things out. Maybe when Tommy got back in a week everything would have ironed itself out. Maybe all they needed was some time apart. They had been so perfect for each other—both college students, the same age... Tommy turned around and found Garrett staring at him.

"You really can't stop thinking about him, can you?" Garret sounded a little annoyed.

"I'm fine."

"Whatever. Let's get another drink and do a lap." Garrett led the way to the back bar.

The night wore into a welcome and comforting blur. Tommy found himself in the company of more beer bottles than faces, but whatever the night offered, none compared to the comfort the slightly slanted bar provided his slouching body. When the condescending bartender hinted that he might be better suited to stand, he ordered a drink and turned into just another warm body. When he looked up to offer a hearty apology, nothing brought him more joy than finding a nice set of soft eyes, framed by a warm face that bore a wonderful resemblance to Kyle.

"You look like you're having a good time."

What kind words, Tommy thought. "It could be better." Tommy felt his confidence skyrocket.

"Yeah? How's that?" The guy moved in closer and Tommy tried in vain to label the cologne that tickled his nose.

"Oh, I don't know." Was his comment funny? *Whatever.* Hopefully, he had made a good impression or the guy would not have stayed to talk to him.

"Who are you here with?"

What that had to do with anything, Tommy could not tell, but he played along.

"Some friends."

"And where are they?"

"On the dance floor, I think, maybe... I don't know actually, I don't live here normally."

"Oh? I'd hope you wouldn't live at a bar." The guy was chuckling, obviously having a good time. Tommy skillfully made his inroads.

"No, no, I mean...here, in this... I live in California. I go to school there."

"Is that so?"

Tommy must have said the right thing, for the guy moved in still closer. *Wow! So this is what reeling someone in feels like.* He really did have the touch. "Yeah, that's so." Tommy tried to figure out what color hair the guy had, but had to settle for brown when too many options swamped his brain. The effort was too taxing. It was the same preppy cut as Kyle's. The polo helped fill out the image and he was the perfect body type—slender build, nice arms, modest stubble.

"Can I buy you a drink?"

"Yes." Tommy got another chuckle out of him.

"Okay, but what's your name?"

"Tommy. My name's Tommy. What's yours?" As he stood up, the light caught the guy's face. He looked a little older, and Tommy wondered if he should have said Thomas, although he hated going by Thomas. Only his dad called him Thomas—oh, sometimes his mom did—but he thought maybe Thomas would sound more mature.

"Scott, Tommy, nice to meet you. What do you want to drink?"

Tommy shook his hand and wondered how that firm hand would feel slithering down his naked body. Not that he had ever been sexually adventurous, but he was willing to act like he was in one of the few porn movies he had tucked away under his bed.

Scott enjoyed the conversation with his pathetically easy target, insofar as it passed the time in a smooth manner. He enjoyed a mild form of amusement by being the only one in the conversation who was able to finish complete sentences. But this kid Tommy was sweet enough. Almost a waste, but what can you do? Sometimes you take what's handed to you. The fact that he was not local only convinced Scott further that he would not be missed by anyone of importance.

"So, Tommy, you having a good time?"

"Yeah, sure."

"How about taking off and having a good time somewhere else?" Scott guessed that a more sophisticated line would be unnecessary. Placing his hand on the back of Tommy's neck, Scott massaged the tense muscles, enjoying watching the head droop. *Hook, line and sinker.*

"Sure."

Sad, this one last fling would not provide more of a challenge. Scott rose first and guided Tommy by the arm. The kid acquiesced, following like a good little dog, but when they rounded the corner and moved towards the door, they had the misfortune of running into one of Tommy's friends. For a second, Scott thought about inviting him along. Two might make it more interesting. But the kid shot Scott a stern look that warranted a slap. The "Good Samaritan" reached in and pulled Tommy to the side, but not far enough away to be out of earshot.

"Hey, you alive in there?"

"Yeah, why you gotta yell?"

Scott needed to wrap this up, to get rest for his busy day that would start early in the morning. Obviously, Tommy had to check in, and Scott kept averting his head to avoid a good look at his face.

"You looked like you were leaving."

What a genius this bitch was.

"Yeah, I'm goi...I'm goi' to my new friend's house for a little while." Then he looked at Scott, who gave the obligatory wave of his hand.

"How about you hang here for a while, then we'll split together?"

"Nah, I'm goi' go, go for a while...don' worry, I'm fine."

"Yeah, you look it."

"Seriousl', Garrett, I'm fine."

The young crusader turned to Scott. "What's your name?" Although Scott found the friend's active role touching, Scott quickly ran through some better uses for the kid's energy. This little fag was being more of a nuisance than he had a right to be.

"I think your friend said he was fine." Scott would avoid playing 20 questions.

"Yeah? I'll be the judge of that. He looks a little soused. Now, if you don't mind, I think I'll watch over him and maybe you two can hook up another time."

"I think he's an adult. Maybe you should let your friend think for himself."

"Not tonight. He's my friend and I'm not letting him make any mistakes he'll regret in the morning."

Since this kid stood his ground, Scott started to feel eyes all around directing their attention towards him, exactly what he was looking to avoid. He had better end this quick. But the little one was not looking to have any more conversation and had taken Tommy by the arm, telling him, "You'll thank me for this later." Scott grabbed the kid by the arm, perhaps a little too hard, for the look he shot back made it clear that he was ready to start something. Although Scott had no doubts about his chances, a fight would only bring him attention he was not prepared to deal with, so he let go, and let the little bitch feel like a savior. Maybe Tommy was not worth it anyway. While they disappeared into the back of the bar, Scott felt his opportunity slip away. Even if he could find another guy, he was actually looking forward to sampling those goods. *Oh well, there would always be ano*...and before he could finish the thought, another guy managed to catch his attention.

Something in his face struck Scott as oddly familiar. Someone from a past group? A missed opportunity at the bathhouse? After a few moments, it clicked—that cop's boyfriend. *The fucking fag cop's gay boyfriend. Now, wouldn't this be interesting?* Before he could navigate his way through the crowd, he and the guy he was with, some queen wearing a loud green shirt, disappeared into the crowd. Scott questioned how much effort he was willing to exert. When he decided he did not feel like bothering, that he would leave that fun to Matt, he decided to call it a night. He had been as lucky as he was going to get for the evening, though he felt a little sting in allowing the cop's boyfriend to pass right through his fingers.

In the back area of the bar, Garrett maneuvered Tommy to an available couch without much of a fuss. When Tommy apparently noticed who the guy on his arm was, he looked around for the other guy, then scowled at Garrett.

"Don't worry about him. He was a little old for you anyway."

"That's not...why did...you asshole." The alcohol prevented any real emotion from being attached to the words. "I was gonna get lucky tonight and you had to go an..."

"Don't worry about it. He wasn't that great. There are plenty more just like him out there and none would be worth going home with tonight. You're a bit of a mess anyway." Garrett did what a few people had been good enough to do for him when he was just getting used to the scene. It was every elder statesman's obligation to return the favor to those just entering the fold. If the community was going to get anywhere, they had to help police each other.

"But I was looking forward...he...he...he looked so much like Kyle. You have no idea..."

When the tears came, Garrett was sure the alcohol was not helping. There was something to be said for letting his friend feel the pain instead of letting him drown his sorrows in other men's semen. That was a nifty little line he had picked up along the way that he reminded himself to repeat to Tommy when he sobered up. He was sure he would get a kick out of it. When he felt like Tommy had gone on enough, Garrett decided that they had also had enough out of the night. Getting Tommy home sounded like a good idea.

They would stop for Mexican food, of course, so when Tommy got around to puking he would have something solid in his stomach to keep the liquid coming out of his throat company, then they would go back to Garrett's apartment and chill for a bit. Then, when Tommy had emptied out his stomach and pumped himself with enough water, Garrett would make sure that he got home safe and sound, whether that night or the next morning. Tommy was going to make a good addition to the community, as long as he paid attention and had a good friend looking out for him, someone who, in the future, would look out for Garrett. You can never have too many of those friends.

Chapter 27

Kevin found that once he took up his pen to commit his feelings to the page, his thoughts fell just out of grasp, taunting him with their reluctance to leave his mind. Maybe he imagined them being there in the first place, figments of a conscience he pretended to have, one he created once he took his first step outside of San Diego—the new him—touching down into Philadelphia for the first time, steps away from who he was, the one that all too easily found him once again. Words used to flow easily for him, yet now, when he needed them most, they failed him, refusing to surface when he called out for them. Perhaps none existed to do his heart justice. His teachers saw potential for him as a writer, but like everything in his life, Kevin had failed to follow his abilities up. Maybe karma finally caught up to him. The empty page laughed at him. The more he wallowed in his own sadness at the state of his life, the more he felt sorry for himself. Josh had been a sort of bottoming out for him. Ah, a pun, maybe he should write that down for John, but John would not appreciate the humor in it. He would take everything literally, like he always had, and only focus on the act of what happened and not appreciate that Kevin was confessing a wrong-doing, accepting that he was sorry, trying to find where their relationship might go after they were able to address all of their problems.

But what were their problems? Here, Kevin stumbled. He wanted to make a list of things to address, but none came to him. Kevin felt like he was waiting at a stoplight that would never change. Maybe that was why he allowed himself to fall in with Josh. Maybe he was forcing a change he was not man enough to make on his own. That sounded a little too harsh for him to write down. Plus, did he believe it? He felt like he had been put into a room as a child and forced to write five reasons why he committed whatever it was he had done that compelled his parents to punish him. Whatever he came up with was not really a reason for much of anything, just something concocted to not only make it sound like he had considered the consequences, but also to get him out of the room as quickly as possible. He wondered if his parents even took the time to read what he had written down all those times.

Then a phrase crossed his mind: *Do we have a future?* It seemed to fit, but did he really need to be that dramatic? Maybe they were just going through something. Would time take care of the rest? Maybe all couples went through this over the course of a relationship. Maybe everyone, except for Eric, who was no real help. Maybe it was best to just go out, have a few drinks and forget what had happened. Somehow he knew that what he had done with Josh would always be in the back of his mind, knowing the only way to put it to bed would be to get it off his chest, regardless of the ramifications to his relationship. *Was this maturing?* Maybe telling John would be a good test, a test to see just how much Kevin meant to him. *Was that the right thing to do?* Should he be testing his boyfriend? Maybe they just saw things differently.

Maybe Kevin should blame everything on his boredom. No, there had to be more than that. Maybe Kevin just was not in love with John anymore. Kevin cast his pen aside, the phrase "Maybe he did not love John anymore" running out-of-control through his head. No, he could not contemplate that possibility. *Of course I still love John.*

His lack of choices brought on a headache instead of relief. He needed some experience in order to find any worthwhile solution. All of his prior relationships were short lived—as long as he allowed them to continue, that is—but meeting John created a convenient way out of the monotony that had overtaken his life in Southern California. He itched for a change and for more opportunity. Maybe John had served his role and it was time to move on, but did he need to stay in this part of the country? Maybe San Diego was not as bad as he thought. Maybe he just needed a new perspective, and now that he had it, he could be happy there. What he would not give for a wise ear to listen and impart some worthwhile advice. Too much time had passed for him to reach out to the friends in San Diego he had left so abruptly, ones that told him he was making a big mistake, ones that had never left San Diego and did not know what life could be like more than 15 miles from the beach. Since they all hated John, they would tell him to come home. Eric? No help there. He had become all high and mighty all of a sudden, as John's champion. He must have had some morals fucked into him recently and Kevin was not enjoying being on the other end of that guilt trip. Why did the answer not just fall into his lap, telling him what to do? Confess to John and hope that sparks some renewed interest? Just up and leave and go back to California? Leave John and stay in the area, making something of himself on the East Coast? Bide his time and wait for things to settle down, wait for him to get used to "married" life? Kevin now saw why he had avoided long-term relationships so successfully. Kevin missed the life that only required a stiff drink and a good lay to make your week.

The phone snapped his train of thought. How long had it rung? He paused as he reached for the receiver. Might John be calling? His hand shook a little. What was he afraid of? Would John hear something—the thing—in his voice and ask what was wrong? Would Kevin have an answer? Or did the fear that he might spew out all that had been stored in his heart, thereby committing himself to a decision he felt incapable of making? The answering machine decided for him. When the beep sounded, he was relieved to hear, "Ya screening bitch, pick up the damn phone!" Eric did not feel the need to keep talking. Why waste the air or effort? If Kevin neglected to answer, Eric would keep calling back. Resistance proved futile.

"Hey." Eric's enthusiasm for a sale bounded through the earpiece, offering Kevin subtle relief. Even if Kevin did not have the money to shop, watching Eric hand his credit card across the sales counter the way most people offer Kleenex would distract Kevin long enough for his anxiety to ebb. Kevin jumped at the first meeting time Eric suggested.

John stepped back into Dr. Riles' office—reaching Kevin would wait—walking in while Glenn ran down the day's plan.

"Now you'll be in his car with us right on your tail. If for some reason you lose sight of us, good. You shouldn't be able to spot us anyway. Once you get to where you are going, follow along, and we'll move in when we can. See what exactly is going on there."

"Shouldn't I be wearing a wire or something?"

"You watch too much TV, Doc." John enjoyed letting Glenn do all the talking for once.

"Relax, Doctor. You're going to be fine. This will all be over soon and you can go back to your wife, given that you really were a stooge in all of this. While I find it hard to really believe that someone of your presumed intelligence could be that stupid, your paperwork seems to look legit so you might be off the hook even though I don't know how you could not know that several missing persons ended up on your table. Good thing your school committee is thorough." He wanted to say he was pissed to learn the doctor was walking away from all of this, given what he contributed, but such was his job—such was the law.

"Or at least better at covering their own ass." John could not have said it better himself. Watching Glenn get worked up proved even more amusing, seeing him gun for the last word. Having a gay partner compelled Glenn to assert himself in the most amusing ways.

"Cheer up, Doctor. You really think you have something to be nervous about?"

"Wouldn't you be upset, Detective, if you were in my situation? Not knowing what you were involved in?"

"I wouldn't be in your situation, Doctor." The doctor's vacant eyes never left Glenn's stare. You could see the wheels turning in his head and John wondered, for a moment, what he must be going through, but quickly abandoned that unfounded compassion.

"You need to understand something, both of you. I am not some malevolent person, with his head buried in the sand. I'm here to do research in the hopes that what I find can help people. That is what I do. If someone comes to me with an offer, and their documents are in order, why would I question them further? Sure, hearing the word 'church' come up can be odd, but you must understand, I hear a number of odd things. If I were to pass judgment on every one of them, I would be nowhere. Everyone has his or her own agenda, and whatever I can use to further my own is fine with me. Sometimes you just have to trust the person on the other end. As long as the paper work is in order, that is. The notion that people would take their own lives because of their sexuality sounded plausible. I didn't need to question any further." At least the doctor dedicated enough time to concocting a useful speech that might sway a jury. His energy would have been best spent elsewhere though.

John avoided countering with his own speech, choosing to accept the rhetorical nature with which the doctor offered his. The doctor would have his conscience to live with, and that might have to be enough. "All right, Doctor. Don't forget, we'll be right behind you. Just try to relax." The doctor nodded like a good patient.

"Oh, the guy's name again who's picking you up?" John wanted to know if the name would come out the same.

"Scott."

"Good. Now sit tight and wait."

John and Glenn exited out the back of the building. "You think he'll crack?"

"Don't care. As long as he cracks around this Scott character, I could give two shits about him. Once we nail him we can find the trail ourselves if we have to." They made themselves comfortable in their car in the faculty parking lot and waited for Scott to arrive. Hopefully, they would not have to wait long.

"What do you think they'll get the doc with?"

"My guess is that he'll skate through it. The paperwork will check out if it's real. If we find out that it's not, there's no way of proving that he thought otherwise. So as far as I'm concerned, let the guy live with knowing that he contributed to a bunch of murders. He wouldn't last in jail anyway."

"Yeah, I guess you wouldn't see getting it stuck to you from behind by some big ugly guy as punishment." Glenn really did need some new material.

Time crawled. John wished he had brought a book, but when he could not, for the life of him, recall the last book he had glanced at, much less picked up, he buried that idea. Maybe one of Kevin's magazines, though Glenn would have had a field day if he pulled out *People* or *Us*. You could tell when Glenn gave in to his boredom, for he just stared out the window, tapping his finger against the glass to no particular rhythm. Sitting on your ass for two hours will do that to you. Just before the third hour hit, the radio sputtered. "Go for Thompson." Dr. Riles had left the building and entered a tan sedan. They had a description of the driver called in and the car was now in motion. He listened as the officer relayed the car's direction. "Copy that. Follow them over the bridge and have someone else pick them up at 21st, over."

John stowed the radio. "They're heading across the river, down South Street." John put the car in reverse and plotted a route in his head.

As five different cars took their turns tailing the car, after waiting for them to finish whatever it is they were stopping at the gas station for—and pausing to get a paper at a newsstand—the car pulled onto Broad Street, trekking down the main drag of the city at a leisurely pace. John and Glenn picked them up around the sports complex, thinking they would be near their destination at some point. When the car headed towards the expressway, John guessed that they were headed towards the airport. When they headed north instead, he stopped trying to predict. He had another car follow them onto the on-ramp and they turned off on a side street, moving north on their own. He was hoping they would not lose him on the highway. Although they had a make and model, plus a description of the suspect, if they lost them John did not know what they would miss out on. Although he had spouted off about not caring when Dr. Riles cracked, he knew that they needed the evidence to which Riles would lead them.

When his team called in their exit number, John took a deep breath; he could taste what was coming. They had about seven minutes to get their game faces on for show time. They would reach their position by the time the traffic light changed. That off ramp had a tendency to keep you waiting forever.

John and Glenn caught up to the suspect a few blocks away. With two cars separating them, John could barely hold his fingers still on the steering wheel. They followed the car through a left turn, and then a right, until they coasted on their way to the waterfront. When they turned down an alley, John kept going, making his next right, coming around through the other end of the alley. They followed on foot, and when he saw the car idling in front of a warehouse door, he called for back up. They waited for the car to enter the building before they dashed forward.

In a matter of moments, squad cars converged on the scene. Glenn administered the obligatory hard knock on the steel door, gave it a few moments, and when there was no reply, they broke through the door and swarmed into the building. Startled by the crash of the door, the driver—some yards away, leading the way to the back of the warehouse—spun around and unloaded a shot into Dr. Riles, then took off running. John followed after him, shoving boxes out of his way to the same exit door.

John fumed at not finding backup stationed at the back door, but then again, the tight alley must not have allowed for a car. The moment John scouted in each direction, he quickly saw that no outlet would provide his suspect a means by which to escape. John had him; he only needed to flush the bastard out.

John darted towards the rustling, snagging a glimpse of the driver, who had a good lead. John would have to run too fast to catch up, making a successful shot too difficult. If John stopped to shoot, no telling where the prick might hide, but the driver had thought of shooting first, not bothered by stopping, apparently. John ducked behind some dumpsters for cover and waited for the bullets to stop. After the third shot there was a long pause. The next audible "thud" told John that the perp must have gone in through a door. *Great. A chase through a building.*

John took a deep breath and thanked himself for wearing his vest. He darted his head in and out of the doorway. When no more shots followed, he took off up the alley. Without anyone in view, he spied a door, partially opened. He called in his location and when he heard the sirens in the distance, he proceeded in with caution.

With water on the other side, his guy would have to go for a swim, and no one would swim in these waters, no matter how desperate. Though they had the guy cornered, John did not want to chance it. John wanted to be the one chasing him. As he entered the building, he felt for a light switch, threw it on, then planned how he should navigate through all the freight. From a safe vantage point in a corner he noted the stairs along a wall and the catwalks above. This was going to be a pain in the ass.

John inched along the hallway created by the row of boxes and stuck to the perimeter of the building, making his way to the back staircase. He would try and overshoot the driver's position, coming at him from behind if he could. The door opened and he saw four officers, including Glenn, enter. Avoiding any contact, he watched as they took off in different directions through the rows of boxes. The din of sirens in the background offset the squeaking of his shoes on the rusted metal steps. *This part of the job sucks.*

He paused every ten feet, listening for any sign of the driver's position. When he saw a fellow officer take to the stairs, he knew they were zeroing in on their man. They must have completed their sweep, although John was not confident that he was not tucked away among the high pallet-stacked boxes, ideal for tucked away hiding spots. A second officer joined the first; together, they kicked in the doors on the upper level. John paused in between some doors down the walk to cover their backs. When they hit the third door, a round of shots rang out from the inside. They braced themselves against the wall in anticipation of more fire, but the shots ended. Two officers charged the door. John quickly brought up the rear, entering the room with the suspect holding a gun to his head.

There was a long silence; the officers, with their guns trained on the driver, the driver glaring back, only determination in his eyes. "Drop the gun. No one else has to get shot here today."

The driver's eyes floated in John's direction. "You'll never understand, John."

John felt his breath flutter, but he resisted the temptation to take the bait. "You're right, but put the gun down anyway."

"You knew I was waiting up here." His voice chilled, settling into an eerie calm.

"I'm not interested in what you were waiting for. Just know that you're going to put down that gun and take a walk with us."

"I was waiting so you could see this, see my eyes. You'll never appreciate how close we came." He took a deep breath, the vein on the side of his neck swelling. John slowly raised his gun for what he knew was coming. He would wound him in the hopes of the gun dropping out of his hand. "One day, perhaps sooner than you think, you'll wish you were the one pulling the trigger."

John watched as the muscle in his hand tensed. John did not bother discouraging the act. His brains exploded out of the side of his head, dribbling down the side of the wall. As his lifeless body slumped to the ground, John felt not one ounce of pity, ignoring the incoherent drivel spewing out of his mouth only moments before. John had learned to block that shit out. Still, he had to cover his nose as he knelt down to fish for the guy's wallet. The other two officers had already left to get a cleanup crew. John found a license in the wallet. The world would be a better place without Scott Everett in it.

John joined Glenn and some of the other officers as they combed through the original warehouse. An ambulance had already carted Dr. Riles away, John learned on his way up the stairs to where Glenn and another cop were digging through the files.

"What'd you get?"

"This is crazy. They have all these records of bodies moved in and out of here. All given numbers and blood type, and get this, their HIV status. The ones they marked as "positive" were "dumped." Real discreet language. Some of the guys found a couple bodies down there that have tags. All we have to do is either match some photos or run their prints, but this looks like it. It's all right here."

"Any names of the people involved yet?"

"Nah, checking but...holy shit! Would you get a load of this shit?" John walked over and peered over Glenn's shoulder.

John gazed down of a stack of pictures of him and Glenn standing at a window. "What the fuck are these from? When we were checking out that Townsend apartment?"

"Guess so. I seemed to recall that hideous shirt of yours. Why the fuck would they be taking our picture..." Glenn's voice trailed off and John quickly returned his attention to Glenn from the activity on the floor. But

320

what Glenn handed over was not something he had prepared for: the picture of John and Kevin from the beach in San Diego. The photo had been in their apartment. *How the fuck would they have...* Only one thought entered his mind and found its way to his mouth, "Kevin."

He was out the door and down the steps as fast as he could go. Somewhere in the background he heard Glenn calling out some names and a gallop of support sounded from behind. What if they were at his house and Kevin was home all alone? How fast could they make it home? 15, 16 minutes from this end of the city? Please, God, let Kevin not be home and all this just be John's instinct. John checked his watch as he jumped in the front seat of his car, and at 3:18 he hoped that he would be in time for whatever his heart told him had already happened.

He tried the phone as he merged onto the expressway but when he tried to get through to the home line, it rang and rang and rang without going through to the machine, which meant that Kevin was at home and no matter what John did, the gas pedal would not go down any further. John had too much to concentrate on to try his cell phone.

Fuck. Almost 2:30. Matt entertained a hundred different options as to better places to be at that moment. *What a waste of time.* More and more, getting the fuck out of Dodge, distancing himself from the inevitable coming down on all that he had been a party to bothered him more than he cared to admit. Experience told him to put the car in gear and drive away—*get while the getting's good*—but something

321

compelled him to leave the car in park. *Give him another minute or two.* Reminding himself that he had chosen to be there, in that car, parked outside the cop's apartment—not that Scott ordered him—that he could move out as he wished, cooled his heels. *Patience. What's one more to the pile?* William seemed to vanish, which proved odd, since Matt thought he never left the warehouse. *Must have something to do with Scott going off the deep end.* Matt checked his watch again... *This is a bad idea, bad idea. Split now, while you can*...though taking care of this end of things just seemed like a fitting closure to this chapter in his life. All in all, the hour he had spent sitting in his car, in sight of the building entrance of the cop's apartment, was getting less romantic and more boring by the minute. Not to mention stupid.

Fuck it. He's not going to show. He hunched over and put the car in gear, lowering the window to let some fresh air in before he signaled to enter traffic. Then a shriek echoed down the street, his hand freezing in place on the gearshift. Two obvious fags strutted past his car, swinging shopping bags. It had to be who he was waiting for. They stopped at the front door and exchanged kisses. *Stay or go, stay or go, decide now.* His hand loosened on the gearshift. *Fuck him and his pig boyfriend. Five minutes for you to settle inside before I make my move.* Matt figured that he would have to wait for the elevator and he wanted to avoid catching him in the hall or on the same elevator. He already knew the apartment number, and Scott had told him there was no back exit, so he would have enough room to work without having to chase anyone around. He would do this as quickly as he wanted, without depriving himself of any fun along the way, yet still have enough time to head south before work traffic clogged the streets. *Too easy.* Matt rolled up the passenger-side window.

The hall, blessedly empty with all the yuppies at work, allowed him to stroll leisurely to Room 816 unnoticed. He stopped, listened for voices, and when he heard none, he gave the door a few knocks.

"Yes?" When the door opened, the fag looked confused, but not put off.

Matt utilized his endearing voice. "Hi, my name is Ralph. I just moved in a few doors down. I was wondering if I could use your phone to order a pizza. I haven't had a chance to get my phone hooked up yet and I forgot to charge my cell at my old place."

"Yeah, sure, come on in." He let Matt walk into the apartment while he held the door open for him. *Stupid and kind, what an unfortunate mix*, Matt thought.

"The phone is on the counter over there and I'll get you the phone book." As he handed the phone book to him, he said, "I'm Kevin, by the way."

Matt took the phone book and quickly opened it to avoid shaking hands, but Kevin did not seem to mind. He just disappeared with his shopping bags into the bedroom. Matt dialed a number that he knew, and quickly hung up. He waited a minute, then made like he was ordering. After his order, he said, "Hey, ah, Kevin, what's the address here again?" Kevin called it out. When Matt was done, he pressed the dial button and left the tone running. He turned the volume down and set the phone back on its base. He did not want it to ring or let Kevin be able to make a quick call. For further assurance, he reached on the side of the base and carefully pulled out the connection. In either case, he would have enough time to do what needed doing.

Kevin trotted back in. "On its way?"

"Yeah, hey, thanks again."

"Yeah, no problem, I remember what a hassle it was when we moved in. The phone company takes forever."

"You have a roommate?"

"Yeah, I live with my boyfriend." He did not even have to think about it. Why would you volunteer that information so freely? Kevin's brazenness impressed Matt.

"Oh, cool." It seemed like the neighborly thing to say. "What does your boyfriend do?"

"He's a cop. He usually puts in long hours."

"Oh. Having a cop as a boyfriend must come in handy." Good, so he was not expected any time soon. "So, any advice about the building? Thin walls? Nosey neighbors?"

"Walls are pretty thick; can't remember the last time I heard a noise from anywhere. The neighbors tend to stick to themselves. I really couldn't even tell you the last time I ran into one on this floor."

This was just too easy. Matt almost wanted to leave and come back to make it interesting, but he needed to beat the traffic. "Cool. I'm looking forward to living here. Seems like it'll be nice."

"Yeah, it's a good building. But listen, I'm glad you were able to use the phone, but I was going to hop in the shower, so if..."

"Oh, sure, I won't bother you anymore." When Kevin turned to open the door, Matt came up behind him, wrapped one hand around Kevin's mouth and the other around his arms. Matt had him. "Now, listen," he whispered in Kevin's ear, "I'm going to move my hand, and the moment you make a noise, you're dead. Got it?" Matt removed his arm first, reached in his back pocket for his gun and pulled Kevin away from the door with his hand. While pointing his gun at Kevin, Matt dead bolted the door. He did not look like he was going to put up much of a fight. The fag probably thought he was going to get raped and was going into the passive, just-don't-hurt-me mode. *Stupid, to the last.*

"On your knees, now." Matt checked to make sure the silencer was on tight. Kevin followed directions well. *Good fag.*

"Now, you watch movies, Kevin?" Having the gun to his head would keep the voice low and relatively quiet.

"Yes." You could hear the fear in his voice, almost too pathetic.

"You ever see *Pulp Fiction?*"

"No, I haven't."

Oh, Christ, goddamn fag has no taste in cinema. There goes my fun. "Oh well, then what I was going to say will be lost on you." Matt tried to think up something other than a Samuel L. Jackson imitation. He surveyed the room. Looked cozy enough, the way these fags lived. He thought they might have a mirrored ball hanging from the ceiling and Liza Minelli posters everywhere. Who would have thought? Then his thoughts drifted to the cop boyfriend. That was his in. "You love your boyfriend?"

"Yes." *Oh great, a crier.* Just what he needed, to have Kevin start bawling like a chick. *Oh well. Hmm.* What could he do? Kevin wore a watch. He pulled the gun back from Kevin's forehead. "All right, tell me what time it is."

His arm shook as he brought his watch down in front of his eyes. It was like seeing a dog that had just been doused with water in the shower.

"3:03."

"Good, 3:03. I want you to remember that time. Can you do that for me?"

"Yes."

Matt stood Kevin up and led him into the bedroom.

Adrenaline drove the car as John sped through traffic, vacillating between sides of the road and jerking around corners. Drivers picked the best day to heed a siren zipping past them. What should have taken 15 minutes took eleven. He left the car parked in the street as he bolted into the lobby of his building. When the elevator doors did not open immediately, he dashed to the stairs. He hit the eighth level and cursed their choice in floors as he sprinted down the hallway, drawing his weapon as he paused for a moment at his front door. When he saw the door cracked open, he took a deep breath. *Kevin, please, for the love of God, be all right.* He kicked the door open, but when he heard a guttural moaning, he turned towards the bedroom and saw Kevin dragging himself out along the carpet, trailed by a stream of blood. John dropped his gun and ran to him. He got on the floor with him and flipped him over, trying to find out where he was hurt, but the blood gushed from everywhere; his clothes were saturated with blood.

"Kevin! Kevin!"

John held Kevin's head still and looked into the eyes that were rolling back into his head. They focused when he said his name, managing for a moment to hold John's gaze. Kevin tried to talk, but he choked on his own blood. John held his head up so he could try to say something.

"Kevin! Fuck! Fuck! Fuck!"

His body grew cold and limp in John's grasp. "Kevin!"

He stared down at him, lying in his arms, blood spilling out of his mouth.

Kevin managed something that sounded like "John?"

"Yes, I'm here. Just hold on, baby. Help is coming. Just hold on."

"John...J...I'm sorry...I'm so sorry, I'm so sorry...J..."

"Kevin, don't talk, just hold on...don't talk, just hold on..." John couldn't let go of him to reach the phone.

"I'm so...J, I'm so...I'm so..."

"Kevin, it's not your fault. Oh God, please, Kevin hold on, hold on..."

By the time the other officers arrived, within minutes, Kevin had already let go.

Matt stepped out onto the street. He checked his watch. *3:20, not bad timing.* He had just enough time to get going. He strolled to his car and got behind the wheel. He could leave town with a clean conscience. He had fulfilled all of his obligations to Scott. Some time into his drive, as he coasted along the freeway, he caught sight of the 18-wheeler jackknifing right in front of him, followed by his own roof collapsing right on top of him. He heard a lot of crashing after that, and then everything got real quiet, real soft, and real white.

Chapter 28

When something in him stirred, William delved into the depths of his brain to locate the words to describe his state. These were the times when he reached for his Bible, thumbing through the pages to find the explanation for his mind. Driving along the desolate streets in the early morning, he felt like he was experiencing the inevitable product of the prolonged threat of seasickness, that receding dryness tickling his tongue. The glints of sunrise as they pricked his cheeks offered little warmth for the chill that had overtaken his body since before he even visited the hospital. Hard to believe that was just the day before. All that sat in front of him: the sky, once black, then purple, now turning to hues of pink, even a touch of orange. His car crawled alone on the road, driving away from the future that lay behind him in the city that had long since passed out of his rearview mirror.

As the blooming trees announced their enviable vibrancy with the help of the rising sun, William found himself easing up on the accelerator, loosing his grip on the steering wheel. He coasted down the next off-ramp, reading the sign to determine just how far his journey had taken him. Along the side of the road, he looked down at his odometer when the street name offered no useful information. A few hundred miles. If he turned back now, he could make it back by the afternoon. Make the turn or keep driving? Yes, he would leave; extricate himself from the undeniable mess brewing, but not without tying up some loose ends first. He had learned at least that much. But first he needed to locate the off-ramp to find his way back south. Why did engineers in this part of the country feel the need to complicate things by not make an on-ramp for every off-ramp in case you made a mistake and needed to turn around on the same road?

Some hours later, his eyes stinging with the lack of rest his body rejected, William wound his car through the side streets that led up towards the warehouse, barely registering the color of the stop lights that offered permission to turn or stop. His autopilot guided him within a few blocks of the warehouse, but his senses snapped back the moment his strained pupils noted the first cop car pulled off to the side of the road. He managed a deep breath, casting his nerves to his weary condition, but the yellow tape strewn across the alleyway entrance produced recognition that no amount of denial could shake. Someone, several ones, had apparently tied up some loose ends for him, forced his hand. But how many ends had they managed to tie together?

He pulled the car alongside the nearby curb. The cops had discovered the warehouse. But how? He immediately went to his cell phone and dialed Scott's number. His voice mail answered. There were no messages on his own phone either. He did not know what to make of the situation. Had they gotten to Scott too? Did that mean that they were after him as well? He needed to go somewhere and collect himself. The morning had been filled with too many events to rationalize, something the afternoon was doing nothing to ease.

His speculations quickly encountered facts when he took a booth at a local coffee shop, finding the details in the morning paper. There, in black and white, some reporter spelled out all of the available details. Scott had taken his own life in a shoot-out with police in a nearby warehouse and the doctor whom they suspected of involvement was wounded, and was in recovery at a local hospital. Investigators were still piecing together the information they uncovered in the raided warehouse, but all they could confirm was that they had thwarted the ring responsible for several disappearances and deaths of members of the gay community.

The story ran a companion picture, depicting the interior of the warehouse, with cops lingering, rifling through all their work. In related news it said that lead detective John Thompson, was mourning the loss of his boyfriend, who had been killed in an apparent connection with the murders. They had yet to put together a suspect, or figure out how the murder took place, as there were no witnesses, and neighbors neither heard nor saw a thing.

It must have been Scott...or Matthew. But they made no mention of finding Matthew. Perhaps he fled the city and would try and contact William, or merely escape altogether. Better that he get away too, rather than try to contact William, which only made his own situation more precarious. There was nothing to trace anything back to him—unless they apprehended Matthew. No, he was far too clever for that. But the doctor.... The doctor would not have known what William looked like. In fact, did he even know his name to offer to the police?

If they found the warehouse, what else did the police know?

But no, no one would come knocking on his door, the one that did not even exist at the moment. He would be far away from here by the time the possibility of his involvement materialized. But in easing his own fears, his eyes settled on the snapshot of John on the front page. Just a head shot of him in his uniform. It said how he had cracked everything wide open with the help of the doctor, and what a decorated officer he was. *His son, a grown man.* Then what had passed under his eyes returned: *boyfriend.* He returned to that section of the story. *Yes, right there: boyfriend. My son—gay? No, there must be a mistake. John, my son?* His mind circled like this for William knew not how long. There must have been a message in there for William to heed, and what he took it to mean was that he needed to disappear. Seeing the photo of his son after all those years the other day sparked something in him. Learning that his son grew to be a homosexual produced a different reaction. All of a sudden the wheels stopped turning in his head. His heart paused and his breath turned in on itself. For those moments while he sat in silence, just staring at the photo of his grown-up son, he felt neither sad, nor pain, nor guilt, nor anything at all. Just hollow. Real hollow.

His mind drifted, recoiling back to that cold winter day where William saw his whole life torn asunder. The snow that covered the trees, the air that scorched his nostrils as his lungs heaved forward and his legs plunged through ten inches of snow at a time to reach the lake too late to do anything. He stared down at his oldest son, standing over the gouged hole in the icy floor. His son, who stared off after his younger brother, the one who should have been there, the one who fell through the ice's floor. William collapsed, knowing he should have been there.

When he realized that he had failed to be there, he committed himself to never being there again, to save his family the anguish that his inability to be a man had caused. This moment froze in his mind. With his back turned to his wife and son, he eased into his overcoat and adjusted the scarf his now dead younger son had made for him. He turned for an instant, a subtle moment, as he reached for his hat on the coat-rack. His oldest boy appeared in the periphery of his vision. Those eyes told him to run, those eyes of judgment that William knew would never forgive him, eyes that were too young to comprehend, but old enough to demand some reason. William saw those same eyes alive again in the photo of the paper, those eyes looking away, yet staring him down, and condemning his actions. In those eyes, William relived his failure as a man, as a father, all over again, his son once again connected to his shortcoming, and this time, more deaths accompanying his inability to succeed.

He did not know what to feel. Should he be dwelling on the collapse of his work? What was there for him to do, now that his position at the Church was gone? He could not go back there. There was no one to go to. Of course he knew those who were under Monsignor Drollings, but what good would that do? No, he was ruined in this town, and now all he could do would be to flee, to start again somewhere else, somewhere where his name was not yet known.

His thoughts drifted back to his son. His gay son. The phrase repeated over and over in his head, like the ever-present wind against a thin pane of glass in a snowstorm. Did William's failure turn his son? Did William's failure as both a man and a father somehow do this to his son? Was that possible? Guilt collected in his throat. In leaving his family, he thought to spare them further misery, but perhaps his leaving had brought on a new misery for which he would have given anything to have avoided. But what did that mean for his work? Did that suggest that his son was like all those that he had counseled, tried to heal through his life's work through the Church? Was John no different than Scott or Isaac? Was there no hope after all, and everything they had been pursuing was nothing more than a fool's errand? William would not permit himself to feel that way. There had to be hope, had to be a way to help all those who needed a kind hand out of the darkness that had descended over their souls.

William refused to let his failure detour him from picking himself up and trying again. One day his own son would have a way out, even if he would never know who was giving him this gift. William would find it, no matter what the cost or the effort. This much he owed his son. If his son, and millions of others, could be turned by some influence—some faith, *his* faith—then science could find a way to correct it.

As the newsprint dampened from the sweat building in the palm of his hand, William stared down at the smearing image of his son. A burst of inspiration beckoned him to dare to contact him, but the flash flamed out as quickly as it had started up. He would cause his son no more harm, bring him no more grief until he had found the cure for all his misery. Contact would only undoubtedly cause some unforeseen distress, and William was not one to repeat his mistakes, but he could not pass up a final goodbye of some kind. Having a conversation was pointless, but to be able to see his son, even from afar, would be a fitting end to this chapter in his life. What better place than at the funeral for his son's boyfriend? To attend the ceremony that maybe some day John would say was a good thing.

William again heard Monsignor Drollings' words in his head: "It is never too late to fix the past." Maybe the most Christian thing for him to do would be to turn himself in to the authorities, to confess his sins and let justice be done. But William knew better. His life could still be a benefit somewhere else, something being jailed would hinder. His purpose operated above such archaic laws. Asking his son for forgiveness would be an exercise in futility as well. William understood that the world was not ready to understand the scope of his work, not for possibly years to come. Now, with accomplishments yet to realize, the road looked clear before him, but his journey needed a symbolic goodbye in order to commence properly.

"Mrs. Riles, you can see him now." Barbara had paced about the waiting room, with her son watching her. The phone call had come out of nowhere and she pulled herself together to get to the hospital, but quickly fell apart when the impact of having her husband shot engulfed her. Tommy at least offered his support. Still, sitting in the waiting room, subjected to the constant news cycle, "facts" of a crime ring with her husband tied somewhere in the middle. The nerve of these stations, to splash her husband's picture across the screen! She had no idea what her husband had been doing there, but there was no way for all of these allegations to be true. Every minute felt like a year, watching the sand blow off a mound as she waited for the chance to hear her husband's voice. When she and Tommy walked into the private room in intensive care, seeing all the tubes coming in and out of Stephen, she felt every inch of her husband's pain, pain that threatened to buckle her knees and send her to the floor. What about those lies the television spewed mattered in the face of this? Those reporters could not see what pain he was in and how much he must be suffering.

"Stephen?" Her hand trembled as it inched across her husband's brow.

His eyelids crept open and his mouth struggled to smile. Seeing him conscious cast aside any desire to curb her tears, giving way to a flood of tears reserved for every fear she had stockpiled in her mind. Tommy rubbed her back and held her hand.

"It's okay, Mom."

She collected herself, waiting for Stephen to stir once again. Even through his grogginess, Barbara knew that her husband felt his family's presence. That had been what she had wanted most—for him to know that they were there with him. As she stared down at her husband, she resisted thinking about those reports and how much of them could be true. Then she wondered what the connection to his school would be. But she could not wrestle with all of that at the moment; that would come in time.

She bent down and kissed his forehead. "Get some rest, Stephen. We're right here for you, and we're not going anywhere."

John declined to speak, as if any words to express what he had to say, the will to find something to utter existed, as if he even possessed the voice to make it happen. A healthy amount of humor and tears in between the mild laughter gave some life to most of the ceremony. Kevin would have been proud that his friends paid him such an appropriate tribute, but he would also understand that John could not express his grief in such a public way.

As the group filtered out of the church, John wandered past the well-wishers and out near the breeze that swept in from the river, coming off the choppy water. Here, he found a moment of solitude that the past few days had deprived him of. Everyone had been good enough to offer their support and love, but this was the moment when he needed his space. As he looked back at the church, his mother greeted people, while Eric made his way towards him. Just off down the road, near the caravan of parked cars, he saw a man with gray hair, standing under a tree that offered little shade, studying him from afar. For a moment he entertained the bizarre feeling that it was his father, staring at him. All of his grief had caused him to reflect, and he found himself, in the past few days, thinking about the man who had walked out on him all those years ago. That must have been what put the image in his head.

When Eric caught up to him, he turned from the man and nodded when Eric paused. It had even been comforting to have Eric calling every day and stopping by the apartment, going through Kevin's clothes, doing some of the wash, then folding up some of Kevin's shirts and organizing them in Kevin's drawers as if tomorrow he would get out of bed and need something to wear. John could not bring himself to tell Eric to stop these past few days. John welcomed any memory of Kevin. Even so, today he was not up for a conversation.

"John?" He paused. When he got no response, he continued. "I just wanted...I know we never really got along, but I just wanted..." You could hear the pain in his voice. "John, I just wanted you to know that he loved you. He really did. That's all." When John turned to say something back, Eric had already walked off.

He did not feel like calling after him, or anyone for that matter. When he searched the crowd to see if he could place the man again, he too was gone. What did he expect to find? His father come back, after all this time? John wondered when the last time his imagination had gotten the best of him in such a big way. His emotions were all riled up from losing Kevin, and he was reflecting on the other losses in his life. He was supposed to be there for Kevin, to protect him, just as it was his job to protect every other person in the city; yet he had failed at that—failed Kevin, just as he had failed his little brother all those years ago.

When he was alone again, alone with his thoughts, the cool breeze running through him felt like the thing he needed. His thoughts drifted to Kevin and their time together and all the moments they had shared—the times they laughed at bad movies and days where they bickered about money; days when they wanted to give up and days that seemed like they could rest in each other's arms without thinking about the clock. Kevin had taught him how to feel the breeze as they walked on the beach holding hands and encourage him to take a little more time in life, something he would force himself to get good at now. Had he added to Kevin's life? In this moment, Kevin's last words ran through his head, words he could not shut out even if he had wanted to. The fact that Kevin blamed himself was too much to take. John was the one who should have been there to protect him, the same way he should have been there to protect his little brother all those years ago. The tears trickled down his cheeks, but decided not to fall from his face, instead coasting down his neck and into his collar. He hoped that Kevin knew how much he had loved him.

He turned, giving the dream of seeing his father one more shot. Gone, just a figment of his grief. As he continued to think and remember, he wondered how good a boyfriend he had been. Had he been everything to Kevin that he should have been? He thought back through everything, contemplating what he might have done differently if he had been given the chance.

He turned his attention to the clouds, shifting in the sky. Kevin would have come up with some clever way of conveying the sight before John's eyes. In his head, he heard the whispers, scraps of words passing through his mind, words used by victims to describe people who would become John's cases. In the clouds, they told John that they saw a hat, a long coat, side-burns and a cropped moustache. The wind shifted a mass of white into a portly man with flat feet, and in the clouds he watched as an image of Kevin's smile took shape. The wind whistled Kevin's laugh and a numbness pricked John's toes on its way to his heart. He had discovered how best to describe the clouds that day; they were painted with his failures and his regret.

About Brad Windhauser

Originally from Los Angeles, Brad Windhauser moved to Philadelphia after attending college in San Diego in 2000 to pursue his M.A. in English/Creative Writing, which he received from Rutgers-Camden in 2002. He is currently an instructor at Temple University.

He lives in downtown Philadelphia where he spends his down time reading, scribbling down new story ideas, and enjoying the occasional bottle of medium-bodied, slightly spiced red wine. *Regret* is his first major work to be published.

Printed in the United States
89815LV00003B/139/A